Praise for Connie Briscoe

P.G. County

"This romp of a read combines lush settings, humorous dialogue and outrageous behavior with a raucous finale."
—*Ebony*

"Briscoe's quick wit and obvious love of language shine brightly in this twisted tale."
—*Black Issues Book Review*

"Bestselling author Briscoe presents a comic satire on the African American upper crust of Prince George County. The author demonstrates consummate skill as she reels the characters into a hilarious denouement."
—*Library Journal*

Praise for Lolita Files

"*sex.lies.murder.fame: A Novel* is brilliant. Lolita Files has delivered a true page turner with remarkable characters."
—Eric Jerome Dickey

"Author Lolita Files sizzles… this thriller takes on the world of book publishing… and society's obsession with fame and fortune."
—*Ebony*

Scenes

"A sas

CONNIE BRISCOE,
LOLITA FILES and
ANITA BUNKLEY

YOU ONLY GET *Better*

THREE BRILLIANT, NEW NOVELLAS

YOU ONLY GET BETTER

ISBN-13: 978-0-373-83059-6
ISBN-10:   0-373-83059-9

© 2007 by Kimani Press

The publisher acknowledges the copyright holders of the individual works
as follows:

THE PERFECT LIFE
© 2007 by Connie Briscoe

THREE FOR THE ROAD
© 2007 by Lolita Files

THIS TIME AROUND
© 2007 by Anita Bunkley

www.kimanipress.com

Printed in U.S.A.

CONTENTS

THE PERFECT LIFE

Connie Briscoe

CHAPTER 1

The brass headboard thumped against the wall as he rolled off of her and onto his back. Maxine gritted her teeth and lowered her flannel nightgown back down to her knees then stared up at the ceiling and began to count silently. One, two, three... When she reached ten, she turned her face against the cotton pillowcase and glanced at her husband. Just as she'd predicted, he was sound asleep, his fifty-year-old, sepia-toned face looking as contented as a baby's after feeding. In another ten seconds flat, Curtis would be snoring loudly enough for the neighbors to hear. Whereas it would be hours before she would be able to get even a wink of sleep.

Maxine tossed the bed quilt aside and stood with enough force to shake a mountain, even though she knew Mr. Romantic After Sex wouldn't feel the bed move. You would think she'd be used to this dull-sex routine by now. She was forty-five, they had been married for twenty years and this wham, bam, good night ma'am routine had been going on for ten of them. For years it had been tolerable. She would just roll onto her side, fume for a few minutes and doze off herself. But for the past year or so, Maxine had been having a lot of trouble falling asleep. She was also gaining weight, having hot flashes and losing her eyesight. Not only was her sex life more depressing these days, her whole life was also messed up.

She grabbed a pair of black slipper socks from the floor near the bed and put them on. This getting older was no walk in the park. In fact, it was more like a walk through hell. It certainly didn't make life's ills any easier. She opened the door and marched out of the bedroom. What she needed was a good stiff drink. A nice glass of sherry, or better yet, Tia Maria.

She made her way down the carpeted hallway without bothering to switch on a light. No need to make everyone else in the house miserable, too, by waking them. Besides, she had enough misery running through her pores at this moment for the entire household. She stopped abruptly at her daughter's closed bedroom door and stared at the orange neon Keep Out poster for a second, then twisted the knob and threw the door wide open.

Earlier that evening she had reminded Brandi for the hundredth time not to close her door as the fifteen-year-old rudely hopped up from the dinner table and stormed off because Maxine refused to let her go to a party that Saturday night. Maxine didn't like teenagers closing their bedroom doors. No telling what they were up to behind them. She hadn't allowed Brandi's older sister, Naomi, to close her door unless she was getting dressed and she wasn't going to start allowing it now.

Maxine hastily flipped on the light switch and walked up to Brandi's twin bed as the girl lifted her head and squinted against the bright ceiling light. Brandi rubbed her eyes, frowned deeply and looked up at her mother, a puzzled expression on her young tan face. She was clutching an off-white teddy bear, and a few strands of dark brown curly hair peeked out from a pink cotton scarf tied around her head.

Maxine struggled to keep her cool as she stared into the young girl's face, a face that her mother and others always said was the spitting image of her own. Maxine didn't see it. She thought Brandi was a lot cuter than she had ever been. "Didn't I tell you not to close your bedroom door?" Maxine said, hands planted firmly on her hips as she towered above the bed.

"What?"

"I've told you a thousand times to keep this door open," Maxine said, straining to keep her voice calm. Why did kids suddenly become hard of hearing when they reached the teen years? Naomi had been the same way.

Brandi glanced from her mother to the clock on her nightstand and back at her mother. "It's one o'clock in the morning, and you woke me up to tell me *that?*" Brandi tightened her clutch on the teddy bear and buried her head beneath the pillow.

"If you kept the door open like you're told, I wouldn't have to wake you up."

"It's just a damn door!" Brandi yelled, her voice slightly muffled by the pillow.

"Don't you curse at me, young lady." Maxine smacked her lips, bent over and yanked a pair of blue jeans off the floor. "And why can't you ever hang your clothes up when you take them off?" she snapped. She held the jeans out at arm's length. "I pay too much money for this stuff that you *have* to have, for you to be throwing it on the floor. I'm tired of telling you that over and over again."

Brandi yanked the pillow off her head and sat up abruptly. "Get off my back, will you? I'm trying to sleep here. You have no right to do this to me just because you're having one of your senior moments."

Maxine glared at Brandi for a second and debated what to do. She was tempted to grab the girl and drag her out of bed. But Maxine *did* feel a twinge of guilt for waking her daughter in the middle of the night, at least partly because of her frustrated sex life with her husband and partly because, well, Brandi was right. She was having a senior moment, one of those awful episodes where it felt like all the blood in her body was rushing to her head and it would burst wide open any moment. Maxine knew what that meant. A hot flash was coming on. Still, Brandi had no right to talk to her mother that way.

Maxine wiped the perspiration from her forehead with the back of her hand and threw the jeans across the seat of Brandi's desk chair. She backed out of the room and switched off the light. If there was anything more aggravating than getting older, it was having a smart-mouthed, ornery teenage daughter. Maxine had gone through this once with Naomi, now thankfully away in her freshman year of college at Hampton University, Maxine's alma mater. Maxine didn't like to admit it to anybody ever but she had actually breathed a sigh of relief when Naomi left home. One less ungrateful brat to deal with.

She walked down the short flight of stairs of the split foyer and across the family room carpet to the kitchen. She opened a cabinet, reached up for the bottle of Tia Maria and poured herself a drink, then walked back into the family room and sat on the stuffed leather armchair. She put her feet up on the footrest, took a sip and leaned her head back as the warm liquid floated through her body. Liquor seemed to make her hot flashes come even more fast and furious, but so what. It also helped her to relax.

What a chore her life had become, she thought as she glanced out the patio door. It was pitch black, but she didn't need to be able to see to know exactly what was going on out there in this cookie-cutter suburban neighborhood. Nothing. Every house, every yard, every driveway was the same, down to the little nondescript trees planted at the curb in front of each dwelling. It was the typical Maryland suburb. It was quiet, it was safe. It was also dull, just like her life.

Sometimes she missed the danger and excitement of Washington, D.C., and the early years of their family life. She and Curtis were struggling to save money to buy this house and better cars, but they were young and vibrant and always made time for dinner, dancing and outings with the girls. He regularly brought her roses and chocolates for no reason, and she made the effort to cook his favorite meals.

Somewhere along the way all of that had changed. She couldn't remember the last time Curtis brought home flowers or candy, and she hated to cook. It was hard to get up the motivation to prepare a big meal when it went unappreciated. And no one appreciated her around here anymore. Not Curtis. Not the girls. All they cared about was having clean laundry and getting three hot meals a day. If she walked out of this house tomorrow, they could find a cleaning woman and never even miss her. Curtis could pop one his precious Viagra pills and hire prostitutes for his sex life for all the romance he showed his wife.

Her weight had fluctuated a lot since she reached her forties, as she fought against regaining the extra pounds she had carried around in her childhood. Curtis used to notice whenever she gained or lost a few pounds. He generally preferred her when she had a little more meat on her bones and was more "full-figured," as he called it. But over the past year she had slowly ballooned to one hundred forty-five pounds for the first time in her life, and Curtis hadn't said a word. Not one word. She had become invisible to him.

She had had a good relationship with Brandi until about two years ago. They used to shop together, cook together and laugh at each other's jokes. She had had good relationships with both of her daughters until they turned thirteen and discovered boys. Then they seemed to think they didn't have to listen to their old, hot-flash-having mama anymore. What a pity. She had worked so hard to develop open relationships with her daughters and not to be too controlling. But if Naomi and Brandi thought that meant they could run over her and do whatever they pleased—whenever they pleased—they were dead wrong. She was still their mother and as long as either of them lived in her house, her word was law.

Which is exactly what her mama used to tell her. Maxine exhaled loudly. Sometimes she felt that she had become a watered-down version of her mother despite all her effort not to. Even her mother was telling her to lighten up with the girls these days. Just last week, Brandi brought her report card home with a D in history. Her grade in math had dropped from a B to a C, so Maxine took her cell phone and grounded her until the next marking period.

Apparently, Brandi called her grandmother very soon thereafter, because less than an hour later Maxine picked up the
phone to hear her mother's voice. "Don't you think you're
being too hard on Brandi, Maxine? I don't think I ever punished
you for longer than two weeks and never for a report card."
Maxine listened politely as her mother went on and on. She
didn't remind Francis that she was never grounded for her
report cards because she hardly ever brought home any grades
below a B. She was too scared of what would happen if she did.

Maxine lifted her head to take another sip of Tia Maria just
as the phone rang. She blinked and her thick eyelashes fluttered
rapidly as she hastily placed her glass on the coffee table. Who
would be calling at this hour? she wondered as she jumped up,
ran into the kitchen and grabbed the phone sitting on the
kitchen desk.

"Maxine," her mother said, her voice sounding high and
anxious.

"What is it, Ma? Is everything okay?"

Maxine heard her mother sigh loudly and a chill ran up her
spine. "Are you all right?" she asked anxiously.

"I'm fine. It's your Aunt Cassie. She had a heart attack.
She—" Francis paused and sniffed. "She didn't make it,"
Francis said softly.

Maxine caught her breath. "Oh, no!"

CHAPTER 2

"Oh, no," Maxine repeated as her mother sobbed softly. Maxine slowly sat down at the kitchen desk.

"Your cousin Vernon just called from the hospital in Newport News."

"Was Vernon with her when it happened?" Maxine asked.

"No. He said he stopped by her apartment after dinner and found her there on the floor. He's having a rough time. Oh, Lord. I can't imagine finding anyone dead on the floor."

"That's awful and Aunt Cassie's not that old. She's only..."

"She had just turned seventy-five last week," Francis wailed. "Just ten years older than me. I spoke to her on her birthday. We talked about getting together later this month over the Thanksgiving holidays. I can't believe this is happening."

"I'm so sorry to hear this, Ma. Do you want me to come to your house tonight?"

Francis sighed. "No. It's late and I'm fine."

"You sure? I know the two of you are close."

"Not just me. She was your favorite aunt."

"Yes, but I haven't talked to Aunt Cassie since she moved from Atlanta to Newport News five or six years ago. Now I regret not keeping in touch."

"You were real close to her daughter, Tonya, too, at one time."

Maxine swallowed hard and squeezed her eyes shut. "Yes."

"Remember when you were both little and how she used to stay with us for weeks at a time when Cassie traveled? Vernon was grown by then and living on his own. He and Tonya had different fathers and were never all that close, more like distant cousins than half brother and sister. But you and Tonya were always together, just like sisters. You were both so cute. You even looked alike."

Maxine opened her eyes and grabbed a pencil. She rolled it back and forth across the desk. How could she *not* remember? Tonya, her cousin and best friend. Tonya, her college roommate. Tonya, the man stealer.

And she and Tonya looked nothing alike. She was paper bag brown, and Tonya was café au lait, the product of a white father and a black mother. *She* was always plump as a girl, and Tonya was slim and exotic looking. *She* had short, dark, nappy hair, and Tonya's was long and curly and naturally jet black. Funny what a mother could see, or couldn't.

"That was a long time ago, Ma."

"I know. I talk to her once in a while but I haven't seen her since she moved to Bermuda a few years ago myself. I'm sure she'll be coming up for the...the funeral. Vernon said he was going to call her." Francis paused. "I still can't believe this has happened."

Maxine shook her head. "Neither can I."

"Well, I guess we have to make plans to go to Newport News on Monday or Tuesday. Vernon said we could stay with him and his wife. Do you want to drive down together?"

Maxine cleared her throat. She knew this was coming. She hadn't been back down to the Tidewater area of Virginia since she graduated from college and she had no intention of going anywhere near Tonya. She was going to have to be firm about it, because her mama could be quite persuasive when she wanted something. "I don't need to go. I haven't been in contact with them for years. And besides, Brandi..."

"But this is your aunt, Maxine. Your favorite aunt. My sister."

Maxine let out a deep gust of air. "So much is going on with

Brandi now. Her grades are slipping, and I think it's got something to do with this boy who's always calling up here. I just don't think I can leave her now."

"Bring her with you. Curtis, too."

"She can't go. She's got a history exam coming up next week."

"Well, Curtis can stay there with her then. This is important. Look, I know you had your differences with Tonya, and you all had that...that thing, that falling out. But this is family, Maxine. You have to go."

"I don't have to do anything of the sort."

Francis gasped. "What is wrong with you?"

"Nothing. I just have no interest in going down there and seeing her again. That's all."

"You mean Tonya? For goodness' sakes. That happened almost twenty-five years ago. You all were babies. I'm sure she regrets what she did, and this will be a good time to..."

"Babies?" Maxine said as she frowned into the phone. "She stole my fiancé from me, Ma. How could we have been babies?"

"You know what I mean. And I always thought she did you a favor in a way. What if you had married him? What was his name? I can't even remember now."

"Aaron. His name was Aaron. And how can you think she did me a favor by having an affair with my fiancé and running off to Las Vegas with him to get married? She was my best friend."

"Well, they never actually got married, right?"

"No. She caught him cheating on her in Vegas and called it off. At least that's what Debbie told me years ago." Debbie was her closest friend. She had also gone to Hampton University and always went to the class reunions. "She keeps up with all that stuff."

"See? They couldn't even get to the chapel before he cheated on her. Better you both found out how he was sooner rather than later. The man was obviously a bum."

"Actually I heard that he went to law school after they broke up. He was practicing at a big firm in Chicago last I heard."

"He's still a bum in my book. You know how I feel about men who can't keep their drawers up."

"Ma, please!" It always embarrassed Maxine when her mother talked bluntly about men like that.

"Humph! Don't get me started."

Maxine scoffed. "Why are we even talking about this? I don't want to go to Virginia."

"Fine. I'll just have to tell the family that you couldn't make it to your favorite aunt's funeral. And I guess I'll have to drive all the way from D.C. to Newport News, Virginia, alone since I really don't like to fly anymore. If your father was still here, he would drive with me, but he's not, so…" Francis's voice drifted off.

Maxine smiled wryly into the phone. She didn't remind her mama that that would have depended on whether her father was shacking up with one of his other women, and if they were even on speaking terms. Her daddy had passed away more than ten years ago—God rest his soul—and her mama's memory about all the ups and downs during their thirty-five years together before he died was very selective. Since her father's death, Mama had somehow managed to weed out the other women, and all that remained was the wonderful husband and father of the early years of their marriage.

Now Mama was playing the sympathy card. Well, Maxine supposed that if ever there was a time to do than it was after the death of a sister. Her mother needed her, and she was being selfish, all over something that happened aeons ago. Maxine smacked her lips. "All right, Ma. I'll go."

As soon as Maxine said it, she remembered the last time she faced Tonya and how she had slapped her across the cheek, just before she and Aaron ran off to Vegas together. She remembered telling Tonya that she hoped the two of them and all their kids and grandkids rotted in hell for all eternity.

Maxine pushed the eraser end of the pencil against the desk, and it snapped and broke in two. She could feel another hot flash coming on as a wave of heat rushed through her body. Tension always seemed to trigger them. And nothing was more tense than remembering those last days at Hampton Institute—as it was then called—and getting the fateful news from Tonya and Aaron.

CHAPTER 3

Maxine descended the steps of the student cafeteria in Virginia-Cleveland Hall two at a time as a feeling of elation washed over her. She had just eaten her last dinner in the cafeteria at Hampton Institute, and tomorrow afternoon she would march triumphantly across the stage to accept her bachelor's degree. Her emotions had been like a roller coaster the past few days. Down at the thought of leaving the college after four years. Up because she was finally graduating and moving on to start a brand-new life working as an elementary school teacher.

And in a little more than a month, on June 20, she was going to marry her sweetheart of the past three years. She felt so lucky. The only thing bothering her was the extra twelve pounds she'd gained over the past few months, as she had just explained to her roommate, Dee Dee, in the cafeteria.

"I'm gonna start working out right after graduation tomorrow," Maxine said. "I *have* to get into that size-ten wedding gown even if it kills me. Mama and Daddy spent a fortune on that dress."

Maxine turned her head and looked at Dee Dee, walking beside her as they crossed the circle in front of Ogden Hall. The expression on Dee Dee's pale pretty face, with its lips turned down, was the polar opposite of the way Maxine felt at that moment.

"Come on, girl," Maxine said as she playfully nudged Dee Dee's arm. "What you looking so glum for? In less than twenty-four hours we're out of this place for good. It's time to celebrate!" Maxine skipped across the grassy area in her high platform sandals, and her bell-bottom jeans flapped in the breeze as she twirled around in happiness.

"You gonna fall over on your face running around like that in those shoes," Dee Dee said.

Maxine giggled and ran back toward her friend. She hugged Dee Dee's slender frame, smashing the side of her short brown Afro against Dee Dee's big, curly do.

Dee Dee smiled thinly. "Okay, okay. Jeez, girl."

Maxine let Dee Dee go. "You're going to miss this place. Is that it?"

Dee Dee shrugged and twisted her mouth, and the little black mole just above her thin upper lip disappeared. "I guess."

"I know. Me, too. But look at it this way." Maxine took Dee Dee by the arms and turned her until their faces were inches apart. "We're starting a new life together," Maxine said as she looked into Dee Dee's saucer-shape hazel eyes. "And we're homies. We'll still be able to see each other and hang out. It's just that we'll be doing it in the real world now. And I'll be a *Mrs.—Mrs.* Aaron Robinson." Maxine giggled. She loved how that sounded. "All I have to do is lose some of this weight so I can get into my dress. You don't have that problem, naturally. You should still be able to fit into your maid of honor dress."

Dee Dee looked down toward the ground. "Uh-huh."

Maxine touched Dee Dee's chin and tilted her head back up. "Oh, girl, would you please cheer up? You'll find yourself a man one of these days."

Dee Dee pulled her chin away. "It's not even about that. I...I guess I just keep thinking about all the people we're leaving behind, people we might not see anymore."

Maxine nodded in agreement and squeezed Dee Dee's arms. "This isn't about Douglas, is it?"

Dee Dee blinked and stepped out of Maxine's grasp. "Nah. I'm way past that."

"Good, 'cause that dude was definitely not right for you," Maxine said, planting her fists on her hips. "He's such a dumb ass."

"He wasn't that bad."

"He wasn't good enough for you, always standing you up and making you go to him. Later for that. You need someone who treats you good. Like Aaron. Everybody deserves a man like Aaron. I know you get tired of hearing me say stuff like that, but I can't help it. It's true." Maxine laughed as Dee Dee rolled her eyes skyward.

"So you're always telling me," Dee Dee said.

"Maybe you'll even meet somebody at our wedding. A lot of Aaron's friends will be there. A couple of them are *fine,* too, girl."

"Enough with the pity party, please," Dee Dee said. "I'm doing okay." She glanced at her watch. "Speaking of Aaron, we should get going. Isn't he meeting us in front of the dorm in, like, two minutes?"

"It's just across the way. And for some reason, he's always late picking me up these days. I don't know what's up with him sometimes."

Dee Dee nodded just as Maxine spotted a black Chevrolet Stingray in the distance pulling up in front of the coed dorm. The car was an early graduation gift from Aaron's folks. Maxine had been more excited when he got it than Aaron was. She loved cruising around campus with him. "Look," she said excitedly, pointing in that direction. "There's Aaron now."

"See? I told you we needed to get moving," Dee Dee said as they walked briskly toward the dorm.

"I'm shocked," Maxine said. "He's hardly ever on time anymore. Come on, let's get this party started." She tugged at Dee Dee, and they picked up the pace. "You should call Melvin and ask him to come with us."

Dee Dee turned up her nose. "I don't think so. He's not my type."

Maxine shrugged. "I just thought it would be cool to have another dude with us, make it a double date. Melvin's not as fine as Douglas but he really digs you."

"Like I said, he really isn't my type."

"Fine. You can just hang out with us. I'm sure Aaron won't mind."

When they reached the coed dorm, Aaron was standing at the top of the steps waiting. He smiled and Maxine thought he looked so cute in his bell-bottom jeans and red, black and green dashiki. He had one of the biggest Afros on any guy at Hampton Institute and his black platform shoes extended his height to well over its natural six feet. Maxine ran up and stood on her toes to plant a big kiss on his lips. Dee Dee stood off to Maxine's side and lit a Salem Light.

Maxine tucked an arm around Aaron's waistline, and he casually slung his arm around her shoulders. "Did you turn the English paper in to Dr. Lutz yet?" she asked.

"Yeah, I got that done," Aaron said.

"So you'll graduate on time tomorrow?" Dee Dee asked.

Aaron smiled broadly and gave a thumbs-up. "It's in the bag, baby."

"Cool," Dee Dee said.

Maxine frowned. She wondered how Dee Dee even knew that Aaron had a paper to turn in before he could graduate. She couldn't remember discussing it with Dee Dee. She made a mental note to ask Dee Dee how she knew later. Right now, it wasn't that important. Celebrating was.

"So, where do y'all want to go?" Maxine asked, looking from one to the other. "I heard about this party over in Norfolk. It'll be tight in the Vette, but we've done it before." Maxine laughed at the thought of the three of them piling into Aaron's two seater.

Dee Dee took a long drag off her cigarette. "Um…listen. Maybe I should stay…"

Maxine held up her hand in front of her friend's face. "Uh-

uh. You're not backing out now, Dee Dee. This is our last night here, and you are the two people closest to me on campus. I want us all to be together, whatever we decide to do."

Dee Dee blinked. She stomped her foot and looked past Maxine directly at Aaron. "Well?"

Aaron took his arm from around Dee Dee's shoulders and shoved both hands into his jeans pockets. "Um…" He paused and the most puzzling expression crossed his face.

Maxine frowned as she ran her hand across the top of her Afro. What was going on here? 'Cause something was unsettling as heck, like when you hear a soft sound in the house and don't know where it came from.

She looked up at Aaron. "What is it, honey? What's going on?"

Aaron glanced at Maxine then quickly cast his eyes away. "We need to talk."

"So fine. Let's talk."

"Not here." He gestured toward the dormitory building behind them. "Let's go up to your room first."

What could be so important that he wanted to talk to her in private right this minute? Maxine wondered. She hoped he wasn't getting cold feet. Just last week, he had expressed reservations about getting married so soon after graduation, but she managed to put him at ease. Or so she thought.

"It's messy up there now with us packing, but, okay, if that's what you want." Maxine started toward the door and glanced back at Dee Dee. "We'll be right back."

"You should come up with us," she heard Aaron say from behind her.

"Ah, I think I'll just…"

"I *need* you to come up," Aaron said firmly.

Maxine froze in her step. *I need you to come up.* What did that mean? And why was Aaron talking to Dee Dee that way? Suddenly the soft sound was more like a loud thud.

Dee Dee stomped her cigarette out as Aaron ran up in front

of Maxine and held the glass door open. Maxine tried to catch a look from Dee Dee as they entered the building, but Dee Dee avoided looking directly at her. Maxine swallowed hard as the three of them walked past the front desk and headed for the elevator. As they rode up to the room that Maxine shared with Dee Dee, each of them stood in silence with their backs to a different wall, and Maxine noted with alarm that neither Aaron nor Dee Dee seemed able to look directly at her. She fidgeted with the wooden beads around her neck.

Something odd was going on here and Maxine didn't like the feel of it one bit. Her mind raced back quickly over the past several weeks. She had thought that Aaron was acting a little weird but brushed it off as anxiety about the upcoming wedding. He was a man, wasn't he? And marriage made all men nervous, even when they were in love. For the most part, Aaron was still his old sweet, loving self. He was late more often than usual, and that was exasperating, but otherwise he was pretty much the same.

Dee Dee also had seemed off over the past weeks. She was distant and easily agitated, especially whenever Maxine talked about the wedding. But Maxine thought she was just emotional about coming to the end of her stay at Hampton Institute. She also thought that maybe Dee Dee hadn't quite gotten over her failed relationship with Douglas even though it had ended months ago, and Dee Dee swore she was past it. It probably didn't help that she was always blabbing about her upcoming nuptials and the elaborate wedding plans while her friend was having man trouble. Dee Dee probably felt it was being rubbed in her face. Maxine made a mental note to try not to talk about the wedding so much.

Still, she wondered if she had brushed those uneasy feelings off too easily, and Aaron and Dee Dee were about to tell her that the two of them were... Maxine took a deep breath and shoved the nasty thought out of her head. No way would the two people she loved most in the world outside her immediate family do something like that to her.

She had met Aaron at a Groove Phi Groove party in their sophomore year just before he pledged, and the two of them had been a couple ever since. Whenever anyone saw one of them in public, they saw the other or knew that the other was somewhere close by. Whenever someone mentioned one, they mentioned the other. *Aaron and Maxine did this. Maxine and Aaron are going to do that.* Dee Dee was always joking that they were joined at the hip, like Siamese twins.

If anything, Maxine was even closer to Dee Dee than she was to Aaron. They had known each other all their lives, from the moment their mothers stuck them in playpens together. They were cousins and lifelong best friends and lived within a few short miles of each other. If for one moment Maxine could imagine that Aaron would deceive her—and she had a hard time imagining that—she was positive that her cousin would never do anything to hurt her.

It had to be something else. But what?

The elevator door opened and Aaron stood aside as Dee Dee and then Maxine exited. Maxine deliberately stayed behind the two of them as they walked down the hallway toward the dorm room. She was looking for a sign, anything that might give her a clue as to what was going on. She studied Dee Dee's face closely as her roommate removed the door key from her blue beaded shoulder bag and inserted it into the lock. Dee Dee's face was expressionless, and that in itself was odd given what a happy time this should have been for all of them.

Dee Dee opened the door, and Maxine stepped into the room first and tossed her leather shoulder bag onto the patchwork quilt neatly covering her twin bed. As usual, Dee Dee's bed was still unmade, and it was piled high with clothes that Dee Dee hadn't gotten around to packing just yet. Maxine stood in the middle of the narrow room, now filled with packed boxes, and turned to face the two of them as they entered.

"Okay. What's this all about?"

Dee Dee strode past her and dropped her beaded shoulder

bag on the small desk at the end of her twin bed. She pulled out the desk chair, and the legs scraped loudly as she dragged it across the floor and placed it in front of the lone window in the room. "Do you want to sit?" she asked Maxine, indicating the chair.

Immediately, Maxine wondered if someone close to her had died. But that didn't sit right. Why would Dee Dee have waited so long to tell her something that serious when they had been together all afternoon? Why would they both have stood on the stoop in front of the dorm talking casually and joking around if someone close to her had died or taken ill? "No, thanks," Maxine said tersely. "I'll stand."

Dee Dee sat in the chair herself, crossed her legs and looked up at Aaron. Maxine stood near her bed and followed Aaron with her eyes as he paced slowly up and down the tiny room, walking from the chair where Dee sat to the door at the other end. He paused suddenly at the door and turned abruptly to face Maxine.

"Just say it," Dee Dee blurted out from behind Maxine. "She's got to know."

Maxine turned to Dee Dee, then back to Aaron. "Say what? Damn it! Will somebody please tell me what the hell is going on?"

CHAPTER 4

"Maybe you should tell her," Aaron said suddenly, looking sheepishly at Dee Dee. "You've known her all your life."

"But you're the one engaged to her."

Maxine walked up to Aaron. "Is this about the wedding, Aaron? Are you getting cold feet?"

Aaron looked down at the floor, and Maxine whirled around and faced her cousin. "Somebody talk to me, for God's sake. What is going on here? Dee Dee?"

Dee Dee stood up and squared her shoulders. "You could say that he's getting cold feet. Right, Aaron?"

Aaron nodded. "Sort of."

Maxine nodded, too, and touched his arm gently. "Well, that happens, baby. You and me can talk about it. Last week, we…"

"It's really more than that," Aaron said, interrupting. He looked down at Maxine with the saddest expression she had ever seen on his face. "I'm sorry, baby. The wedding is off."

Maxine's eyes grew wide. It felt as if he had just taken his fist and knocked her upside the head. "I…I don't understand. We've been planning this for almost a year. We're going to get married in June. Then I start teaching in September and you…you start law school at Georgetown. Right, honey?"

Silence.

"Talk to me, Aaron," Maxine said impatiently. She was sick of all this hedging. "Is there someone else? Just come out and tell me."

He tightened his lips and looked at Maxine. "I'm sorry," he said. "We didn't mean for this to happen. It just did."

Maxine caught her breath. Oh, no. She turned and looked straight at Dee Dee.

"Like he said, it just happened. One thing led to the next and…"

Maxine's mouth dropped open, and the room began to spin. "No, no. Are you telling me that you two…" She shook her head to clear it and stumbled as she took a step back toward her bed. The room was spinning madly now, the floor twirling round and round beneath her feet. She flopped down on the bed and put both hands out to steady herself.

Suddenly she realized that her breathing was blocked, as though someone was holding a plastic bag over her head. "Oh, God." She grabbed her throat and opened her mouth widely. Her chest heaved in and out as she tried to suck in some air. Aaron ran to the window and opened it as Dee Dee jumped up, took a step toward Maxine and placed a hand on her shoulder.

"Are you all right?" Dee Dee asked anxiously.

Maxine slapped Dee Dee's hand away and yelled at her. "Hell, no." She stood, still heaving as she tried to catch her breath. "Get away from me."

Dee Dee held her hands out and backed off as Maxine ran to the window and stuck her head out. She inhaled deeply as the two of them stood behind her and watched. As soon as she got a good mouthful of air, Maxine clenched her fists, turned and glared at them both.

"This is disgusting. How the hell does this just happen? Will you please explain that to me?"

"I…" Aaron paused, unable to continue.

"How long has it been going on?"

"About three or four months," he said. "I tried to tell you a few weeks ago, but I couldn't."

"I wanted to tell you, too, but…"

"Oh, please," Maxine said, interrupting Dee Dee. "I don't believe either one of you. And what about us, Aaron? Did you just stop loving me?"

"I still care about you, Maxine. But not in that way. Not anymore. With Dee Dee I..."

"Shut up!" she yelled. "Don't say that to me!" She ran up to him and pounded his chest with her fists. "You no-good bastard! How could you go and screw around with my best friend?"

He grabbed her by the shoulders and held her back. "It just happened."

"Stop saying that. Stuff like this doesn't just happen." She wiped the tears from her cheeks with the back of her hand. "Three years, Aaron. I gave you almost three years of my life. I thought you loved me. I thought we would be together forever. And what about all our wedding plans? I have a dress, the invitations have been printed. Oh, God."

She sobbed and turned to face her roommate. "And you. I...I don't even know what to say to you, Tonya." She shook her head and stared at her cousin, speechless for a moment. "Why? Why?"

Tonya closed her eyes then opened them. "I wish I could tell you. We would have stopped it if we could have."

Maxine snarled. "You make me sick to my stomach."

Tonya gritted her teeth, and Maxine's eyes traveled to the mole above her lips. She had once loved that mole. Now she wanted to reach out and rip it off Tonya's face. "Get out."

"What?"

"I said get out! Both of you."

Aaron backed toward the door. "Come on, Dee Dee."

"Hell, no, this is my room, too," Tonya protested.

"I don't give a damn," Maxine said. "I want you both out of here. Now."

Aaron opened the door. "Dee Dee, we should go. We can finish this later."

"This *is* finished as far as I'm concerned," Maxine said, glaring at Tonya.

Tonya glared back. "I'll meet you downstairs in a minute, baby," she said, never taking her eyes off Maxine.

Maxine rolled her eyes to the ceiling as Aaron left the room and shut the door. The two of them stared each other down for a minute.

"I'm going to go for now," Tonya said finally. "But I just wanted to remind you that this is still my room, too. I can come and go whenever I want."

"Over my dead body. I can't stand the sight of you now. I trusted you. You and me were like sisters. And you pull this crap."

"You always say we're like sisters but you have never treated me like your equal. It's always about you, you, you. What *Maxine* is doing and what *Maxine* wants. So don't throw that sister crap up in my face."

"I don't know what you're talking about. I always treated you like a sister. We all did. My mother, my father and me. My parents helped you with your tuition here. Hell, half the time my mother is more concerned about you than she is about me. She treats you like her daughter."

"And you can't stand that, can you?"

"Get out," Maxine said quietly between clenched teeth.

Tonya placed her hand on the doorknob. "I'll be back tomorrow. I still have things to pack."

Maxine ran up to Tonya's bed and grabbed an armful of clothes.

"What the hell are you doing?" Tonya asked, her eyes wide with alarm.

Maxine didn't say a word as she ran toward the open window. Tonya flew across the room, jumped in front of her and reached for the clothes. They wrestled and bumped into an open box perched on the edge of Tonya's desk. It tumbled over, and paper, pencils, erasers and books fell out all over the floor.

Finally, Maxine grunted and shoved Tonya into the desk. Then she leaped for the window and tossed the clothes out. She turned around with a smug look on her face. "Not anymore, you don't." She marched toward Tonya's closet and threw it open.

"Stop it!" Tonya yelled in protest. "Who the hell do you think you are? You can't do this."

"Watch me." Maxine reached into Tonya's closet, grabbed another armful of clothes, hangers and all and raced to the window.

"You're crazy!" Tonya yelled. "Okay, listen. I'll leave if you stop this."

Maxine paused a few feet from the window. "Fine. Go."

"I just need to come back at some point to get my things."

"Just go." Maxine turned her back to Tonya.

"I'm gone. If you need to reach me, I'll be in Aaron's room." The door slammed shut.

What had she done? She had just sent the bitch straight to her fiancé. Correction. Her *ex-fiancé*. Maxine stomped her foot, marched up to the window and threw the clothes out.

CHAPTER 5

Maxine jumped and opened her eyes to find her husband standing above her dressed in khakis and a ribbed pullover. He gently shook her shoulder.

"Max, wake up, honey. It's almost ten o'clock."

"Huh?" She blinked sleepily and sat up. She stretched and a sharp pain traveled down her back. That was when she realized she was still in the leather armchair in the family room, her feet propped up on the footrest. She had been having a nightmare about Tonya.

In less than an hour's time that day at the dorm her life had been turned upside down. The next afternoon, when she walked across the stage to get her degree, she was in a daze, unable to believe what had happened the day before. She didn't tell anyone, not even her parents when they arrived for the graduation ceremony. Her mother knew something was up as Aaron was nowhere around. But it wasn't until she had been safely back at home for a week that she could talk about it and a year before she began to date again.

She had spoken to Tonya only once after that disastrous day in the dorm room. Tonya had returned to the room, and when her parents went down to load the car, Maxine told Tonya that she hoped she would burn in hell for all eternity. She had never talked to Aaron again.

"Ouch," Maxine said as she placed her bare feet on the carpeted floor. She arched her back to stretch out the pain.

"Don't tell me you slept down here all night," Curtis said.

"Okay, then I won't tell you."

"Very funny," he said, chuckling as he walked through the archway into the kitchen. "You want some bacon and eggs?"

She shook her head. "No, thanks. Is Brandi up yet?"

Curtis scoffed. "Before noon? No way."

Maxine stood. "I'm going to wake her up."

"Let her sleep."

"She sleeps too much."

"That's what teenagers do."

Maxine put on her slipper socks, then entered the kitchen as Curtis removed a cast-iron skillet from a base cabinet. The enticing aroma of fresh coffee filled the air. Curtis made coffee every night and set the timer for the following morning.

"I can't believe I fell to sleep down here. I'll be sore for two days."

"You'll live," he said as he placed two mugs on the counter-top.

Maxine bent over and touched her toes. "You didn't even realize I wasn't in bed?"

"Not until this morning. I was knocked out."

"That figures," she said sarcastically.

"What's that supposed to mean?"

"Nothing," she said as she stretched her arms above her head. "Just that sex is like a drug for you."

He shrugged. "What can I say? It relaxes me."

"Wish I could say the same."

"So do I. But nothing relaxes you lately, Maxine. I keep telling you to take up yoga or tennis or something to relax. You're almost always wound up about something or other. That's going to get harder on your body as you get older, you know."

"You trying to tell me that I'm getting old?"

"Trying?"

Maxine put her hands on her hips in mock anger, and Curtis laughed.

"You know I'm playing with you."

"My body is changing, and it's driving me nuts. It's harder to knock off the weight. And these hot flashes. Ugh!"

"You still look good to me. I just wish you would take better care of yourself."

She shrugged. "I probably could do a better job of that." Maxine sighed dismissively and stopped stretching. "Mama called last night."

"I heard the phone ring. Is everything all right?"

"She's fine. But Aunt Cassie passed away sometime yesterday evening."

Curtis paused as he cracked an egg over a ceramic bowl and looked at her. "Oh, no. What happened?"

"Heart attack. Ma wants me to drive down with her for the funeral."

"That's a three-hour drive. Why don't you all fly?"

"I would, but Mama doesn't really like to fly."

"Do you want us to come with you?"

Maxine shook her head. "No. You never met Aunt Cassie, and Brandi has an exam next week. I don't want her to miss it, given her grades recently."

"I agree with that."

"I don't even really want to go myself, but Mama's counting on me."

"Weren't you close to your aunt and her daughter when you were growing up?"

Maxine nodded.

"What was the daughter's name? Dee or something."

"Tonya. But everyone called her Dee Dee. I haven't talked to Aunt Cassie in ages and not to Tonya since we graduated from Hampton."

Curtis nodded and chuckled. "Oh, yeah. I remember now. She's the one who ran off with your old college sweetheart."

"Yes, and it's not funny. She was my best friend."

"When it happened, I'm sure it wasn't funny. And I don't mean to make fun now, but it was so long ago. Kid stuff."

"You sound like my mother. We weren't kids. I was engaged to him. It was a horrible time and now it's all being dragged up again."

"It was pretty rotten of them, I admit. But look at it this way." He turned to face her, spoon in one hand, and his brown saucer-shape eyes smiled as he touched her nose gently with his fingertip. "If you had married him, you would never have met me."

"True, dear. But I think you're missing the point here."

"Am *I* the one missing the point?"

Maxine let out an exaggerated gust of air and poured herself a mug of coffee. "Oh, you. You're impossible. I'm going to get dressed and get Lazybones up." She turned toward the doorway with her mug then doubled back. "On second thought, maybe I will have some breakfast after I get dressed."

"I knew you were going to change your mind," Curtis said as he poured a bowlful of eggs into the pan. "I already got you covered. Brandi, too."

She walked up the stairs and into Brandi's room and tapped her on the shoulder. "Breakfast will be ready in fifteen minutes," she said.

Brandi opened her eyes and rolled over on her back. "I smell bacon. You mean, *you're* cooking breakfast on a Saturday?"

"Don't be ridiculous," Maxine said, chuckling. She hadn't fixed a big breakfast since Brandi entered high school a year ago. These days, her idea of cooking breakfast was placing boxes of cereal on the kitchen table, along with bowls and spoons. She was really whipping it up if she placed the milk in a pitcher. "Your father is cooking."

"Figures," Brandi said, wiping her eyes sleepily. She pulled the scarf off her head and tossed it onto the bed.

"Smart mouth," Maxine said as she sat on the edge of the bed. She placed the coffee mug on the nightstand and gently tapped Brandi's leg. "Sit up. I have something important to tell you."

Brandi stretched leisurely and sat up.

"You've heard me talk about Aunt Cassie, right?"

"Uh-huh."

"You never met her but she passed away last night, so I'll be driving down to Newport News with Grandma next week."

Brandi nodded. "Sorry to hear that, Ma. How long will you be gone?"

"We'll probably leave Monday or Tuesday and come back around Friday. That will give us a day or two to visit with relatives down there. Uncle Vernon and his wife and some other cousins."

"That's where Grandma is from, right?"

Maxine nodded. "She moved up here to go to college at Howard University. But then she met my father and—"

"Got pregnant with you and dropped out," Brandi said, interrupting. "That's why she had to settle for being a secretary in the government instead of becoming a teacher. Blah, blah, blah."

Maxine smiled wryly. "Which is exactly why I always tell you not to let that happen to you."

"Yeah, yeah. I know."

Maxine noticed a window was open and went to close it. "Why on earth do you have a window open in November? All the heat is going out of the house."

"I was hot."

As soon as Maxine shut the window she noticed an unpleasant odor just beneath the aroma of bacon and coffee filling the house. She faced Brandi and eyed her suspiciously. "Were you smoking cigarettes in here last night?"

Brandi raised her eyebrows. "Me? No."

Maxine marched back toward the bed and stood above Brandi. "Don't you lie to me."

"I haven't been smoking."

"Then why do I smell smoke?"

Brandi shrugged insolently. "Beats me. You started back smoking?"

"Don't you sass me, young lady. I haven't had a cigarette in five years." Maxine yanked the covers off Brandi. What was she ever going to do with this girl? She was positive that she smelled cigarette smoke and that this had something to do with that boy who was always calling up here lately.

"Get up out of that bed this minute and get dressed. After breakfast I want you to start studying for your exam. And if I ever, *ever* even think I smell smoke in this room again you are grounded until you're eighteen. You got that?"

"I hear you."

"You know that smoking is bad for…"

The phone rang and Maxine paused while Brandi reached out to her nightstand and grabbed it. "Hello?" Brandi said, suddenly sounding like she had been awake for hours. "Just a minute." Brandi covered the mouthpiece. "It's for you. It's Debbie."

Maxine nodded. "I'll take it in my bedroom," she said as she retrieved her coffee mug. "I want you up and dressed."

Maxine took a deep breath outside Brandi's room to calm herself then walked to her bedroom and picked up the extension. She was planning to call Debbie and tell her about Aunt Cassie. Although she had known Debbie in college, they hadn't become close friends until after graduation. Debbie never knew Aunt Cassie or Tonya but she knew all about them, thanks to Maxine. Debbie was the kind of friend one could confide in, and Maxine needed to confide in someone now.

"Hi, Debbie. I was about to call you," Maxine said as she sat on her bed.

"Hey, girl. I was calling to see if you wanted to go to the mall this afternoon. They're having some great sales."

"I don't think so. Things are too crazy around here. I just caught Brandi smoking—or least I caught the smell in her room." Maxine sighed loudly.

"Oh, no!" Debbie said. "Cigarettes or pot?"

"Cigarettes. I already went through the pot smoking with Naomi."

"I remember. Did you talk to her?"

"I tried to. Or yelled at her is more like it." She would certainly have to have a much longer talk with Brandi at some point. "But you know how that is. Sometimes I think teenagers go through a period of deafness."

Debbie chuckled.

"Enough about that for now. My aunt passed away last night, and I'm going to have to drive down to Newport News with my mother for the funeral."

"I'm so sorry to hear that. Is this Aunt Cassie? The one you always used to talk about?"

"The one and only."

"You were so close to her at one time. I'll say a prayer for you and your mom tonight."

Debbie was a big-time prayer and she attended church most Sundays. She didn't go around wearing religion on her sleeve and try to convert everyone or anything like that. She didn't even really stick to a particular denomination. One year she would attend a Baptist church, the next a Catholic one. Currently, she was into her nondenominational phase. But regardless of which church Debbie was attending, she really believed that prayer worked and she had special prayers for just about everything. "Thanks, Debbie."

"I hate to even mention this, but will you-know-who be coming up from Bermuda?"

"Most likely."

"I just read her latest novel, *Lonesome Life*."

"Did you now?" Maxine asked with more than a little sarcasm in her voice.

"Uh-huh. It takes place in Bermuda, and I have to admit it was interesting. The way she described the settings was so romantic, and there's this one hunk in it who…"

"Thanks a lot, girlfriend," Maxine said, interrupting.

"Oops. Sorry. Guess I got carried away. You've never read any of her novels? She must have written six or seven of them by now."

"Never. But I'm not surprised that her descriptions are nice. She wrote a lot of poetry when we were in college, and it was actually pretty good. But that's enough talk about Tonya's novels for one day if you don't mind."

"Oookay. Moving on then. When are you leaving for the funeral?"

"Probably Monday or Tuesday. I want to be there for my mother and I look forward to seeing some of my relatives, but I definitely have no interest in seeing her again. And that's putting it mildly."

"I don't blame you after what she did to you. Do you think Mr. Big Shot Lawyer will be there?"

Maxine paused and closed her eyes. Aaron! He had never entered her mind. "Oh, hell. I never even thought about that."

"Well, you better start thinking about it. Your aunt was almost his mother-in-law."

Maxine swallowed hard. "Oh, hell."

"You said that already. Girl, you need to get your mind wrapped around this."

"God, Debbie. I don't want to deal with this. I thought I had put all that behind me."

"Obviously, you haven't put it all behind you. This is probably happening for a reason."

"And what would that be? To torture me?"

"No, silly. You know what I mean. God always has a purpose."

"Fine, Debbie, but meanwhile what am I going to do if Aaron shows up? I can't face him. He dumped me for my best friend, and I'm sure everybody down there knows it. I'll be the laughingstock of the whole funeral."

"A woman just died, Maxine. Do you honestly think people at the funeral are going to be looking at you and thinking about something that happened more than twenty years ago?"

"Yes. You know how people are. They won't say anything to my face but they'll be whispering behind my back."

"You're probably right, now that I think about it. But..."

"Oh, God."

"You gotta stay cool, Maxine. You're a married woman now with two beautiful daughters."

"Right."

"Just act like it means nothing to you."

"I can't do that. They screwed me good. I can't pretend it never happened."

"What else are you going to do? Go down there and kick both their asses?"

Maxine sighed into the phone. "I'm tempted."

"Want me to come with you? I can put some of my old karate chop lessons to good use."

Maxine laughed. Trust her girlfriend to cheer her up. Despite her wayward teenage daughter and something as dreaded as meeting up with Tonya and Aaron, Debbie could still put a grin on her face.

"No, really, Maxine. You just gotta play it cool. Wear something sharp and expensive looking. Get your hair done. Make sure you look like a million dollars. Then go there acting like you're at the top of your game. Brag about Curtis and the kids. Curtis has a nice steady job and he treats you well. You got a good man there."

"Good, yes," Maxine said. "But he's a boring accountant. And my daughters are like the teenagers from hell."

"You didn't think Curtis was so boring when you met him. I remember you thought he was fine. You couldn't stop talking about his sexy brown eyes."

Maxine smiled at the memory. "Well, yes. He was a drummer in a band then, and he looked sexy sitting behind that drum set. Kinda short, but cute. He's changed since then. He hasn't touched those drums since Naomi was born."

"We've all changed, Max. Don't be surprised if Aaron and Tonya aren't what you expect, either."

CHAPTER 6

Maxine walked into Brandi's room Monday evening to find her lounging on her bed talking on the telephone, her books and papers scattered out beside her. Maxine strode to the foot of the bed and folded her arms across her waist.

Brandi covered the mouthpiece and looked at her. "Yeah?"

"Girl, I just know you've finished your homework if you have the time to run your mouth on the phone."

Brandi smiled sheepishly. "Just about."

"Just about isn't good enough. Who is that?"

"Eric."

"Get off that phone this minute and finish your homework. It's almost ten o'clock."

Brandi let out an exaggerated breath of air. "I have to go," she said into the mouthpiece. "I'll see you at school tomorrow."

"Do you think life is all about boys and parties?" Maxine said as Brandi hung up the phone. "Because it's not. I've told you a hundred times no talking on the phone until your homework is done."

"Eric called to ask about our English homework."

"I bet."

"Well, he did, and Daddy said it was okay for me to talk to him for a few minutes."

"Well, Daddy was mistaken. The rule is no talking on the phone until your homework is done, especially to boys."

"Well, Daddy said I could," Brandi repeated snidely. "I can't help it if somebody calls me. You want me to be mean and hang up on 'em? Just 'cause you would do that doesn't mean I would."

She slapped Brandi hard across the face. A rash of pink flowed across Brandi's cheek as she clutched it. Tears welled up in her eyes. For a second Maxine hated herself. She had slapped Naomi across the cheek a few times during her teen years and always felt badly afterward. No matter how difficult her girls got, it never felt right when she hit them, whether a spanking on their buttocks when they were young or smacking them as teens, and she had promised herself never to slap Brandi. Now she had just broken that promise. But she was feeling more stressed than usual with the death of her aunt, and this ornery child had it coming.

Brandi turned away from her mother, her face filled with resentment.

Maxine closed and opened her eyes. "Why are you so difficult? You always got something smart to say."

"I won't open my mouth ever again. Will that make you happy?"

Maxine clenched and unclenched her fists. The sassy comments never stopped coming, but she decided to ignore them for now. "Look, I don't want to argue anymore. I came up here to tell you that I'm leaving early tomorrow morning before you get up."

"When will you be back?" Brandi asked, not looking directly at her mother. But Maxine couldn't help but notice the expression of relief on her daughter's face. What Brandi really wanted to know was how many days of freedom she would have until her mama's return.

"Probably Friday. The funeral is on Wednesday, day after tomorrow. But Ma wants to stick around on Thursday to visit with relatives down there."

"Fine."

"You behave yourself while I'm gone. And definitely no smoking. Understand?"

Brandi nodded silently without looking up. Maxine walked to the door, paused and turned back to face Brandi. "I'm sorry I hit you. But you can be so trying at times."

"Likewise," Brandi said.

Maxine rolled her eyes to the ceiling with resignation and walked down to the family room where Curtis was sitting at one end of the tan leather couch watching CNN. She flopped down on the other end of the couch, leaned back and closed her eyes. She could hear the voice of a reporter interviewing someone about terrorism. But Maxine had a lot of personal things on her mind—the death of her aunt, the drive down to Newport News the following morning, Brandi's impossible behavior, seeing Tonya and possibly Aaron again for the first time in years—and the reporter's voice was getting on her nerves.

She looked at Curtis out of the corner of her eye. She was leaving early tomorrow morning on a road trip, and she would have thought that her husband would realize that she needed to talk to him. "Do you see me sitting here?"

Curtis glanced at her and blinked with surprise. "What?"

She gestured toward the television. "Do you have to have that so loud?"

Curtis picked up the remote from the coffee table and turned the volume down. "Sorry. I didn't realize it was bothering you."

She scoffed loudly. "I'm leaving at six a.m. and I have a million things to do. I have to finish packing, and we need to talk before I go. Or did you forget that I was leaving?"

"C'mon, Max. There's no need to be so sarcastic. What you got on your mind?"

"Right now, Brandi. I just slapped her."

Curtis shook his head sadly.

"Well, say something," Maxine said. "I know you don't approve."

"Do you care whether or not I do?"

Maxine folded her arms defiantly. "I can't stand it when she gets smart with me."

"I don't like it either, Max, but I haven't hit her since she was about ten years old and that was an occasional tap on the butt. Naomi, either. I talk to them now."

Maxine sat up abruptly and glared at him. "Well, I'm not you," she said sharply.

Curtis gritted his teeth. "I don't like you smacking them. You did it with Naomi almost up until she left for college. You don't have to be so tough on them. They're good kids."

"Maybe if you weren't so lenient, letting them do anything they want when they want, I wouldn't have to be so tough on them. Brandi was just on the phone with some boy, but she still hasn't finished her homework. Then she tells me, 'Well, Daddy said I could.' You let them get away with murder."

"One of her classmates called to ask about the homework. I was in her room when the call came and told her she could talk for a few minutes."

"That's just the point, Curtis. Didn't we say *no* phone and *no* TV until her homework is done? No, means no, at least it does to me. That's a terrible way to raise a child."

"Are you saying I'm a bad parent? You have to have some flexibi—"

"Making rules and then allowing her to break them is wrong," Maxine said, interrupting him, her voice rising. "Any idiot knows that."

"That was uncalled for. And you don't have to shout. I'm sitting right here."

"Well, why don't you get that?"

"Why don't *you* get it. You're too rigid. Any parent needs to have some flexibility."

She stood with exasperation. "You have too much damn flexibility."

"Okay, okay," Curtis said, obviously struggling to calm himself. "Sit back down and let's talk it out calmly. We won't get anywhere if you jump up and run off."

"I don't need to get into this now. I have too much to do."

"Fine," Curtis said and picked up the remote. He turned the volume back up.

Maxine threw her hands in the air. "Will you turn that thing back down?"

Curtis turned the volume down. "I thought you just said you were done talking."

"About the kids, yes. But I wanted to tell you that I'm leaving at six a.m. to pick up my mother. We'll be staying with Vernon, and the phone number is on the desk in the kitchen."

Curtis nodded. "Is that it?"

"Yes," she said with finality and walked off to finish packing for the trip. She hated the idea of leaving for a long trip after arguing bitterly with her daughter and especially with Curtis. But they could both be so infuriating at times.

She went to the closet, picked out her black dress shoes and slipped them inside a cloth pouch. She walked to the bed, flipped open the top to her Tumi bag and placed the shoes inside. She needed to put all that had just happened with Brandi and Curtis on a back burner for now and focus on what lay ahead. Getting packed, picking up her mother in the morning, driving to Newport News, the funeral. Meeting with Tonya and maybe even Aaron.

She flopped down on the edge of the bed. How was she ever going to get through these upcoming days? She was going to be embarrassed out of her mind. Her fiancé and best friend had both deceived her in the biggest way possible. She had been dumped by her fiancé only weeks before her wedding day.

She would never forget the humiliation of having to call all her bridesmaids, all her friends and neighbors to tell them that the wedding was off. Her mother was forced to sit down and call the family. She didn't go into detail about Tonya and Aaron running off to Vegas together. It was too raw and embarrassing to talk about then. Mama said it was really none of anyone's business anyway. But Maxine had no doubt that the news eventually got around. She and Debbie had become friends when

Debbie called to ask her if the rumors about Tonya and Aaron were true.

Maxine had gone over in her mind how to deal with Tonya when they met and decided that it would be best to ignore her as much as possible. She would speak and then move on. But what would she do if she saw Aaron? She hadn't spoken to him since he broke up with her that day in the dorm and had hoped she never would.

She sighed and stood up. She was probably blowing this all out of proportion. Like Debbie, Curtis and her mother all said, it had happened so long ago. They had all moved on, and given the circumstances of her aunt's death there wasn't much she could do except show up and try to get through it.

CHAPTER 7

As Maxine merged the Volvo onto Interstate 95 heading south, she glanced quickly at her mother dozing peacefully in the passenger seat. She smiled, then turned back to face the open road and braced herself for the long drive ahead. Only about two hundred more miles to go on what had to be one of the most boring interstates in the country. No scenery, few trees—just miles and miles of flat dull pavement.

Maxine planned to do all the driving to Newport News with only one stop for breakfast at about nine. Last time she was in a car on the highway with her mother driving, she'd been tempted to tell the woman to slow down as the speedometer slowly crept past eighty miles an hour.

Mama was in her midsixties but very sharp. She had recently lost some weight and was the same slender size ten that she had always been and still kept her hair neatly trimmed in a short pixie cut. She was such a strong and independent woman. She'd had to be, with a husband who drifted from one young chick to the next, often leaving his family for months at a time. Mama had never talked about it much and rarely complained, at least not to her daughter.

But Maxine had seen her mother slowly harden over the years. She had vague memories from childhood of a young mother who laughed and sang as she worked around the house and looked after her daughter. Mama would sometimes tickle her mercilessly when she braided her hair before school and she regularly took her and Tonya to movies, shopping and the theater.

Then one day when she was in her early teens, Maxine realized that the outings were fewer and much further between. Daddy was out more often and when he was home, Maxine could usually feel the tension in the air as he and Mama argued almost nonstop behind closed doors. Maxine couldn't understand the words being said, but the angry muffled tones were hard to miss. She would run into her own bedroom and slam the door shut. When they stopped arguing, Daddy would often storm out of the house, and Mama would shut herself in their bedroom for hours, then come out and try to put on a cheerful face as she cooked or cleaned.

Mama only began to soften again after Daddy died ten years ago and she chose to remember the good things about him, like his gentle manner with people, his stunning good looks and his wonderful sense of humor.

Her relationship with Curtis was nothing like her parents' relationship had been, and for that Maxine felt blessed. Curtis was so levelheaded, she could never imagine him cheating on her with another woman. She could remember them having a big argument about a year after they were married, just before Curtis went away to a conference in Atlanta. He was gone for only two days, but Maxine had tossed all night like a tissue in a tornado, worrying that he would meet some cute, skinny thing and have a fling. Someone who would never argue or disagree with him.

She knew better now. Curtis was so brutally honest and straightforward that if he so much as felt an attraction for another woman he would probably come and tell her so they could "talk it out" as he often said whenever they disagreed about something. She smiled. Sometimes she found herself toying around with the idea of having a fling of her own just to add more drama to their relationship.

Mama stirred and sat up straight. "You getting tired yet?" she asked as she lowered the passenger-side mirror. She patted her hair neatly into place.

"I'm fine."

"Let me know if you get tired. I can drive some." Mama opened the glove compartment, removed a map of Virginia and studied it for probably the tenth time on the trip.

"Ma, I told you before we left that I printed the directions out on MapQuest."

Mama waved a hand at her nonchalantly. "I don't trust those things."

"I don't know why not. They always get me where I want to go."

"Maybe, but it's not always the best way."

Maxine shrugged. "So you might lose five, ten minutes, max."

Mama scoffed. "They have you going around in circles. I don't like anybody wasting my time. I only got so much left."

Maxine shook her head and remained silent. She had long since learned to choose her battles wisely with her mama. She only persisted when something was important to her. Otherwise she let things slide since she was going to lose most of the disagreements anyway.

"Are you okay?" Maxine asked. "Do you need to stop?"

"I'm fine. I don't want to stop until we get ready to eat. We need to get there before dark since I don't know my way around."

"We'll get there. We have plenty of time."

"We would get there faster if you would pass that truck in front of you."

"What?"

"You been driving behind that truck too long. Go on and pass it." Mama flicked her wrist as if to show Maxine where and how and pass the truck.

Maxine widened her eyes in disbelief but didn't say a word. This was not a battle she wanted to fight. She silently crossed over to the next lane and passed the offending truck.

Mama settled back as if she had decided that things were under control to her satisfaction, at least for the moment.

"Mama, why did Aunt Cassie move from Atlanta to Newport News?"

"Oh, you know Cassie. She couldn't sit still in one town for a minute. And I think she wanted to be near Vernon and his family as she got older, since Tonya was all the way down there in Bermuda. The longest Cassie ever lived in the same place was when she was living with Tonya's father in Washington, D.C. They were there for about ten, eleven years at the most, and after they got divorced, Cassie was always moving around—Chicago, Philadelphia, Houston, Atlanta. Even lived in Las Vegas for a while. When Tonya was little, she would take Tonya with her, but once Tonya reached school age Cassie mostly left her with us since she didn't want Tonya to keep changing schools. You remember all that, don't you?"

Maxine nodded silently.

"Poor Dee Dee. That couldn't have been good, with her mother always coming and going, especially when she was young. But I never said anything to Cassie. She was head-strong, so I kept my mouth shut. We both married womaniz-ers—good-looking men but no good to us. 'Cept Cassie's womanizer was white, and she eventually got fed up with it and left him. *Men.* They're all the same." Mama chuckled at the memories. "Can't say I blamed Cassie, but I felt sorry for Dee Dee."

"Why? She seemed happy enough with us."

"She was fine living with us, but a child needs her mama close by, her daddy, too—especially when they're young. That's one reason I stayed with your father."

"Do you know what happened to Tonya's father?"

"No, and I don't think Cassie ever heard from him again after they split up."

"I always kind of thought of us as Tonya's family anyway."

"Me, too. That was a bad situation for her all around. I always figured that all I could do was to make her feel that our place was her home."

"You did a good job of that, Mama. I swear at one time I thought we were sisters and not cousins."

"You were just like sisters. Always together and cute as could be." Mama looked at Maxine. "You've never talked to her since college? Not even once?"

Maxine shook her head. "No."

"Well, be civil towards her when you see her. What she did to you wasn't right, but we all make mistakes and we're still family."

"Mama, you should know you don't have to tell me that. What do you think I'm going to do? Whack her upside the head?"

"*Humph.* I don't know. You were mad enough to do that when it happened and you always were one to hold a grudge."

Maxine blinked. "I am not."

"Yes, you are. I remember when the two of you were about thirteen. Somebody told you that Dee Dee had kissed some boy you had a crush on, and you didn't speak to her for weeks. Come to find out, it wasn't even true."

Maxine nodded as the memory came flooding back. "I had forgotten all about that. You're talking about Ralph. He was as cute as he could be." Maxine shook her head at the memory. "And I'm not so sure it wasn't true. I think Tonya did kiss him but she kept insisting she didn't. I was too scared to ask him if it was true, and he wasn't even really interested in me. I finally decided that one little kiss with a boy who hardly knew I existed wasn't worth ending our relationship."

"I don't think what happened with Aaron was worth the two of you ending your relationship."

"That was different. I was engaged to Aaron. How could I ever trust her again after that?"

"People change. You all were very young then and young people can be foolish, especially when it comes to love and sex. We never talked about it, but I'm sure Tonya regrets what she did."

Maxine shook her head firmly. "I wouldn't want her around Curtis."

"Curtis? Oh, shoot. Curtis is a keeper. You wouldn't have anything to worry about with her or anyone else with Curtis. He would never do something like that."

"It's not him I don't trust, it's her. The thought of her even flirting with him would make me mad."

Mama nodded. "Well, it's your life and your marriage. But you're being silly if you ask me."

"Why do you always take up for her, even after what she did to me? And think of all the money you lost when the wedding was canceled."

"I just feel as if my two daughters aren't on speaking terms, and that's hurtful."

"You don't *have* two daughters, Ma. You only have one. Me." Maxine pointed at herself.

"I know that, Maxine. And you know what I mean."

Maxine was silent. Yes, she understood in a way. Tonya was like a daughter to Mama. But she was the *real* daughter, and what Tonya had done was vile, disgusting and cruel. She would never, ever be able to forgive her or to forget it. But she had given up trying to understand why her mother and others didn't see it that way.

"Let's drop it," Maxine said.

"Fine. But I hope you're not going to be rude to her."

"I'm just going to go down there and act like it never happened. I'll be cordial but I ain't going to be chummy. Those days are over."

"Suit yourself, Maxine. And could you please pass that car in front of you or we'll never get there. I can't believe how slow that old man is driving."

CHAPTER 8

Vernon lived with his wife, Viola, in a large colonial style house on a tree-lined street in Newport News, Virginia. Each house on the block was different, and all the lawns were neatly trimmed. It was a far cry from her own cookie-cutter neighborhood, and it felt refreshing to get out of the suburbs.

As soon as Maxine and her mother pulled up in front of the house, Maxine spotted her cousin Vernon sitting on a glider on the front porch, smoking a pipe. As Maxine parked the car at the curb, Vernon bounded down the stairs two at a time. He had always been a tall, slender man with a quick step, and Maxine could see that hadn't changed, even though he must be well into his fifties by now. He was still quite attractive, too, aging with a distinguished gracefulness that seemed to be common on her mother's side of the family.

Vernon was down on the sidewalk helping Mama out of the passenger door before she could get a foot on the pavement. Once Mama stood up straight, he wrapped her in a big bear hug.

"Tough times," Mama said as she patted Vernon's cheek warmly. "How are you holding up?"

"I'm hanging in there, Aunt Francis. It was such a shock to find her. I'll never forget that."

Maxine walked from around the car, and she and Vernon hugged warmly.

"It sure is good to see you," Maxine said. "It's been so long. I'm just sorry it's under such difficult circumstances."

"It's been too long," Vernon said. "I swear, Maxine, you get prettier every time I see you."

"Oh, go on," Maxine said, hitting him playfully on the arm. "You're looking pretty good yourself."

Maxine popped the trunk, and they followed as Vernon carried their bags up the narrow path leading to the front door, where Viola was standing behind the screen door. Viola threw the door open and greeted them both with big lingering hugs as Vernon walked upstairs with the luggage.

Viola, a petite woman who always looked ten years younger than her age, smiled as she took their jackets and hung them in the hall closet just off the front door. Then as Viola and Mama chatted in the hallway, Maxine looked around. It had been decades since she was last here, but things were coming back to her now. It was a comfortably decorated house, with graceful arches off the central hallway leading to a good-size living room and dining room. If memory served her right, farther down the hall was a big old-fashioned country kitchen.

Viola led them through the arch and into the living room. "Come on," she said. "Y'all sit down. You must be tired after that long drive."

Mama sat in one of two big easy chairs, and Maxine headed for the couch under the window just as Vernon came back down the stairs. He sat in the other easy chair, and Viola excused herself and walked off toward the kitchen.

Maxine saw no signs that Tonya had arrived and she breathed a momentary sigh of relief. She wasn't even sure that Tonya would be staying here at the house or whether she would choose to stay elsewhere.

"So, how was the drive?" Vernon asked.

"Oh, I thought we would never get here as slow as this child drives," Mama said jokingly as she gestured toward Maxine.

Maxine rolled her eyes to the ceiling. "I got us here in one piece, didn't I?"

Vernon chuckled. "Now that I think about it, Aunt Francis

always did have a heavy foot. I can remember hiding on the floor of the backseat when I was a kid riding with her."

Mama waved her arm. "Oh, shoot. It wasn't that bad."

Viola returned with a tray and handed each of them a tall glass of iced tea. "How long will you all be staying?" she asked as she sat on the couch next to Maxine.

"Until Friday, I think. Right, Mama?"

"At least until Friday. We want to spend some time visiting. It's been so long since we were here."

"Too damn long," Vernon said.

Viola nodded.

"Tonya said she might come by the house this afternoon," Vernon said.

Mama stole a quick glance in Maxine's direction. Maxine took a long sip of iced tea.

"Will she be staying here?" Mama asked.

"No, she's staying at a hotel," Vernon said. "She got in last night and stopped by for a few minutes."

"I see," Mama said. "It will be good to see her again."

"We offered to let her stay here, but her boyfriend is with her and when she heard that you all were staying with us she said they would get a room nearby," Vernon said. "She thought it would be too crowded with all the other company we'll be having after the funeral."

Maxine nodded but wondered if that was the real reason Tonya had decided to stay elsewhere.

"She's probably become used to a certain amount of luxury," Viola said. "Cassie told us a few months ago that she's living with some rich dude in Bermuda."

"Now don't get carried away, Viola. Mama didn't say he was rich. He just owns a few properties down there."

"She said he was well-to-do. Same thing."

Vernon grunted. "I still thought she'd want to stay with family. We got plenty of room for everybody here."

Maxine crossed her legs. It sounded like Tonya was doing

all right for herself in Bermuda, she thought, but all this talk about her was making Maxine uncomfortable. She knew it had been more than twenty years since their fallout and others may have forgotten all about it, but she hadn't. And she was willing to bet that Tonya hadn't forgotten, either.

"Will you all be having many people here after the funeral tomorrow?" Mama asked. Maxine could have kissed her mother for changing the subject.

"Everybody is coming over here afterwards," Viola said. "We got people coming from Atlanta, Chicago, everywhere, since Cassie lived so many places. The phone's been ringing off the hook."

"Is there anything we can help you with?" Mama asked. "We're ready to work."

Viola shook her head. "The neighbors have everything under control. They're going to come over while we're at the funeral and set the food and everything up."

"That's nice," Maxine said.

Vernon stood up. "Why don't you show them to their rooms, Viola? Then we can go and sit out on the front porch and talk."

"Isn't it kind of cold to be sitting outside?" Mama asked.

"This is the best time of year to be sitting out there," Vernon said. "It's too hot and humid in the summer, too cold in winter."

"He sits out there all the time," Viola said. "Since I don't let him smoke that pipe in the house."

"Just get a sweater," Vernon said. "You'll be fine. I'll be out here waiting." He opened the front door and walked out.

Viola led Maxine and Francis up the stairs and showed them two bedrooms. The first had two twin beds, and Viola said they used it as a guest bedroom. The other bedroom was Aunt Cassie's, and had one double bed. Maxine and her mother insisted on sharing the room with twin beds. With so many people coming from out of town, someone might need a bedroom at the last minute.

Viola sat on the edge of one bed as Francis unpacked a few things and hung them in the closet. Maxine had just placed her bag on the other bed when she noticed a recent framed photo of Aunt Cassie with Tonya sitting on top of the bureau. She picked it up.

"That was taken the last time Tonya was here in the states, about a year ago, I guess," Viola said. "She stayed for about a week."

Maxine nodded and placed the photo back on the bureau. Mama picked it up and looked at it. "She looks beautiful in this picture, even younger than she did when I last saw her several years ago," Mama said. "I wouldn't have recognized her. I'm surprised you did, Maxine."

She would recognize that face, with the mole and the curly black hair anytime, anywhere, Maxine thought. No matter how much it changed.

"I think she had a face-lift," Viola said.

Mama put the photo down. "She looks stunning."

"I hope Vernon didn't make you too uncomfortable going on and on about Tonya," Viola said with an apologetic smile. "Men can be so forgetful about some things."

Maxine nodded. Obviously, Viola remembered what had happened between the two of them. She shrugged. "That's okay. I expected that coming here."

"How has she been doing?" Mama asked. "I talked to her a few months ago but only briefly."

"She doing good as far as I know. Of course, Francis's death was a terrible blow to her. But she's been with that man down there for about eight or nine months now, I think. He's a developer of small vacation properties or something like that and he's building a house for them on a hillside near the beach."

"Sounds nice," Mama said.

"Did she ever have children?" Maxine asked as she began unpacking.

"No, she never had children," Viola said.

"Too bad," Mama said.

"Doesn't sound like a bad life to me," Maxine said.

"I can't imagine never having children," Mama said.

"Neither can I," Viola said. "But to each her own, I guess. She seemed happy enough last time we saw her."

Single and childless had its charms, Maxine thought. No sassiness, defiance, back talk, worrying, disagreements about child rearing, and a million other things that came with teenagers and spouses.

"Anyway, enough about all that," Viola said. "How are the girls, Naomi and Brandi?"

Naomi was finally out of her hair, and Brandi had her pulling out her hair, was what Maxine wanted to say, but she gave the stock response instead. "They're fine."

"Naomi is in college at Hampton," Mama said proudly as she sat in an armchair. "Brandi is a handful, but they all are at that age."

"What are you talking about?" Maxine said as she shook out a black nightgown. "I was an angel."

Mama scoffed. "I remember you breaking your curfew, sneaking out of windows late at night. Scared me half to death when I found your bed empty."

Maxine grimaced at the memory. "That happened only once."

"Yes, since I put alarms on the windows and doors."

Maxine smiled. "You were so strict. I couldn't even have boys over until I was sixteen. I try to be more lenient with Brandi but that doesn't seem to be working. I think some boy who's always calling the house has got her smoking. I smelled it in her room."

"Cigarettes?" Mama asked.

Maxine nodded.

"At least it's not drugs," Viola said.

"And the mouth on her is enough to drive anyone insane."

"You had quite a mouth on you, too," Mama said. "Teenagers will be teenagers."

Maxine shook her head. "Only a few more years to go. I just hope I can make it."

"It will be over before you know it," Mama said. "And then you'll be wishing you could have those years back."

Maxine looked at her mother doubtfully.

"Y'all coming down or you going to stay up there running your mouths forever?" Vernon yelled from the base of the stairs.

Viola giggled as she walked out of the room and stood at the top of the stairs. "Why? You miss us down there all by your lonesome?"

"I just wondered 'cause Tonya is pulling up."

Maxine gasped and dropped the shoe pouch she was removing from her bag on the bed. She glanced in her mother's direction. She felt about two years old and completely helpless. Mama patted her arm reassuringly as Viola reappeared in the doorway.

"Tonya's here. You all ready to go back down?" Viola turned and headed out the door.

"Don't worry," Mama whispered. "It's going to be fine."

"Yeah, right," Maxine said.

Mama walked toward the door, but Maxine's feet suddenly felt like blocks of cement. Mama turned and looked in her direction. "You coming?"

"You go on without me."

Mama gave her a look of disapproval.

"I'll be down in a minute, Ma."

"You sure?"

"I'm sure. I just need a minute to collect myself."

"Try to remember that she's probably as nervous about this first meeting as you are, maybe even more."

Maxine scoffed.

"Come on now. I'm sure she regrets what she did, especially given how it turned out between you two."

"You always make excuses for her. Even now, all these years later."

"I'm trying to be objective."

Maxine still didn't understand why her mother felt a need to be objective. *She* was her daughter, Tonya was not. "Go on down, Ma," she said with finality. "I'll be down in a minute."

Mama took a deep exasperated breath of air and walked out. As soon as she left, Maxine ran to the window, lifted the curtain and looked out, trying to spot Tonya and her boyfriend. A late-model black Lincoln sedan sat at the curb, and its driver leaned on the hood smoking a cigarette. The passengers had already disappeared into the house. So Miss Thang had a car and driver, Maxine thought. How lovely.

Maxine dropped the curtain and sat on the edge of the bed. The last thing she wanted to do was go down there and face a rich, glamorous, face-lifted Tonya, with her raggedy hard-working, mommy-looking self. She had been nervous from the get-go about this and after arriving and hearing the news about Tonya's lifestyle in Bermuda she felt even more reluctant.

She jumped up. Might as well go and get this over with. But first she was going to freshen up and change out of her wrinkled jeans. She rifled through her luggage, pulled out a turquoise silk suit and held it at arm's length. No, she thought. That would be going too far. She tossed it aside on the bed and dug deeper into her bag. She finally settled on a pair of crisply ironed black jeans and a mauve colored top with an empire waistline and flowing sleeves. She slipped a pair of black mules with a sexy low heel on to her feet.

She touched up her makeup and felt a little better after checking herself in the mirror. But if that bitch started acting high and mighty, she was going to walk straight out of the room and back up here. She wasn't about to put up with any crap from Tonya.

She walked to the top of the stairs and squared her shoulders. She had one thing going for herself that she didn't have all those years ago while at Hampton, and that was experience. She was a much stronger woman now. She could take care of herself.

CHAPTER 9

Maxine was surprised that her mother hadn't come back up to see what was taking her so long. As she walked down the hallway in her heels, she could hear voices and laughter drifting up from the living room. She straightened her back and gripped the rail as she descended the stairs. If she could just get through this without throwing up.

She paused at the landing, and all eyes turned in her direction. Maxine spotted Tonya immediately, seated on the couch between Mama and her male friend and going through a wallet full of photographs. Vernon, sitting in an armchair closest to the archway, stood first as Maxine entered the room, followed by Tonya's friend. Mama, Viola and Tonya remained in their seats.

"Here she is," Vernon said. "Tonya, you remember Maxine, don't you?"

Maxine took a step forward as Tonya stood. She noticed that Tonya looked even better in person than she had in the photograph upstairs in the guest bedroom. Her ivory complexion was flawless and radiant with the glow of true happiness. She was wearing a navy pantsuit that hugged her figure and she looked slim and well toned as always. Her jet black hair was now sleek instead of curly and fell softly around her shoulders.

What wonders a rich and generous lover can work, Maxine thought wryly. Tonya took a step forward as if she was going to embrace Maxine, and Maxine quickly extended her hand at arm's length. Tonya paused, smiled and they shook hands.

"This is Mark," Tonya said, gesturing toward the man standing behind her. He was short for a man, about the same height as Tonya in her heels, and was brown complexioned and a bit on the stocky side. Although immaculately dressed in slacks and a sport jacket, he was not at all what she would have expected Tonya's man to look like, Maxine thought. She reached out and they shook hands, and Maxine noticed that his warm brown eyes twinkled when he smiled.

Vernon insisted that Maxine take his armchair and then he went into the dining room and got a hardback chair for himself.

"Francis was just showing me pictures of your girls," Tonya said as she and Mark sat back down on the couch. "They're beautiful. How old are they now?"

"Eighteen and fifteen."

"Brandi looks just like you," Tonya said.

Maxine raised an eyebrow. "That's what everyone says, but I think Brandi looks more like her father and that Naomi looks like me."

"Well, Brandi looks like you in this picture."

"I think they both have a little of Maxine in them," Francis said.

Tonya nodded and looked at Maxine. "It must be fun having two teenage daughters. That's probably my one regret, never having children. I would have loved a daughter."

"She would have made a great mother, too," Mark said. "I've seen how she is with my daughter."

Maxine was silent. What about stealing your best friend's fiancé right from under her nose? Seems that would be something you would regret, considering all the pain and suffering it caused. Or how about when Aaron later went and dumped her after they ran off? Or had Tonya completely and conveniently forgotten about all of that?

"You seem to be doing okay for yourself," Mama said to Tonya. "You all are building a new house in Bermuda?"

Tonya glanced at Mark and smiled. "It's finished. We moved

in last week. It's in an exquisite setting on a hillside. And you can see the ocean from my office on the top floor. It's just beautiful."

"I wanted her to have the perfect setting for her writing."

It was all Maxine could do not to roll her eyes straight to the ceiling. It's in the most exquisite setting…blah, blah, blah. What was with that? Tonya had been hooked up with this dude for less than a year and already sounded like a snob. Maxine was tempted to remind Tonya of the time when she was just Dee Dee, man stealer.

"How many novels have you written?" Viola asked.

"I'm working on my seventh. But it's taking longer because we've been so busy building the house. I'm way past my deadline."

"I have every one of 'em," Vernon said.

Tonya smiled. "Do you really read them, Vernon?"

He waved an arm. "Nah. They're too mushy for me. I just buy them 'cause you wrote 'em."

"I read them," Viola said.

"So do I," Mama said. "All of them."

"How many have you read, Maxine?" Vernon asked.

Mama and Viola exchanged glances as Maxine cleared her throat. "None of them, actually."

Vernon jerked his head back with surprise. "Don't you like to read?"

"I love to read," Maxine said coolly. Just not that junk, she thought. Someone could hold a gun upside her head, and she would never read one of Tonya's novels.

"Too mushy for you, too, huh?" Vernon said as if in answer to his own unasked question of why she didn't read Tonya's novels. Maxine left it at that.

"I have a lot of devoted fans, but my novels aren't for everyone."

"Maxine reads mostly nonfiction, don't you, Maxine?" Mama said.

"No, I read more novels than anything."

Mama cleared her throat.

Viola stood up. "Can I get you folks anything to drink? Tea? Soda? Something stronger?"

"I'll take tea," Tonya said.

"I'll have a drink," Mama said. "What you got?"

"Vernon made margaritas."

"I'll take that," Mama said.

"Nothing for me, thanks." Maxine said. She seriously doubted she was going to be down here long enough to finish a drink.

Viola scurried off to the kitchen, and Vernon took Mark down to the recreation room to shoot some pool. An awkward moment of silence hung in the air as Maxine crossed her legs and turned slightly away from Tonya and Mama seated on the couch. Mama looked as if she was desperately trying to think of something to say that wouldn't inflame her daughter— probably an impossible task—and for a moment, Maxine felt guilty about the way she was behaving. She didn't want to make her mama and the others feel bad. But she didn't feel guilty enough to change her behavior.

"So, tell us how you met Mark," Mama said finally.

"We met when friends of mine came down to Bermuda and stayed at one of his hotels. He says it was love at first sight for him, but I wasn't interested at first. I was just coming out of a bad relationship with a guy from Houston."

"It was a long-distance relationship?" Mama asked.

Tonya nodded.

"Those things are hard to keep going," Mama said.

"Tell me about it. Anyway, Mark kept calling and asking me out, sending me the most exquisite flowers…"

If Tonya used that word one more time, Maxine thought, she would puke for certain. *Beautiful* this and *exquisite* that. Maxine couldn't stand how everyone was pretending like everything was normal. Like this woman hadn't destroyed her wedding plans and nearly destroyed her life. Mama had lost a small fortune when they had to cancel everything at the last minute. Had she forgotten that? It seemed so, the way Mama was sitting around and acting like Tonya could do no wrong. It was disgusting.

"I finally agreed to go out with him and the rest is history."

"You both look very happy," Mama said as Viola reentered the room with a tray. She placed the tray on the coffee table and began handing glasses out.

"Why were you so reluctant?"

"Excuse me?" Tonya said, looking at Maxine as she accepted a glass from Viola.

"I said, why were you so reluctant to go out with Mark?"

Tonya blinked. "Well…"

"What was the problem?" Maxine continued, interrupting, the tone of her voice rising. "He wasn't engaged or married? Was that it?"

The room fell silent. Viola sat down quickly and took a long gulp of ice water.

Mama sipped her drink and stared at Maxine with wide eyes.

Maxine jumped up. "Isn't that your thing? Going after men you can steal from another woman?"

"Maxine, I don't think you…"

"Never mind," Maxine blurted before her mother could finish. "I'm out of here. You all can sit around and pretend everything is all hunky-dory if you want. Not me."

She stormed out of the room and ran up the stairs. In the guest bedroom, she kicked off her heels and threw herself on the bed, face down. She pounded the bed with her fists.

She sat up abruptly and gritted her teeth. She couldn't remember the last time she had felt this angry. If she were in her own house, she would scream at the top of her lungs. She jumped up and paced the floor, her arms folded tightly across her waist.

She tried to go down there and be civil. She really did. But there was just no way, not after what that woman had done to her. Maxine couldn't stand being in the same house with her, let alone the same room. Beautiful this and beautiful that. Who the hell did she think she was? If she had stayed down there even one minute longer, Maxine was sure she would have become a murderess.

She heard footsteps walking quickly up the hallway, and she clenched her fists. She hoped it was Tonya, 'cause right now she was ready to strangle someone—anyone—with her bare hands.

CHAPTER 10

Mama appeared, looking both upset and worried at the same time. She stood in the doorway, her fists clenched at her side as she watched Maxine pacing the floor. "Maxine, what was that outburst all—"

Maxine held a hand up. "Don't start, Ma. Just don't."

Mama sighed deeply and entered the room. She reached out, took Maxine's hand and tugged her toward the bed. "Come. Let's sit down and talk."

Maxine snatched her hand away. "I don't want to sit down."

"All right. All right," Mama said, her voice beginning to sound weary as she sat down. "Then just talk to me."

"I don't want to talk, either." Maxine pounded her fist in her hand as she paced. "Right now, I want to hurt somebody so bad."

"No, you don't and stop talking like that. You need to sit and calm yourself down."

Maxine stopped pacing and looked to see her mother sitting on the bed, her eyes filled with concern. Mama was right, of course. She didn't really want to hurt anyone. Well, she did, actually. But she would never do that. She just wished her family understood how she felt. She sat on the bed next to her mama.

"It's just that everyone is sitting down there acting like nothing happened and everything is normal. It's not."

"Well, what do you want us to do, beat her up?"

"Yes!"

"Maxine."

"Okay." Maxine paused and sighed loudly. "I just want...
I'm not sure what I want."

"What Tonya did was wrong. We all know that."

"*Pfft*. Vernon has completely forgotten."

"Well, he's a man. He can't help it. But you don't have to
act like this. I would love to see you and Tonya make up and
become friends again, but I know that's not going to happen.
Still, by holding on to all this anger all these years, you're only
hurting yourself. Trust me, I know about feeling bitter because
you feel you've been wronged by someone you loved and
trusted. I lived with a womanizer for thirty-five years, and he
couldn't be trusted as far as you can spit. I didn't get my sanity
back until after your father passed away. Fortunately, that
didn't happen to you and you went on and married a wonderful man with good character. You need to let all that stuff that
happened in the past with Tonya go, Maxine."

"But I can't. I'll never be able to forget what she did to me."

"I didn't say to forget it, just let go of the anger. Look at it
as a lesson learned in life."

"It damn sure was that. I learned that I hold on to anger for
a long time."

"I'm sure there's more to learn from it than that, but you're
so busy being angry, you can't see straight."

Maxine lowered her head, and Mama touched her chin and
held it back up. "She's about to leave and go back to her hotel.
Why don't you go down and apologize? Or just go down and
say goodbye."

Maxine gently shook her head from her mother's grasp.
"No, I'm not doing that. I hear what you're saying but I'm not
ready to do that."

Mama stood up. "Fine. Well, I'm going to go down and
say goodbye."

After Mama left, Maxine buried her face in her hands. Mama
was right. She needed to let go of this anger. But it was so hard to
do that. If anything, being so close to Tonya made her feel worse.

CHAPTER 11

Wednesday morning the air was filled with the quiet hustle of a household preparing to attend the funeral of a beloved family member. Everyone spoke in hushed tones as they dressed and checked last-minute funeral preparations. Mama had just slipped on her black church hat when Vernon announced softly from the bottom of the stairs that the limousine had arrived and was waiting at the curb for them. Maxine, her mother, Vernon and Viola all piled into the car and rode mostly in silence to the small church, not far from the house.

The four of them walked up to view the body with Vernon leading the way, then they sat in the front pew, along with other cousins, aunts and uncles. Many of the faces in the church were familiar to Maxine from years past.

About five minutes after they were all seated, Tonya walked down the aisle with Mark at her side and approached her mother. Tonya spent several minutes with her mother, then joined Vernon at the entrance to the pew. Somehow Maxine managed to be civil and even to nod as Tonya entered the pew and glanced in her direction.

Within thirty minutes after the family was seated, the church was packed with family and friends. They came from Newport News and as far away as Las Vegas, Nevada. In her short time living in the Newport News area, Aunt Cassie had become well-known and liked. From what Maxine knew of her aunt, that was generally the case wherever she had lived.

After the burial many of the funeral participants rode back

to Vernon and Viola's house, where the neighbors had prepared a spread big enough to feed a city. There were hams and fried chicken, sweet and mashed potatoes, fruit and green salads and all sorts of rich chocolaty desserts.

Maxine went upstairs to hang up her suit jacket then came back down and stood in a long line at the buffet table for a bite to eat. The line moved quickly, and she walked down to the basement area with her plate of food and a glass of white wine. The house was crowded enough that she could avoid direct contact with Tonya, but she was taking no chances.

She sat in one of several folding chairs that had been set out around the pool table and mingled with long-lost relatives while she ate. Just as the sun was setting, Vernon walked to the basement area with Viola, and they both stood next to the shelf holding his CD player and speakers. Vernon got everyone's attention by clapping his hands together, and the room went silent.

"I want to thank everyone for coming to pay their last respects to my mother. It's wonderful to see so many of our family members and friends here today from all over the country. I especially want to thank my neighbors for preparing this delicious feast for us. Ma always loved a big gathering and good food, so she is surely smiling down on us. If she were here, she would be walking around telling everybody to get more food and drink, and I want to do the same. There's still plenty of everything left, so please, go get seconds or even thirds. Forget about your weight for a change and take some of that good fried chicken home with you. Now, something else Ma loved is missing from this gathering. Music! And I'm planning to fix that right now by playing some of her favorites."

He turned and flipped a button on the CD player, and the sounds of Aretha Franklin singing "Chain Of Fools" blared out over the speakers. A loud cheer went up as Vernon grabbed Viola and spun her around. Soon the recreation room floor was full of bodies pumping to Aretha.

Connie Briscoe

Maxine sat and watched as she tapped her foot to the beat. When the song changed to "Respect," one of Maxine's male cousins crossed the room and grabbed her hand. She couldn't even remember his name, Kenny or Benny or something. She smiled and shook her head. "No, thank you."

"C'mon, Maxine. Don't tell me you don't dance."

Maxine laughed. "It's been so long. I don't want to embarrass myself."

"Nobody here cares what you look like. Just come on out here and have fun."

"Oh, okay. But just one dance."

She got up reluctantly, trying to recall what to do with herself. She could remember a time when she and Curtis loved going to parties and nightclubs. Hopefully, dancing was like riding a bike—something you never forget.

She soon found herself warming up to the music and the upbeat crowd. But one dance was more than enough, and she politely thanked her cousin and excused herself. She picked up her glass of wine, walked around a bit and chatted. She was talking and laughing with two of the neighborhood women when she felt a wave of heat travel through her body, the early sign of one of her dreaded hot flashes. She quickly excused herself then stepped through the sliding glass doors onto the patio.

She closed her eyes and lifted her face toward the sky, letting the clear November air cool her off. She hadn't spoken to Curtis or Brandi all day. As annoying as they could be at times, she was beginning to miss them. Viola mentioned that Curtis had called while they were out. She would be sure to get in touch with them before she retired that night.

She had just sat down in one of the patio chairs and placed her glass on a small nearby table when she heard the door slide open behind her. She turned to see Tonya shutting the sliding door with one hand and holding a glass of red wine in the other. Maxine turned back and stared out into the night. Now, what the hell did she want? Maxine wondered.

"I had forgotten how pleasant fall nights can be in the South," Tonya said as she lit a cigarette. She sat in the chair next to Maxine and held the pack out toward her. "Stick of poison?" Tonya asked, a coy smile playing around the corners of her mouth.

Maxine shook her head and picked up her glass. "No, thanks. I'm surprised that you still smoke after all these years."

"I quit several times but I always go back. So, Francis tells me that you all are leaving on Friday."

Maxine nodded.

"So am I. Maybe we can get together sometime tomorrow. Catch up with each other."

Not likely, Maxine thought. She was having a hard enough time sitting here now acting civil. "Hmm."

"You ever go back to the campus after we graduated from Hampton?"

"No." And she had no intention of going back, ever. Too many bad memories. She stood and prepared to leave.

"I see," Tonya said as she stomped her cigarette out on the patio. "Listen, before you go back in, um, I hate to even bring this up after all this time, but..." Tonya paused and Maxine squared her shoulders. What was this going to be about? Whatever this woman was about to say, Maxine was sure she didn't want to hear it.

Tonya stood up and faced her, and the patio light shined on her face, illuminating her dark eyes and accentuating the small mole above her lips. Maxine had forgotten just how beautiful Tonya looked under certain types of lighting.

"I want to apologize," Tonya said. "What I did to you back then was terrible, and I felt awful about it. Still do. I don't know how many times..."

Maxine shook her head, and Tonya paused. "Why are you bothering to apologize to me now? I mean, it's been more than twenty years, and I don't..."

"I thought about calling you at least a hundred times to

apologize," Tonya said before Maxine could finish. "I even wrote you a letter once but never mailed it. I was too ashamed."

Maxine swallowed hard but kept her mouth shut. She was tempted to tell Tonya again to just drop it. She didn't need to have all this old stuff dredged up. But then she remembered that it was right there on the surface anyhow, and had been since her mother told her that Aunt Cassie had died. At least Tonya wasn't still pretending like nothing happened.

"You should be ashamed," Maxine said.

"You're right and if you can never forgive me, I understand. But an apology was way overdue."

"I don't think I can ever forgive you, Tonya. I never understood how you could do something like that to me. I still don't and doubt I ever will."

Tonya sighed deeply. "I can't explain it except to say that Aaron and I thought we were in love, and I was naïve enough to think that you would eventually get over it and forgive me."

Maxine's eyes widened. "You're kidding, right?"

Tonya shrugged. "I was young then, and stupid."

Maxine took a sip of wine. "Do you have any idea how much you hurt me? I was so in love with Aaron, and you knew that. He was like this black Adonis walking around on campus. All the girls wanted him, but he wanted *me,* and I couldn't believe how lucky I was. A lot of girls on campus were cuter and skinnier and sexier, including you, but he liked *me.* Before Aaron came along, you were the one who always got the hunks. I got the brainy nerds, except we called them squares back then."

Maxine paused briefly. "You know, I wouldn't have allowed myself to even think about becoming attached to any of your boyfriends. Sometimes you hear about best friends or sisters dating each other's boyfriends after they break up, which is bad enough in my book. But this was my fiancé *while* we were engaged."

Tonya nodded sadly. "I know."

"You just don't do that."

"You're right, and I have no excuses."

"You say you don't even know why you did it, except that you fell in love with him." Maxine scoffed. "Well, so did I and I had him first. He was the love of my life *for three years*. He was the first man I ever slept with. I was crazy about him. I thought we would be together forever."

"And I was so damn jealous of you," Tonya said softly.

Maxine blinked. "What? You were jealous of *me*? But why? You had guys tripping over you."

"I was meeting one no-good man after the other. They might have been hunks but most of them were jerks. Women have always looked at me and hated me, and men just wanted to bed me. And you were so happy with Aaron."

"Yes. Why couldn't you have been happy for me?"

"I was at first. But then I got sick of it. It was always Aaron this and Aaron that with you. 'Aaron is so wonderful and every girl should have a man like Aaron.' You never stopped talking about him for three years. You made *me* fall in love with him."

Maxine was speechless for a moment. She had no idea that Tonya was jealous of her back then. "That's crazy."

"It's true."

"I don't get it. We were like sisters. My family treated you like one of us."

"I know and I loved you all for it. Really. You meant the world to me. But I couldn't shake this…this nagging envy I had of you from the time we were little girls. It got worse after you met Aaron."

Maxine shook her head. "I still don't get it. We were so good to you. My mother doted on you. Dad loved you, too."

"I know. Your mom and dad were always there for me while my mother was running off to another city chasing some dude or looking for her dream job and leaving me behind. A part of me was happy to spend time with you and your parents, but another part of me hated it when my mother left. I always blamed myself for her leaving. I thought if I was a better kid she would like me more and take me with her. And I never even knew my dad or even much about him except that he was white. But you had it all, Maxine, all the time. You had a mom and dad who never left you. And then you got Aaron."

Maxine shook her head. "If you felt that way, why didn't you ever say anything to me?"

Tonya shrugged. "I remember mentioning to you that I missed my mother once or twice, but it was difficult for me to talk about it, and I didn't think you would understand. It's hard to explain how it feels to be abandoned by your mother to someone who's never experienced it. Once I even told you that I was jealous of you, but you probably thought I was joking."

"I honestly don't remember you talking about it at all. But, yeah, I would have had a hard time believing that you were jealous of me."

"Believe me, we talked about it. Not at length but we did. And you're not the easiest person for someone to pour their troubles out to. You can be a little self-absorbed, or at least you were back then."

"Excuse me? I'm having a hard time understanding how you could say that given all my family did for you, including me. I accepted you with open arms. I shared everything with you. I always made sure you were included."

"Yes, you were in control of everything, weren't you?"

"What?"

"You were always the boss. Even though we're the same age, you treated me like a baby sister half the time. It was always *you* who decided what we would do and where we would go. If you wanted music lessons, that's what we did. When you got tired of them, we stopped. No one ever asked me what *I* wanted. I was the helpless little orphan who was supposed to be happy just to be able to tag along."

"That's not fair."

"It's true. You even decided that we would go to Hampton

for college. I didn't have much choice since your parents paid most of my tuition. I never had much say in anything we did, and I always felt like some interloper."

"You weren't an interloper. You..."

"But I felt like one, Maxine. And then you met Aaron and you were so full of yourself. You made me feel like something was wrong with me, because I couldn't find someone like Aaron."

"So that's why you set out to steal him from me?"

"Is that how you think it happened?"

"I *know* that's how it happened. Aaron was totally into me for three years, until you decided to sink your claws into him."

"I...I didn't set out to get involved with him but I didn't try to stop it when I saw it coming."

"What do you mean, when you saw it coming?"

"He started flirting with me in our senior year, making eye contact and..."

"You mean *you* started flirting with him. You couldn't be trusted. Now I find out you were jealous of me, although only God knows why. Well, you said what you wanted to say, and it doesn't really change any..." Maxine paused as Tonya's eyes traveled to something over her shoulder and grew wide with surprise. Maxine turned to see what Tonya was looking at and her heart dropped to the patio floor. *Aaron.*

CHAPTER 12

Maxine almost gagged. Aaron was standing right in front of her, not more than a few feet away, dressed in a dark suit and tie. Gone were the Afro and goatee, and in their place was a tall, handsome, clean-shaven man looking every bit the corporate lawyer he was.

He was smiling and saying something to them, but Maxine had gone numb from her head to her heels and couldn't understand a single word. She was reeling from Tonya's revelation that she was jealous of Maxine and she watched in shock as Tonya approached him and they hugged. He reached out to Maxine, and her body was rigid as he placed his arms around her and squeezed warmly. He let her go, and she glanced in Tonya's direction out of the corner of her eye to see Tonya fold her arms awkwardly, a smile frozen on her lips.

Tonya cleared her throat. "When did you get here, Aaron?"

"About an hour ago. Sorry I couldn't be here for the funeral but I had to be in court this morning. I got the first flight out and came here straight from the airport."

"No problem," Tonya said. "I'm glad you could make it at all. I wasn't really expecting you."

"I wanted to pay my respects. How are you managing?"

Tonya blinked and her eyes misted. "I'm doing fine, considering."

"Good. I lost my mother about two years ago, so I know that it's difficult now, but it gets easier, as hard as that may be to believe." He looked directly at Maxine. "And how have you been?"

"I...I'm fine." Maxine didn't know what else to say at the moment. If she said what was on her mind and started yelling obscenities, they would both think she was crazy.

"Good," he said. "You both look stunning."

A moment of silence hung among the three of them, and Maxine stole another glance at Tonya. The awkward smile was still plastered on her lips.

"So..." Aaron said. "Where are you living now, Maxine?"

"Outside of D.C.," she said abruptly. She hated standing around and pretending everything was hunky-dory. But her feet were stuck to the patio like metal to a magnet.

He nodded. "I think I heard that you got married."

"Yes," she said stiffly.

"Do you have children?"

"Two."

"Boys or girls?" He smiled as he said it, and she glanced away. He was too handsome when he smiled, and she didn't want to think nice thoughts about him.

"Girls," she responded.

He nodded again and shoved his hands into the pockets of his slacks as if he had suddenly realized that a bad vibe was hanging in the air. "I see."

Maxine was still trying to decide whether to stay and let loose some of the things on her mind or to go back inside and forget them both.

"Um, what about you, Aaron?" Tonya asked.

"Two boys, both grown."

"I heard you moved to Denver."

"Yes, I started a practice there with two partners recently."

"That sounds nice," Tonya said.

"Do you live here?" he asked Tonya.

"No, Bermuda."

"Bermuda? Really?"

"I moved there several years ago and just got married recently. My husband is here somewhere. I'd like to introduce you to him before you go."

"Sure thing. Is he from Bermuda?"

"No, but he's lived there for more than twenty years now. We just built..."

"Um, excuse me, but I'm going back inside," Maxine said. She couldn't stand this charade for another minute. She headed for the patio door, but Aaron reached out and touched her arm.

"You're leaving so soon?" he asked.

"I'm not leaving the house. We're staying here, my mother and I. I'm just going back inside."

"Oh, because if you get a minute later on, I'd love to talk."

"Whatever about?" she asked coldly.

"Well, we haven't seen each other since..."

"Why don't you two stay out here and talk now," Tonya said, touching his arm gently as she interrupted him. "I need to get back in and talk to the guests anyway. Some of them I haven't seen since I moved to Bermuda."

"Suit yourself," Maxine said. "But I really need to go back inside myself."

"Please stay and talk to me for a few minutes," Aaron said.

Before Maxine could open her mouth, Tonya had slipped inside and shut the patio doors. Maxine stood there silently and avoided Aaron's face.

"I take it that you're still bitter about what happened at Hampton," he said.

She cut her eyes in his direction. "And you find that surprising? You might feel differently if you had been the one jilted on the eve of your wedding."

He nodded. "Fair enough."

"So what is it that you wanted to talk to me about? Not this,

I hope, because as far as I'm concerned it's over and done with. There's nothing to say."

"Actually, I wanted to find out more about what you've been up to all these years. How you've been doing."

"I told you. I'm married. We have two daughters."

"How old are they?"

"Fifteen and eighteen."

"What kind of work do you do?"

"I'm a teacher."

"Elementary?"

"That's what I studied in school, or don't you remember?"

"Yes, I remember."

"And you're the big-shot lawyer now, aren't you?"

He chuckled. "I don't know about the big-shot part. But I'm a lawyer."

"Well, good for you. I'm sure you must be happy. Was there anything else you wanted to ask me? Because if we're done, I'm going back inside. It's cold out here."

"It *is* rather chilly."

"Excuse me?"

"Nothing, Maxine. Is there something you'd like to say to me? If so, go ahead."

She paused. There was so much she'd like to say to this man. She would start by cursing him out and then ask him how the hell he could do what he did to her. Did he regret what he'd done? It was cruel, inconsiderate and immature. But what good would that do now?

"No, there's nothing."

He nodded and held out his business card. "I'll be here for a couple of days if you'd like to get together and talk. Maybe we could have a drink or something. My cell phone number is on the back."

She ignored the card and looked him directly in the eye. "You're joking, right?"

"No. I'm very serious. The way things were left hanging back then, well, I can't blame you for being upset. We really should talk. Go ahead and take the card."

She snatched the card from him. "Fine. But don't hold your breath waiting for me to call. It's highly unlikely."

CHAPTER 13

Maxine woke suddenly, lifted her head and looked straight at the clock on the bedside nightstand. Ten o'clock. She looked around the room. No sign of her mother. She was probably already dressed and downstairs.

She threw the covers aside and swung her feet to the floor. She hadn't meant to sleep so late but wasn't surprised that she had. It seemed to take her forever to get to sleep the night before. After calling home and speaking to Curtis and Brandi, she kept tossing and turning. No matter how much she tried, she couldn't get Tonya, and especially Aaron, out of her mind. She kept reliving those dreadful last days at Hampton Institute. At one point, Mama even asked her if she was all right and got up to get her a glass of water.

Now that Maxine thought back over yesterday evening with Tonya and Aaron, she felt a little embarrassed about the way she had behaved. What they had done to her was despicable, but it was a long time ago and they were all so much younger back then. They were mature adults now, and Tonya had apologized. She'd acted like a total bitch.

She sighed, stood up and stretched. At least she had gotten through the day. It was over and done with now, and she was ready to get back to her life.

She slipped into her bathrobe and slippers. It was rude of her to sleep so late when she was a guest, she thought, as she made her way down the stairs. She walked down the center hallway and glanced into the living and dining rooms. Then she made her way to the kitchen at the back of the house. She frowned as she looked around the empty kitchen. Where was everyone? Then she spotted the note on the kitchen table.

She picked it up and recognized her mother's handwriting. Apparently, they had all gone out at nine-thirty that morning to visit relatives. They decided to let her rest since she'd had trouble getting to sleep the night before. The note said that her breakfast was in the refrigerator and suggested that she call if she wanted them to swing back by the house to pick her up.

She placed the note back on the table and opened the refrigerator door. She noticed a plate wrapped in foil and lifted the top to find scrambled eggs, bacon and toast. She removed the foil and stuck the plate in the microwave.

As she ate her breakfast, she thought about whether she would call and join them or stick around the house and rest. She so rarely got a chance to spend time alone and relax. After breakfast, she washed the dishes, then walked into the living room and scanned the tall bookshelves lining one wall, looking for something to read.

The first thing she noticed, displayed prominently in the center of the shelves, were what looked like all of Tonya's novels. She removed one from the shelf entitled *Love Among the Breakers,* turned it over and saw an older black-and-white photograph of Tonya smiling out at her. Tonya had obviously had a face-lift or something because she looked years younger in person now than she did in this photograph.

Maxine had never felt the desire to read one of Tonya's novels. In fact, she'd made a point of *not* reading them, even though Naomi and Brandi had read a few of their aunt's novels and her mother had read all of them. But after seeing Tonya, Maxine now found herself a bit curious. Tonya had written some wonderful poetry when they were younger. She sat in one of the easy chairs in the living room and turned to the first page.

An hour later she folded the corner of the page she was reading and closed the book. Not bad, she thought. In fact it was pretty darn good. She often read fiction and when she did she preferred mysteries. She had been prepared to hate Tonya's work as much as she had come to despise the author, especially since she had thought Tonya's novels were mainly of the romance type. There was a lot of kissing and hugging and swooning, but it was more than that. It was about the ups and downs in the relationships of several people living in Bermuda and it even had a little murder mystery going on. Tonya was particularly good at making you feel that you were actually in Bermuda, with her poetic descriptions of the island and its quaint neighborhoods.

The telephone rang and Maxine placed the novel on the coffee table and jumped up. She walked quickly into the kitchen and picked up the wall phone. It was her mother on the line.

"We're at your aunt Freda's and we're about to leave and get some lunch. Then I don't know where we're going, probably ride over to see Allen and Gladys. Do you want us to swing by and get you first?"

Maxine thought for a second and decided not to join them. "I don't think so, Ma. I'll just hang around here. You go ahead and have fun."

"What are you doing there all by yourself?"

"Actually, I was reading one of Tonya's novels that I found on the bookshelf."

"Oh. I'm shocked."

Maxine laughed. "So am I."

"What do you think of it?"

"I like it."

"She's a good writer, isn't she? I bet you're surprised."

"Not really. She was always good at writing poetry. But I'll admit that I'm surprised I liked the novel. So, what time do you think you all will be back?"

"I don't know. Sometime before dinner."

"I'll see you then."

Maxine hung up the phone and made her way back upstairs,

planning to shower and get dressed. In the bedroom, she noticed that she had tossed the outfit she wore the night before across a chair. She picked it up to fold and put back into her suitcase, and Aaron's business card fell off the chair and onto the floor. She picked up the card and read it. "Aaron Robinson, Attorney At Law." She turned it over and saw his cell phone number written on the back.

For a second, she toyed with the thought of calling him and agreeing to meet. They had never talked after that day in the dorm room when he told her that he was leaving her for Tonya, and to this day she had unanswered questions.

She smacked her lips and shook her head. Why dredge all that up again? Sometimes she acted like such a masochist. And after the way she treated Tonya last night, how could she even think of calling Aaron? That would make her as bad as one of those silly women who were ready to kill their girlfriend for screwing around with their boyfriend but were so quick to forgive the man.

She placed the card down on the linen doily on top of the dresser, folded her dress and put it in the suitcase. She showered, dressed comfortably in slacks and a pullover sweater and put her slippers back on. Now what? She glanced at her watch. Almost twelve-thirty. Curtis and Brandi were away, and Naomi was in school. Her mother probably wouldn't return for several hours. She could continue reading Tonya's novel or she could even call Tonya.

Mama said Tonya was staying at the Omni Hotel in town, so it should be easy enough to reach her. For some reason, after seeing Tonya and Aaron yesterday, Maxine felt as if a huge burden had been lifted from her shoulders. She still had her moment, when pangs of anger filled every pore of her body, but they were alternated with feelings of relief. She had built a good life for herself with a faithful, loving husband and two beautiful daughters. They weren't perfect, but she could live with their faults.

She could never go back to being best friends with Tonya and doubted she would ever allow Tonya anywhere near Curtis. She couldn't trust her that way. But they lived in different countries—they could be civil toward each other and talk occasionally.

She sat on the edge of the bed and dialed the operator on her cell phone to get the number to the Omni Hotel, then dialed and asked for Tonya or Mark Harris. She was connected to the room but got the hotel's message service. She left a message asking Tonya to call her if she wanted to get together before they both returned home.

She hung up, walked to the dresser and picked up Aaron's business card. She turned it over to the back, where he had written his cell phone number. Why not? Maybe she wouldn't even bring up the past. They could just talk and catch up. She dialed the number on her cell phone, and he answered on the second ring.

"Maxine," he said, his voice filled with obvious surprise. "I was hoping you would call. Doubtful but hopeful."

"I have to admit, I was doubtful myself. But after thinking it over, I realized that I behaved badly yesterday and I wanted to apologize to you. I'm really sorry."

"There's no need for you to apologize. In fact, it's really me who should be apologizing to you."

True, she thought. But she was going to be mature about this. Mama would be proud of her. "Let's let the past be the past."

"I will if you can. Does that mean you'll have lunch with me?"

She smiled into the phone. She actually felt so much better after doing this. "Why not? It will be good to catch up. Where do you want to meet?"

"How about the Omni Hotel where I'm staying. There's a restaurant downstairs."

So he was staying at the same hotel as Tonya. That wasn't

really surprising, as Newport News was a small city and didn't have that many hotels. "That should be fine. So, say in an hour?"

"I'll be waiting for you in the hotel restaurant."

CHAPTER 14

An hour later Maxine was dressed in her silk turquoise suit and paying the cab driver. She walked through the hotel doors and made her way to Mitty's. Aaron greeted her at the entrance.

"Any trouble finding it?"

"No," she said as he held her chair out for her. "I called a cab rather than try to find it myself."

"I would have come to get you but I flew in and decided not to rent a car since I'm only here for a couple days. I'm flying back to Denver tomorrow."

"Will you see Tonya again before you go? She and Mark are staying here."

He shook his head and sat across from her. "I talked to her earlier. She said they were going to visit some relatives today."

"I see. I tried to reach her myself but she was out."

The waiter stopped by the table and took their orders, and Aaron ordered a bottle of red wine.

"You know, I had forgotten just how pretty you were in blue," he said, smiling after the waiter left. "That shade of blue is definitely your color."

Well, she hadn't forgotten just how intoxicatingly good-looking *he* was, she thought. She was a mature woman, yet she felt ready to swoon right off this chair when he looked at her and smiled the way he was doing now. But she kept those thoughts to herself. "Thank-you, Aaron. I've gained so much weight over the past few years, I usually wear black."

"I think you look sexy."

She glanced down at the table, a little embarrassed at his bluntness. Still, she had to admit to herself that it felt good to have an attractive man tell her she looked sexy. "So, how has life been treating you, Aaron? Last night, you said you have two sons."

He nodded. "Damon, my son from my first marriage is grown, so I know what you're going through during the teenage years. But I'm sure your daughters will be just fine with you to guide them."

She crossed her fingers and held them up. "Naomi is doing well. She's in college at Hampton. So, yeah, one down, one to go. This is your second marriage?"

He nodded. "Going on a year now."

"You're practically newlyweds then."

"You could say that. How about you? You on your first or second?"

"First. Curtis and I met in grad school at American University."

"What does he do?"

"He's an accountant."

"Nice."

"Yes, but you started your own law practice. That sounds so exciting."

"A new marriage and a new law practice all at once." He chuckled. "Maybe I don't have good sense, but it keeps my life interesting, I'll say that."

That was what she remembered most about Aaron. He always had big ideas and something interesting going on. He used to make her look at her own life differently. "I sometimes fantasize about going back to school, maybe after Brandi finishes high school. I like teaching but I could use a change of pace."

"What would you study?"

She shrugged. "Sometimes I think about going to law school."

"You're kidding?"

She smiled sheepishly. "But maybe I'm too old."

He shook his head vigorously. "No, you're definitely not too old. One of the brothers in our practice didn't go to law school until he was in his forties. He's about fifty-five now so he's been practicing law for ten years and will be for another ten, at least."

"That's encouraging. Maybe there's hope for me yet. I also think about studying film and television."

"I think you would be good at that or anything else you set out to do. But if you ever decide to go to law school, look me up. I can help with that. I'm trying to talk Damon into going. He's a manager for a small telecommunications company and he's got a great head on his shoulders."

Their food and wine arrived, and they chatted almost nonstop as they ate. Following dinner, the waiter brought Aaron a glass of sherry and Tia Maria for her. As they sipped their drinks, a moment of silence passed between them—their first that afternoon.

"This has been very nice, catching up with each other like this," he said softly.

She nodded. "I enjoyed it, too."

"I hope you'll keep in touch. It would be nice to hear from you once in a while. And I get to Washington, D.C., a lot."

"You do? Then I'd like that."

He glanced at his watch. "Do you have time to come up for a bit? I could order coffee up to my suite."

She blinked and hesitated. But what was the harm? It wasn't like they were a couple of wild teenagers or even college students. They were both married to other people now, and she had time on her hands. Besides, he was a pleasure to be around. "Sure."

He paid the waiter, and they walked out to the lobby and took the elevators, chatting and laughing all the way up. Maxine realized that part of the reason she was feeling so lighthearted was the two glasses of wine she had with lunch and the Tia Maria with dessert. But it had been so long since she just let herself go and lived in the moment. She was a grown woman. She could have fun without stepping across any forbidden boundaries.

They stepped into the sitting room of his suite, and she draped her leather shoulder bag over the back of an armchair. He helped her remove her suit jacket and draped it over her shoulder bag. They settled on opposite ends of the couch, and he picked up the phone and dialed room service. But in addition to coffee, Maxine heard him ask for a bottle of Tia Maria. She smiled. She was going to have to be on guard with this man.

"So you and your mom are driving back tomorrow?" he asked as he hung up the phone.

She nodded. "Yes." She was brief because she didn't really want to discuss her home life. She got enough of that all year long. While here with Aaron, she wanted to think and talk about the things that always got shoved aside during her everyday life, like her dreams of going to law school or working in the film industry or someday taking a cruise around the world. She and Curtis used to talk about things like that often but lately never seemed to have the time. When they did talk it was about the kids, work, the budget and all the other mundane aspects of their lives.

"So, do you do much traveling?" she asked.

"Not as much as I'd like, at least not for pleasure. I travel all the time for work. My wife is from Chicago so we get back there a lot. How about you?"

"Same here. Not nearly as much as I'd like. As a teacher, I don't even get to travel for work."

"Remember how we used to talk about all the traveling we would do after we graduated from college?"

She nodded. "We even talked about living in Europe or Africa for a while."

"I remember. I wanted to live in London, and you wanted to live in West Africa."

She smiled at the youthful memories. "And I think we both wanted to spend some time in Paris. Did you ever get to any of those places?"

"I've been to London a few times, Paris once."

She sighed wistfully. "That sounds nice. Was it?"

"It was all we imagined when we were in college and a lot more."

Maxine cleared her throat and brushed an imaginary piece of lint from her slacks. "There's something I've been wanting to ask you."

"Go ahead. Ask me anything you want."

"Who came on to who back then?"

He looked puzzled for a second, then it clicked. "You mean with me and Tonya?"

She nodded.

Aaron sighed. "You're not going to want to hear this."

"I can handle it."

"She had always flirted a little with me whenever you weren't around but she started coming on real heavy after we got engaged. I was completely wrapped up into you from the day we first met. You know that. But from the moment we got engaged, whenever Tonya and I were together and you weren't around, she would get real flirty. At first I tried to ignore it but she…"

There was a knock at the door, and Aaron paused. He stood to open the door, and a waiter entered the room bearing a tray filled with beverages, glasses and coffee cups. After he left, Aaron poured them both glasses of Tia Maria and sat down beside her.

"Did that answer your question?" he asked as he handed her the drink.

"Yes," she said then took a sip. "That's pretty much what I thought."

"Any other questions?"

"No. I think we can just drop it. You know, I envy you in a way."

"Why is that?"

"You went and lived the kind of life we always talked about living. Not many of us actually did what we said we were going to do."

"It sounds like you have a good life, a different life from what we might have dreamed about, but a good one."

"Well, yeah, it's a decent life. It's just not as exciting as yours."

"You can always change it," he said in a slightly lower tone of voice. "Make it more exciting."

"And how would you suggest I do that at this point in my life? I have responsibilities, I'm putting on weight faster than I can think and I have hot flashes now." She laughed and took another sip of Tia Maria.

"In Europe, women at your stage of life are considered sexy."

She scoffed. "I'll bet."

"I'm not kidding."

"Why is that?"

"I think it's because you're more mature and experienced. That can be very sexy, you know." He placed his arm behind her on the back of the couch, and she realized that he was sitting much closer to her now than he had been before he got up to let the waiter in. A tingle of fear and excitement raced up her spine. Was he coming on to her or just being ultrafriendly? She decided to believe the latter. After all, he was married and so was she. Surely he wouldn't try anything under those circumstances.

"What do you do to relax or for pleasure?" he asked.

She laughed nervously. Maybe he *was* coming on to her. She placed her glass down on the coffee table. She had a feeling she needed to have her wits about her, and this drink wasn't helping. "Hmm. That's a good question. There's not much. This trip has been relaxing for me, though, just the chance to get away and think."

"Then maybe you should do this more often."

He touched the back of her hair lightly with his fingers. Her body went numb as his fingertips slid from her hair to her cheek and brushed across it softly. Okay, so there was no doubt that he was coming on to her, and coming hard and fast at that. She was surprised but also flattered that he found her attractive. It was all she could do to keep from giggling out loud.

He took his hand and gently turned her face toward his. Something told her to get up and get out of there. But she didn't. Not when he rubbed her chin, his face now inches from her own. Not when he placed his hand on her thigh. And not when he leaned in to kiss her.

Instead she closed her eyes and gave in to the moment, and his warm, moist lips made her feel like a giddy school girl again. It had been so long since a kiss made her feel this way. He squeezed her waist as his lips pulled away from hers and traveled down her neck. She could hear him panting heavily in her ear as his hand traveled back down to her thigh and slipped beneath the edges of her skirt.

That was when the phone rang. Maxine gasped and put her hand on his chest, pushing him away. "Whose phone is that?"

"Don't worry about it," he said, his voice hoarse.

She frowned as the phone rang again. "I think that's mine," she said and quickly stood up. What if it was Curtis or one of the girls? She crossed the room, picked her purse up off the chair and quickly fumbled inside for her cell phone. She glanced at the screen and realized that she didn't recognize the number of the caller.

"Hello?" she said as she put it to her ear.

"Maxine?" said a familiar voice that she couldn't place.

"Yes, this is Maxine."

"Oh, hi. It's Tonya."

Maxine breathed a deep sigh, but whether it was one of relief or regret she wasn't quite sure.

"Hi, Tonya." Maxine stood with her back to Aaron. She was too ashamed to look at him now.

"We just got back to the hotel from visiting relatives, and I got your message. Do you still want to get together? Mark wants to look at some property in Virginia Beach, but I could meet you for a late lunch if you haven't eaten."

Maxine glanced at her watch. "Um, actually I just had lunch."

"Oh, okay. Well…"

Maxine closed her eyes tightly. What was she thinking? Of staying here in this room and making out with Aaron? She must be losing her mind. "How about meeting for coffee instead?"

"That sounds good. Where do you want to meet?"

"Your hotel, in say, ten minutes?"

"It will take you longer than that to get here."

"I'm already here."

"At the Omni?" Tonya asked with obvious surprise.

"Yes."

"I see. Then I'll see you in ten minutes."

"Good. See you soon, Tonya."

She hung up the phone and put it back in her bag, her back still facing Aaron. She felt him stand up from the couch as she reached for her jacket.

"So you're leaving?" he asked softly as he strode toward her to help her into her jacket. She stepped to the side and turned to face him as she hastily slipped her arms into the sleeves.

"Yes," she said with finality.

"Sorry to hear that. I hope I haven't made you uncomfortable."

"You've made me *very* uncomfortable."

"I didn't mean to. I thought you were enjoying this as much as I was."

"I'm not sure what I was doing, Aaron. But this is wrong. In fact, I'm surprised you would do this. You just got married."

He smiled sheepishly.

"Why am I surprised? This is par for the course for you, isn't it? But it isn't for me."

"All evening you talked about how bad your life is and how you wanted to change it. Why not shake things up?"

"Wait a minute. I must have given you the wrong impression for you to say something like that. My life isn't bad. Are there some things I would change about it? Yes. Do I wish it was more exciting? Yes. But it's not a bad life. In fact, I'm thinking right now that it's pretty darn good. At least my husband is faithful."

He shrugged. "That's fine. I'm happy for you," he said sarcastically. "It's your life."

She narrowed her eyes. "You know what? I'm starting to feel real sorry for your new wife if this is how you are when she's not around. Is this how you behaved in college when *I* wasn't around?"

"You don't need to worry about my wife."

Maxine noticed that he avoided her question. "Maybe someone should because *you* obviously don't. I'm getting out of here." She grabbed her shoulder bag, walked quickly to the door and opened it. She turned to face him. "Goodbye, Aaron. It's been...interesting."

He nodded and she turned left. At the elevator she pressed the button and tapped her foot as she waited. What had just happened back there? That Aaron had made a pass at her was surprising enough, but that she had actually gone along with it, even for a hot minute, was shocking. What the hell was she thinking? The man had dumped her for her best friend. Now he was trying to cheat on his new wife with her. It looked like her mama was right, and Tonya had saved her many years of aggravation and heartache being married to that man.

CHAPTER 15

Tonya's eyes widened as she listened to Maxine tell her what had happened less than thirty minutes earlier in Aaron's hotel room.

"I don't know what got into me," Maxine said. "But thank God for your phone call."

"Perfect timing, it sounds like," Tonya said as she stirred sugar into her cup of Earl Grey tea.

"If anything, I wish your call would have come earlier. I can't believe I actually kissed that man. I feel dirty."

"You got swept away."

"*Pfft.* I'm forty-five years old and married. I have no business getting swept away by anyone besides my husband."

"Aaron is a hunk, and he can be tempting when he puts his mind to it."

Maxine leaned over the table in the restaurant and eyed Tonya closely. "He came after you back in college, didn't he?"

"Like a dog in heat. It started slowly at first, with him popping up at our dorm room when he knew you were in class."

Maxine twisted her lips. "The bum."

"Then he would show up outside my classes when they were over and offer to take me to my next class in his Vette. And he suddenly developed this big interest in my poetry."

Maxine nodded. All this time she had believed that Tonya was the instigator, the main culprit. "I think I always assumed that you had initiated the affair, because that meant that the problem was mainly you. If I allowed myself to believe that he was the one who started it, that meant there was something lacking in me, something that would make him look elsewhere. And I didn't want to believe that."

"There wasn't anything wrong with you. Some men just can't be trusted."

"I get that now. But I was very insecure back then. My mother lost my dad to women, one after the other, and the thought that I had lost my man to another woman infuriated me, especially since it was you. You said you were jealous of me, well, I think I was jealous of you."

Tonya frowned. "Why on earth were you jealous of me?"

"You were prettier and more interesting because you were the artsy type. You always got the guys."

"Yeah, all the jerks."

"Still, that was better than the few nerds I attracted. Or so I believed at the time. And I always thought your mother was glamorous and exotic. She was a photographer who traveled and lived all over the country, whereas my mother couldn't even keep my father at home. I know now that that wasn't her fault, and I realize after what you told me yesterday that you were lonely. But I didn't see any of that back then. I was too wrapped up in my own issues, I guess."

"You don't still have feelings for Aaron after all these years, do you?"

Maxine blinked, unsure of how to respond to that. "I have feelings for what I imagined we had, not for him, if that makes any sense. He was my first love."

Tonya nodded.

"But even that just flew out the window," Maxine continued. "How could I have been so blind?"

Tonya grunted. "We both got duped. He's bad news."

"What ever happened with you two after you went to Vegas?"

Tonya took a sip of tea. "Do you really want to hear it?"

"If you feel like telling it."

"Right after graduation we flew to Vegas. It sounds dumb now, but we were going to get married in one of those little chapels you see on TV. After we got out there, he kept putting it off for one more day. Then on about the third night I came down from our room—all the hotels there have casinos on the ground floor—and I saw him standing behind this white chick who was sitting at a slot machine, just a little too close."

"Uh-uh."

"Uh-huh. She was gambling, and they were talking and laughing, but something just didn't look right about the whole thing. I thought about how he had come on to me when he was engaged to you. You know how they say if he cheats *with* you, he'll cheat *on* you? Well, I knew at that moment that he was going to be big trouble if I married him. I broke off the engagement that night."

"Good for you," Maxine said. "Sounds like my mother was right. You showed me what he really is before I got stuck with him. Trouble is, I'm just starting to see it now."

"Better late than never. How are things with you and Curtis?"

"Sometimes I think our life is so dull, but I'm starting to believe that dull is good." Maxine laughed.

"I hear you."

"Things were never as exciting with Curtis as they were when I was with Aaron, but some of that comes from being older and wiser about love and relationships now. And Curtis is the kind of man you can trust one hundred percent. I can always depend on him and he'll do anything for me."

"That doesn't sound dull to me, girl. That sounds pretty damn good."

Maxine nodded. "I would love for us to do more exciting things, like traveling or even just going out for a night on the town once in a while like we used to. Having children changes all that. But Curtis is a good man. If you start with a solid relationship, you can always spice things up if you're motivated."

Things had finally clicked for Maxine. It had taken a disastrous rendezvous with Aaron, but at least she got it now. She knew what was important in a relationship for her and what wasn't.

"When I met Mark, I was coming out of one of a long line of high-drama relationships," Tonya said. "All good-looking men, successful, smooth talkers. Manipulating women was like their part-time job, you know, and they could probably have convinced me to jump off a bridge with them. I wouldn't give men like Mark, who are under six feet tall, aren't drop-dead gorgeous and are nice to women, the time of day."

"I was surprised when I met Mark at the house. I mean, he's kind of cute in a way, but he's shorter than any man I've ever seen you with."

"I have learned to love his looks, 'cause he treats me so good."

Maxine nodded with understanding. "What made you change your mind and decide to give Mark a chance?"

"Frank, the guy in Houston, moved in with a woman living down there. He came right out and told me he was moving in with her and had the nerve to ask if he could keep seeing me on the side. That's bad enough, but the worst is that I actually went along with it for a while."

Maxine shook her head sadly. "A lot of black women are into man sharing."

"Not *this* woman, not anymore. When Frank called me and said he was coming to Bermuda with this other woman and that he wanted us all to meet for dinner, girl, it hit me just how stupid I was being. I told him to go to hell."

"Good for you."

"That was the last time I talked to him. Six months later I was engaged to Mark. Fireworks? No. But I've never been happier or more at peace."

"My girlfriend Debbie once told me that when you meet a man and the fireworks go off, that it will only be a short time before they burn out. But when you meet a man and the feeling you get is more like a steady hum, then you've got something that can last a lifetime. Mama calls them ever-after men."

Tonya smiled. "I like that."

Maxine raised her mug over the table. "Here's to Curtis and Mark, our ever-after men."

CHAPTER 16

Maxine entered the house and set her Tumi bag on the floor near the stairs leading up to the second level. She stood still for a moment and looked around. Curtis had taken Brandi to the mall to meet some friends so Maxine knew that the house was empty. That explained the silence. But something still felt different to her.

She had been away for only a few days, yet it felt like months and she wasn't sure why. She crossed the foyer and walked through the family room to the kitchen. Everything was in its usual place—the remote sat idly on the family room couch, today's newspaper was spread out on the kitchen table and the unused coffee was still in the pot. Curtis had even left a note on the refrigerator saying when he should be back, although she had talked to him that morning just before she and her mother left Newport News.

She walked back across the family room carpet past the armchair and footrest, and suddenly she knew what had changed since she was last here. *Her.* She felt more at peace than she had in years. She was glad to be home and couldn't wait to see Curtis and Brandi. It felt so good to feel that way about her family again.

She would have to wait until tomorrow to see Brandi, though. She and Curtis had called down to Newport News that morning to ask if Brandi could go on her first double date that afternoon and then on to spend the night at her best friend Karen's house. Maxine's gut reaction was to say, no way. Brandi was only fifteen, and she and Curtis had always said she wouldn't be allowed to date until she was sixteen. And her last report card had been disappointing to say the least, especially her grade in history. But Curtis had explained over the phone that Brandi got a B on her history exam the past week and then Brandi got on the line and pleaded with her mother.

"Please, Ma. I promise to do better at school. I just got a B on my history test."

"Your father told me that, and I'm very proud of you. I knew you could do it. Still, we said no dating until you're sixteen. Naomi had to wait until she was sixteen."

"I'll be sixteen in less than a month, Ma. And Karen's mom said she could go. Pleeease!"

"I don't know, Brandi. We haven't even met this boy."

"Dad is taking all of us to the movies. Of course, he'll meet him."

Maxine sighed loudly. Why not? she thought. It was a double date, Curtis was chaperoning and Brandi *was* almost sixteen. "All right, you can go as long as your dad takes you."

Brandi yelled so loudly that Maxine had to remove the phone from her ear for a second.

"Thanks, Ma!"

"How are you getting from the movie to Karen's house?"

"Dad's taking us, I think."

"Let me talk to him."

Curtis got back on the line. "I'm going to pick them up from the movie and take her to Karen's. Then I'll drop the boys off at their houses."

"Fine, Curtis. Sounds like you've got it all covered. I'll see you later this evening."

She picked up the Tumi bag at the base of the stairs and walked up. She placed her bag on the bed and opened it, then she went to a window, lifted the blind and looked out. Before the trip to Newport News she would never have allowed this premature date because, well, just because. She was more rigid then, probably too rigid. Since the trip, it felt like she'd gotten a whole new life. Mama had even commented on the drive back from Newport News that she seemed happier. Mama was naturally thrilled that she had met Tonya for tea and that they were again on speaking terms.

"Why don't you go down and visit her in Bermuda?" Mama had said when they were about an hour outside of Newport News.

"Let's not get carried away now, Mama."

Mama laughed. "You're right. I'm just so happy to see you and Tonya make up."

Make up? Maxine wasn't sure that's how she would describe it but she'd let it go at that. No point dampening her mother's spirits. And she supposed that she and Tonya had made up, sort of. They had exchanged telephone numbers and planned to keep in touch. How much further than that it would ever go, Maxine wasn't sure.

She walked back to her suitcase and removed her clothes, sorting them on the bed between clean and dirty. She picked her black nightgown up out of the bag and held it at arm's length. The floor-length negligee had been a Christmas gift from Curtis many years ago and still had the Victoria's Secret store tag on it. She hadn't even worn it in Newport News.

Suddenly she had a thought. Why not slip into the nightgown and surprise Curtis? He would probably love that. Brandi was spending the night at a friend's house, so it would be just the two of them. And make no mistake about it, Aaron had aroused feelings in her that had been dormant for years. She was still a vibrant, healthy, desirable woman with needs. It was a shame that it had taken a former lover to show her that. But at least he had shown her.

Now to do something about it with the man she really loved and appreciated. She glanced at her watch. Curtis should be back in about thirty minutes so she had some time. She found a pair of scissors in her nightstand and cut the tag off the negligee then she walked into the master bathroom, filled the tub with scented oils and took a quick soak. She slipped into the negligee and walked around the house, picking up every candle she could find. She placed them around the family room on shelves and tables and lit them. Then she found an old Barry White CD that was one of Curtis's favorites and popped it in.

She turned off all the lights and glanced around the candlelit room. It looked very romantic. Not bad for a last-minute job. She sat on the couch, picked up a magazine and waited.

And waited. She glanced at her watch. Curtis had obviously been held up, and she was feeling a little chilly so she went upstairs and put on her white terry-cloth bathrobe then went back downstairs to the couch. She had started to doze off when she heard the key in the back door. She walked into the kitchen to see Curtis entering, his hands filled with brown paper bags.

"Where have you been?" she asked anxiously.

"It's great to see you again, too," he said sarcastically as he placed the bags on the kitchen table.

Maxine checked herself. That was the old Maxine. Always anxious, always worried, usually antagonistic. She smiled. "Sorry. And it really is good to see you, again." She waited until he had finished placing the bags on the kitchen table, then reached out and hugged him.

He squeezed her tightly and kissed her forehead. "Hmm. Maybe you should go away more often if this is how you come back."

"I couldn't agree with you more. I feel great."

He held her at arm's length. "You look different. More relaxed, happier. What happened down there?"

"Pretty much what you would expect at a funeral. I saw a lot of relatives I hadn't seen in years. And Tonya was there." She would tell Curtis about seeing Aaron some day soon and even about the kiss they had shared. But now was not the time.

Curtis raised an eyebrow. "Oh? How is she?"

"She's good. She was there with her new husband and she looks very happy. We had coffee."

He nodded. "And from the looks of it, you two made up?"

"You could say that."

"I'll bet it felt good to bury the old hatchet."

"I admit, it did."

"Great. Now let's eat." He began removing containers from the bags. "I stopped and picked up some Chinese food for us. I'm starving since I..." He paused, holding a container of rice, and cocked his head to the side as he looked at her with a puzzled expression on his face. "Is that Barry White on the CD?"

She smiled at him seductively, opened her bathrobe and slipped it off her shoulders.

Curtis blinked, glanced away and then back at her. "Did I miss something? That nightgown looks very familiar."

"It should. You bought it for me, silly."

He looked her up and down. "*Mmm-mph.* I've got great taste, don't I?"

She laughed. "You certainly do. Still hungry?"

Curtis smiled broadly and dropped the rice container on the table. "Well, you know, everything is a matter of degrees. Suddenly, I'm not *that* hungry."

She reached out and grabbed his hand playfully. "Come dance with me," she said as she led him back into the family room. "We haven't danced with each other in ages."

"What brought all this on?" he asked after they had been slow dancing in the family room for a few minutes.

She looked into his eyes. "You."

"Me? How?"

"Let's just say that being away put a lot of things in perspective for me."

"So you realized just how lucky you are to have me, right?" he said teasingly.

"Exactly," she said.

Curtis looked surprised. "Really? I was kind of joking."

"It's true, Curtis. You are a fantastic father and husband. I'm a very lucky woman, so are Naomi and Brandi. I apologize for not showing that before and being such a jerk at times. But that's going to change, starting now."

He whistled. "I'm going to start sending you away once a month."

She laughed, and he took her hand and turned toward the stairs leading up to the bedroom, but she pulled him back.

"What?" he asked, looking puzzled. "I thought that was where all this was leading."

She put her hands on his chest. "Let's take this slowly—a little dancing, talking, petting on the couch. You know, romance? We've got forever since Brandi's out all night, and I want this to be more like it used to be when we first met and spent hours making love."

Curtis nodded and put his arms around her. "I got you."

"I know you do."

He leaned down and gave a long, passionate kiss on the lips.

"That's what I'm talking about," she said softly. She rested her head on his shoulder and closed her eyes as they moved slowly to the music.

For my mother, Lolita B. Files,
and my late father, Arthur James Files, Sr.,
who always called my mom by her middle name: Belle.

THREE FOR THE ROAD

Lolita Files

CHAPTER 1

9-1-1

The battered buildings were crumbling. People were jumping to their deaths.

"I need my husband!" Lilibelle screamed. "I just need to get ahold of my husband!"

"We understand, ma'am," said the woman on the other end of the line, "but there's nothing we can do. Please try to calm down."

Lilibelle Goldman couldn't calm down. The world was ending. How could she calm down?

She paced barefoot across the living room floor of her sprawling Park Avenue apartment as she did her best to get the woman to understand.

"Do you have a television? Have you seen what's happening here?"

"Are you calling from New York or Washington, ma'am?"

"Yes, from New York. The whole city is coming apart. I need to reach my husband."

"Are you okay?" the woman asked. "Has anyone in your family been hurt?"

"No, but I need my husband. I don't know what's happening. There may be more planes. The city is under attack."

The hotel clerk at the Loews Ventana Canyon Resort in Tucson, Arizona, wasn't sure of what to say. This was the twelfth time the woman had called, asking them to ring the room of Dr. Adam Goldman. But Dr. Goldman hadn't answered, and she had become more and more frantic with each call.

"Have you tried his cell phone?" the clerk asked.

"Of course I have, but there's no reception. I keep getting a message saying service is out. Everybody's probably trying to use their cell phones and it's jamming the satellites. My husband's at a convention at your hotel. Can't someone go and look for him? Perhaps he doesn't know what's happening here."

"I'm sure he does, ma'am," said the clerk. "Everyone here is in shock. All the TVs are tuned to the news channels. People are frightened, some are crying. It's just awful what's happened. Many of our hotel customers are trying to make arrangements to check out and return to the East Coast, but flights have been shut down. Could you hold, please?"

"No, I can't hold!" Lilibelle screamed, but the clerk had already done the deed, placing Lilibelle's hysteria on ice in order to take another call. She was about to hurl the phone across the room when the line beeped. Lilibelle clicked over.

"Hello?"

"Lili."

"Adam! Where are you? I've been calling your cell and your hotel room. Do you see what's happened here? The buildings are on fire! I'm so scared. You need to come home!"

"Calm down, Lili, calm down."

"I can't calm down. Didn't you hear what I said? The buildings are on fire. The whole city's covered in smoke and ash."

She was crying now, her hysteria at full throttle.

"Have you talked to the kids?" he asked.

"They're on their way home. Sam picked up Jenny and Sommer from school and they're all driving here now. But the bridges and tunnels have all been closed. I don't even know if they'll be able to get into the city."

"They'll get in all right," Adam said.

"How do you know that? You're in Tucson, all the way on the other side of the country. You need to be with us, Adam. It's like the end of the world. People are dead. They're jumping out of windows. You can see it right there on TV. What are we going to do?"

Adam Jakob Goldman, M.D., wealthy orthopedic surgeon from a long line of wealthy surgeons in the Brookline area of Boston, listened to his wife as she hyperventilated into the phone. This was Lilibelle's way, had been for all the time he'd known her, which was since her freshman year at Yale some twenty-five years before.

He had fallen in love with the beautiful young black girl the second he'd seen her. So exotic, so delicate, so ultimately high maintenance. He had defied his family for her. It was expected that he would marry a nice Jewish girl, have some nice Jewish kids and settle into the very lucrative family practice in Boston. But Lilibelle had changed everything. She had owned his heart from that very first day and things had been settled, just like that. He married her months later during her freshman year— his family be damned—and they'd eventually had three beautiful half Jewish kids that Adam's very staid family back in Brookline never bothered to get to know. He'd flourished in spite of them shutting him out, building a hugely successful New York practice in the process.

Lilibelle had turned out to be an excellent mom, an excellent wife, an excellent lover and an excellent best friend. But practically everything was a crisis. Everything was the end of the world. Even now, when he knew the sky was literally falling in New York and she had reason to be frightened, it was still very frustrating.

He'd seen this drill so many times, most recently when their youngest child, Sommer, had gone off to college. Lilibelle once again unleashed the hysterics. The crying, the hyperventilating, the falling sky, all in response to the fear of an empty nest.

Adam knew he was partly responsible for her being this way. She had come from an indulgent family that had catered to her—a very beautiful only child—and he had continued to indulge her on an even greater level once they were married. He had tried to assuage her fears over Sommer's leaving for school.

"Next year, when I retire," he'd said, "we'll travel. Just you and I. We'll drive America and see everything you've always wanted to see."

"Even Vegas?" she had asked, delighted at the sound of it all.

"Even Vegas," he had assured her, relieved that he had apparently found the right thing to say. "And after that, we'll travel the world. We'll go to all our favorite places, plus countries we haven't seen. You've always talked about Prague, remember?"

While the thought of going to Prague was cool, Lilibelle was most excited about the Vegas part. For all their traveling over the years, she had never been to Las Vegas. It represented wild fun and abandon to her, a place of neon dreams and fantasy. She wanted to see it all—the shows, the casinos, the high rollers. Even though she'd seen those kinds of things in Monte Carlo, there was something about Vegas that had an irresistible allure. And they had spas there, lots and lots of spas. She was a pampered woman, used to having everything provided for her, including household help and car services. The thought of all those spas waiting under the Vegas sun was exciting. It was enough to divert her mind from dwelling on the fact that her youngest daughter was no longer at home.

Adam had successfully defused her drama that day, but today would not be so easy. In fact, he knew, it would only get worse.

"Have you booked a flight?" she asked. "How soon can you get here? We all need to be together during this. If we're going to die, Adam, we need to die together."

"Stop it, Lili. No one's going to die."

Lili whimpered. He had yelled at her, so unlike him. Adam usually had unlimited patience with her. It was something she could count on. His patience, indulgence and steadfast commitment were the foundations of her entire world.

"I can book the flight if you want," she said. "I'll call the travel agency."

"All the flights to New York have been cancelled."

"Maybe you can fly into Philly," Lilibelle said. "You can get a rental car and drive here from there."

Adam's neck felt hot. Lili could be so determined once she fixed her mind on something.

"There are no flights to the East Coast right now," said Adam. "Everything's been shut down. No one's flying anywhere, at any airport. This thing has got the government in a tailspin, Lili. The thing to do is keep your head. You need to be calm for the kids. The last thing they need is to see you falling to pieces as they walk in the door."

"Then come home," she cried. "Can't you rent a car there? Can't you drive?"

"Drive from Tucson?" he asked. "Come on, Lili, don't be insane."

She was hyperventilating again, she had the phone pressed so close to her ear he could hear her erratic breathing.

"Adam, you have to be here. You need to come home. This is the worst thing that has ever happened. How can you not be here with us?"

Adam was about to answer when a cool hand suddenly rubbed the back of his hot neck. He leaned back into it.

"Is everything okay?" a familiar voice asked.

"Who is that?" said Lilibelle. "Is someone there with you?"

"I'm at a medical convention, Lili. There are lots of people here."

"Oh," said the voice. "You haven't told her."

"Told me what?" Lilibelle demanded.

"Adam! Who is that?"

"It's Robin," he said. "Robin McBain."

"Oh, okay," Lilibelle said. She'd been aware that Robin was attending the convention. Robin McBain was one of the doctors in Adam's practice. "Well, what are you going to do? When are you coming home? I'll call the travel agency and see if they can find you a rental car in Tucson."

"I'm not driving to New York from Tucson, Lili. That's just out of the question."

"Then what are you going to do?" she screamed. "When are you coming?"

The phone was muffled again for what felt like an infinity of seconds, then it opened up.

"I'm not coming home, Lili."

Adam kept his voice flat, full of nothing.

"What do you mean, you're not coming home? What about me and the kids? How are we going to get through this by ourselves, Adam? What if we die?"

"You're not going to die, Lili. Everything is going to be all right."

"Everything is not all right," she yelled. "What's the matter with you? Have you lost your mind?"

"Perhaps," he said in a small voice. "Perhaps I'm finally getting it back."

"What does that mean?" asked Lilibelle. "What are you talking about?"

Adam cleared his throat.

"I'm leaving you, Lili," he announced. "Robin and I...we want to be together. We've been together for a while now. I don't want to have to hide it anymore."

"What?"

"Robin and I. She understands me, Lili. She always has. I know this might not be the right time, but those planes hitting the buildings have made me realize that I have to live my life honestly, not denying myself happiness anymore. I've lived for everyone else for so long. I deserve something good for myself. I want to be with Robin. I want a divorce."

The words clanged loudly in Lilibelle's ear, made even more intense because the phone had stuck from the moisture of sweat that had gathered around it.

"I won't fight you for money," Adam continued. "I'll give you half of everything, even the practice. You can have the apartment and our other properties. The kids all have their trusts. I'll pay you alimony, whatever. I can always make more money. I just want to be with Robin. I'll trade all the money in the world if it means I can be free to be with her."

Lilibelle was silent, her hysteria having abruptly given over to catatonia. She stood in the middle of the living room, staring at the window.

"Lili? Are you there? Did you hear what I just said?"

Lilibelle gazed at the window, assessing the glass. She tried to calculate her weight and dimensions in relation to the thick pane. She was a slight woman, in perfect shape, at the height of health and attractiveness considering the fact that she was forty-three years old. If she ran very hard, with a good rush of momentum behind her, her five foot seven, one hundred and twenty-six pound frame just might break through the glass. And she could jump—just like the people in the towers—out of this burning building that had suddenly become her life, and it would all be over. This very, very bad dream would come to an end. She imagined herself falling, falling, falling from the sky....

She stared at the window.

"Lili? Lilibelle? Lili? Can you hear me?"

She stood there with the phone stuck to her ear.

CHAPTER 2

In Love and War

It was one of the fastest legal transactions she'd ever seen. Adam had filed the required forms with the courts, and less than ten days after that fateful phone call on 9/11, Lilibelle had been served with divorce papers. Adam called in advance to let her know they were coming. He was being so incredibly nice about the whole thing.

He didn't want things to drag on through the courts, he'd said.

"I know how hard this is on you and the kids. It's hard on me, too, Lili. And Robin. It's not like she planned any of this. It's not her fault. But none of us have to suffer needlessly for it. I'm sorry this happened. I really am. I couldn't have imagined it in a million years. But it did, and now we're in it, so let's do what we can to stanch the bleeding as much as possible. We can settle this amicably out of court. I believe you'll agree with me when I say it's the best thing for everyone all around."

Adam was a loving but painfully practical man. He had acted only once in his life with daring passion and risk—when he defied his Boston family to marry a black girl.

Correction. He had acted this way twice. When he left that same black girl—now an older woman—for a woman at his medical practice. On a day of epic devastation, when emotions and fear were running rampant, hand in hand. Lili was accustomed to Adam and his logical approach to effecting solutions. Never once had she imagined that same procedural template would be applied to their union.

Thus, papers arrived detailing Adam's offer to surrender half the marital assets and monies, plus their place in the city and the estate in Sagaponack, while separately assuring the long-term financial security of their children. The courts might not award her half, he'd said. You could never tell what a judge's idea of equitable distribution was, especially now that the children were all out of the house and off in college, practically adults. But he wanted to make sure she had more than enough to live comfortably for the rest of her life. As Lilibelle and her attorney reviewed the documents, it became apparent that Adam had been planning for this for a while.

"We can fight it," said her attorney, Bill Archer, an aggressive litigator with a respectable track record for hefty settlements. "We can take him for everything. We can damage his professional reputation. There are many things we can do to assure you'll never have to worry about money again."

"But he's already offering to give me so much. Both properties, plus forty million dollars, and the kids will be set. It's a lot, Bill. There's no need to ruin the man."

She didn't want to ruin him. She still loved him very much.

"Why not, Lili? Look what he's done to you. He's taken up with another woman, a coworker of his, someone employed by his practice, right under your nose. Is that okay with you?"

"No, it's not okay," she said, "but that's not..."

"I didn't think so," Bill said. "The two of you have been a part of the elite circles of New York society for years. People admired you as a couple. You worked hard to establish the position you've attained. All your charity efforts, what you've done for the museums. Adam has made a mockery of everything. He's made a mockery of you in front of all of New York."

She was in Bill's office, sitting on his couch. He was beside her. The divorce papers were spread out on the coffee table in front of them. The more Bill spoke, the more hushed-yet-disturbed his tone became. He was trying to rile her, she could tell.

"Adam has put a tremendous dent in your reputation, Lili. The abandoned wife always ends up the awkward figure in all this. You'll find yourself the recipient of pity more than anything. Everyone will treat you like a bastard child."

Lili glanced up at him.

"No, they won't. I have a number of friends who I'm sure will stand by me."

"That may be the case," he said, "but realize that once Adam marries Robin, and he's already told you that he will, the two of them will reemerge on the social scene and it will be as though Adam never left. He will be embraced, and eventually, so will Robin. Some of your friends may be standoffish with her at first, but in time she'll be welcomed. Adam's worth over eighty million dollars, Lili. Power and money always prevail. Remember that. Someone of his professional stature and position usually retains his power. He may even be admired for his new younger, stunning wife. That's why we have to make sure you come out on top in all this. You have to retain a sense of power and social standing, and that will primarily come through how much money you get. We can take this to court, and I believe we'll get more than half."

Lili was still, barely breathing. All she'd heard was *younger, stunning wife*. Bill's words stung. Robin was thirty-four, nine years younger than Lily. And she was undeniably beautiful and smart. Lili should have paid attention to that before. In retrospect, the signs were all there. Adam was constantly talking about Robin's tremendous contributions to the practice. Lili had dismissed it as shop talk, something she'd never had much time for anyway.

"Leave work at the office, honey," was her standard line to her husband. "When you're here with me, I want you with me."

Adam had been there with her all right. But his heart was at work, and Lili realized now that she had played a major role in keeping it there.

"So you see," Bill was saying, "you have to do something.

You have to take him for everything. He'll recover. Men like him always do."

Lilibelle stared at the coffee table. She was surprised at herself. The old Lilibelle, pre-9/11, would have been making a grand display. Something in her had changed, as if overnight. She was no longer exploding. Her expression had turned inward. She was very quietly imploding instead.

She still loved Adam, she loved him very much, even more now, it seemed, than she did before he told her he was leaving. He and the children had been the world. But she didn't want to hold on to to someone who didn't want to be with her, nor would she beg for him to come back. Her ego was too frail for that. There was no way she would wake up and lie down with a man who was wishing every moment he was somewhere else.

"I'm going to send these papers back to his attorney," said Bill, "and tell him no deal. We're going to play this tough all the way down the line. We'll contest the divorce until we get him up to an amount that makes the settlement worthwhile. We can drag this out as long as necessary. Trust me, Lili. I'll take care of you. I'll make sure you get exactly what you deserve."

Bill's left arm was around her shoulders now. His right hand was gathering the papers on the table into a pile. Lilibelle noticed the signature page.

"Let's just get it over with," she said.

"What?" Bill asked. "C'mon, Lili, you can't know what you're saying. You're still emotional about all this. It's all so new, I'm sure you haven't wrapped your brain around it yet. I can't imagine how painful this must be for you, but one day the intensity of that pain will subside and you'll be able to operate with a little more clarity. Your rational side will emerge, and that's when you'll realize that what I'm suggesting is right. Let me be your rational side for now. I can see this for what it is. You have to get as much out of this divorce as you can. You're entitled to it. What Adam has done to you and your family is wrong."

Lili shook her head.

"I'm going to sign, Bill. I'm going to accept his settlement. There's no point in me fighting any of this. I'm fine with what he's offering. I just want this to be over. "

Bill pulled her shoulders so that she was now facing him.

"Lili, no. Adam is a very rich man. The least you should do is come out of this a very rich woman."

She couldn't look at him. He lifted her chin with his finger, trying to force eye contact, but she refused to let them connect.

"Lili." His voice was softer now, still hushed, but without the edge. "Don't lay down for this. Adam betrayed you. He betrayed your vows. He abandoned you on 9/11, for God's sake. Don't you see the scope of the indignity you've been dealt?"

"I want to sign the papers," she said. "Just give me a pen. I'm going to sign."

Bill pulled away from her now, no longer the whispering encourager. He became the authority figure. He assumed she needed to be spoken to with a firm tongue. Then she would see the logic. Then she would have some sense.

"I will not let you sign these papers," he said. "I will not watch you sell yourself, and your children, short. I will not watch you be ridiculed by your peers when they realize that Adam not only left you for another woman, he left you with..."

"You will give me a pen." Lilibelle was looking at him now, her eyes piercing, her voice clear. "And you will slide that last page over here and watch me sign it. Then you'll do the job I'm paying you for and get this done as quickly as possible. Otherwise I'm getting up and walking out of here and getting myself another attorney."

Bill was speechless, his heavy, frustrated breathing the only sound in the room. Lili's eyes remained on his. She held out her hand.

He reached inside his jacket pocket and pulled out a pen. He handed it to her.

"You're making a terrible mistake."

"It won't be the first," she said. "I just want this to be over."

Adam was sitting across from Lili, cutting into his medium-rare porterhouse. They were in Brooklyn at Peter Luger Steak House, one of the only reasons Adam was willing to cross the bridge into that borough. Lili watched him carefully slice the meat, as though he were in the operating room. She thought about all the times she'd seen him do exactly what he was doing now. Back then it meant nothing. It was an incidental thing, like the lighting, or the sound of rain against a window. It was a part of the ambience, barely worth giving a thought. Now the way his hands held the knife and the fork, the way a strain of blood oozed onto the plate, and his knuckles—the folds of skin around his knuckles—all of it was center stage. Now that they were no longer a part of the backdrop of her life, they meant everything.

"Thanks for signing the papers, Lili," Adam said as he brought the forked meat to his mouth. He allowed himself to savor the meat, chew it and swallow before he spoke again.

She didn't know why she was here. Yes, she did. She was there because she was crazy. Crazy enough to think that if he saw her again in one of their favorite settings, just the two of them alone—without attorneys, without the kids, without Robin—that he would see her the way he'd seen her all those years they were together. That he would remember that beautiful freshman at Yale, the one he fell for the instant he saw her. Then he would realize how insane he must be to want something different. There was a quarter of a century of love between them. It wasn't just a habit to be dropped. It was a life. It was a way of life they'd made together.

She watched him eating. Adam hadn't even looked up from his plate.

"The steak is pretty good, huh?"

"Superb," he said, finally lifting his head. "Is yours okay? You've barely touched it."

"Oh, yes. It's fine."

"Good."

Adam reached for his glass of wine and took a long swallow. His eyes were on hers as he drank. He was still looking at her when he set the glass down.

"You know what I always loved about us?" he asked.

"What's that?"

"That we were always such great friends. Through everything, in spite of what's happened, I've always felt you were my dearest friend."

"Then why couldn't you talk to me?" Lilibelle asked. "Why couldn't you tell me when you first felt yourself drifting away? We could have done something about it. We could have gotten professional help."

"No. No." Adam was at his steak again. "This was bigger than that, Lili."

"What do you mean? Was our situation that awful? Was I that hard to live with?"

He cut into the meat, sectioning off a piece before he spoke again.

"Well? Was I?"

"It's not as simple as that," he finally said. "I've been changing. I think we both have been changing over the years. That was a big part of it. But then there was Robin. I can't discount her in this equation. There was... I don't know how to say this without it sounding harsh..."

"Just say it," she said, hating herself for wanting to know.

"All right," he said. "There was...an inevitability about us... Do you know what I mean? This wasn't some casual office attraction. There is a tremendous chemistry, no, *synergy*, between me and her. It's undeniable. Even if she and I had never gotten together, I couldn't have continued with our marriage, you see. Just knowing she existed without me being able to have her would have broken me down. It would have debilitated me to the point where I would have been no good to you anyway. The distraction was too great. It was eating away at me. Come to find out it was eating away at her the same way, too."

Lilibelle could see herself watching him talk, even though her head had flown up and away and was hovering above the table on an imaginary string.

"It was chemical, Lili, like she was a drug. I don't expect you to understand this. Hell, I can't understand it myself. But I love Robin. I love her so much."

His hands were waving now, holding the utensils as he attempted to explain himself.

"I rise to my better self because of her. I want to do things I've never done before. You were always complaining about how practical I was..."

"I wasn't complaining."

"I don't mean it that way," he said quickly. "I didn't mean it as an attack. I'm just trying to explain myself. I'm talking to you as a friend."

A friend. That's all she was now. A confidante he could talk to about the woman who finally made him feel real love.

Lilibelle kept watching him, couldn't stop looking at his knuckles as they worked the utensils, this minute moving towards the creamed spinach, the next minute moving towards his mouth. He was a magnificent machine, all wrinkled knuckles and changed emotions and suddenly discarded practicality. He was her magnificent machine once. But then, according to what he'd just said, he wasn't exactly magnificent when he was with her. Robin had brought that out in him. Robin, with her intoxicating, druglike qualities that had made him abandon a quarter century of love.

Lilibelle realized that she was indeed crazy to think that this time alone with him would make him change his heart. Adam's heart wasn't even in the room.

Time caved in on that moment at the table at Peter Luger's. Aeons passed as Adam spoke what Lilibelle assumed were words but they came across as sounds whose meanings didn't register, all between bites of steak, hash browns, creamed spinach and swigs of wine—none of which was touched by her. And, like that, it was over, and they were standing outside, in front of the restaurant and he was hugging her as he said goodbye. Robin was curbside, sitting behind the wheel of a silver Mercedes. What was she doing there? How had she known how long their dinner would take?

Lilibelle suddenly understood that she and Adam wouldn't be riding back to the city together, even though they had come together in her car. He was saying his goodbyes here. At the curb. In Brooklyn. A place he had no love for, other than Peter Luger's steaks.

"Remember, Lili," he was saying, "I'm still your friend, if you'll have me. I'm just a phone call away... Both of us..."

"Both of who?" she heard herself ask.

"Me and Robin," Adam said without the slightest bit of sarcasm. He glanced back at the car, lowering his voice to a whisper, even though the car windows were up. "I know it's hard for you to see her as a friend, but she is. She has a tremendous amount of respect for you."

Lilibelle's head was still on that string, hovering above them, inflated beyond nature's intent, surely about to pop.

"We're here for you for whatever you need. We can still be a family, all of us, just not in the same way."

He clenched her tighter, then kissed her cheek.

"I'm so glad we were able to work this all out. So glad it didn't end badly."

Then he let go and stepped toward the car. He opened the door and got inside. Robin waved to her. Lilibelle was frozen. Seconds later, Adam and Robin were gone.

Robin had pulled off with Lilibelle's man and Lilibelle's life. All she was left with was an empty stomach and an aching heart on the curb at Peter Luger's.

She stood there in a stupor, resisting the urge to clench her fists, her head still floating in prolonged disbelief. She was doing her best to remain a lady. A lady would be dignified, she thought. A lady would not fall apart or show her defeat. She wanted to hurt them both physically, smash their faces, push sharp objects into their flesh, but she'd remained a lady. A laughing couple passed her on their way into the restaurant. Lilibelle wanted to cry. She smiled awkwardly instead.

We're here for you, Adam had said.

We. They were a *we.* How could he do this after having been at her side for more than two decades?

A quarter century. A quarter century. The phrase just wouldn't stop ringing in her head.

A quarter century was a long time. Long enough for two people to fuse into one. She and Adam were the real *we,* not him and Robin. Yet Adam had uttered those words to her plainly, without remorse or consideration.

We're here for you.

Right.

She would never trust another man again.

CHAPTER 3

Life Is a Highway

"Mom, I can't believe you're going to do this."

"I'm doing it, honey. There's no turning back now."

Lilibelle was walking and pulling a piece of Louis Vuitton luggage on wheels into the living room. It was the last of three identical suitcases. She talked on the phone with her daughter, Sommer, as she pulled it across the room.

"But where are you going to go? What are you going to do? You can't just get on the road like this. You've never done anything like this by yourself. Dad's…"

Lilibelle let her daughter's sudden silence hang between them for a minute.

"Sorry, Mom."

"I know, pumpkin. I know I've never done anything like this by myself without your father. Perhaps it's time I learned how."

Lilibelle left the suitcase in the foyer by the front door with the other two pieces, then she walked toward the kitchen.

"I'm actually quite excited about it. I've got the trip all mapped out and everything. Guess what my final destination will be?"

"What?"

"Vegas!"

"Vegas?!" cried Sommer. "Mom! You can't drive to Las Vegas by yourself. That's all the way across the country. This is crazy. You're just acting out."

Lilibelle laughed as she grabbed a bottle of water from the fridge. Sommer wanted to be a psychologist. The girl was only a freshman and already she was diagnosing her mother.

"I'm not acting out, Sommer."

"Yes, you are, Mom. This is totally a reaction to everything that's happened. You're gonna get out there on the road all by yourself, and suddenly you're going to realize that you don't really want to be there. And you're gonna freak, Mom. I know it. You know how easily you freak out over things."

"Is that right?" Lilibelle said, leaning against the island in the kitchen.

"Yes. You freak out over everything."

Lili sipped her water.

"Is that what your father thought?" she asked.

"Mom." Sommer's voice was soft.

"Lili's high-strung, she's a drama queen. That's what he thought, right? That's what you all think, isn't it?"

"No, Mom, that's not what we think. Besides, you can't help the way you are. Dad coddled you. He gave you everything. He helped make you that way."

Lilibelle scanned the apartment as her daughter spoke, her eyes drifting over all the pieces of furniture and family pictures and artwork and antiques and plants and everything that stood for something on its own but had come to reflect the sum total of her life.

"Mom?"

"I'm here, pumpkin."

"You're not high maintenance. Not really."

"Sommer, baby, why don't you quit while you're behind."

They both laughed.

"But seriously, Mom. I'm really worried about this road trip. How long are you gonna be gone?"

Lilibelle made her way back toward the living room.

"I'm not putting a time limit on it," she said. "I've wanted to do this for a very long time. Your father and I were planning to do it together, when he retired next year. But that won't be happening now, will it? Sudden change of plans and all."

The phone was silent on Sommer's end.

"You there?"

"I'm here, Mom. I just don't like it when you wallow like that."

"Was I wallowing? Is that what that was?"

"Yes, it was wallowing. You try to mask it as sarcasm, but it's clearly the pain crying out."

Lili stopped in the middle of the room.

"Really? It's that clear, is it?"

"Crystal."

"Pumpkin, you're going to make one fine psychologist."

"I know."

Lilibelle looked at the suitcases by the door. She realized she needed to make a move. If this was to be done, it was best to do it right now, as planned. Before she changed her mind.

"I've got to get going, honey," she said. "I want to be on I-95 before the traffic gets too thick."

"*Mommmm....*"

"What, Sommer?"

Sommer let out a sharp, frustrated breath.

"Well...um...I mean, like...how am I supposed to reach you? What if I have an emergency or something?"

"I have a cell phone, pumpkin. You'll reach me the same way you've reached me before. It's not like I'm leaving the earth's atmosphere."

"But, but, but what if I..."

"If it's anything pressing, you can just call your father. I'll come back if it's truly an emergency, and by *emergency* I'm talking life-or-death. But, Sommer, honey..."

"Yes, Mom." Sommer sounded defeated.

"I would hope you wouldn't be selfish enough to stage something just to get me to come back. I need to do this. I need to do something for me. Whether you understand that or accept it isn't the issue for me right now. I just hope you can respect my decision and respond accordingly. You and your brother and sister."

Her daughter didn't answer.

"Can you promise me you'll do that?"

"Yes, Mom."

"Good. I'm hanging up now, pumpkin. I love you. Be happy for me. I think this trip is going to be fun."

"I'm happy for you, Mom. Just be careful. I love you, too."

Lilibelle clicked off the line before her daughter could say anything more. If she talked to Sommer long enough, the girl would psychoanalyze her out of making the trip. Lilibelle wasn't going to let that happen. No matter what, she was getting on that road. She was going to find out who she was, and she was going to see Vegas.

Even though it meant she'd be anxious every mile of the way.

An hour later, Lilibelle was on I-95.

It was 1:20 p.m. in the afternoon and she was in her dark blue Mercedes CLK, cruising towards wherever. She was only going to be on I-95 for a few short miles, less than five. After that, she would be on I-80 West for nearly a thousand miles before changing roads. She had the route laid out, but she didn't have any specific plans as to where she would stop first or when she would stop. Maybe she'd even venture off the planned path, if the feeling hit her.

She would do whatever felt natural, even though this was the most unnatural thing she'd ever done.

She suddenly felt very lonely. She turned on the radio. It was tuned to a smooth-jazz station. Pieces Of A Dream's old hit, "Please Don't Do This To Me," came pouring out of the speakers. It was a sweet, sad, mournful song that Lilibelle hadn't heard in years. A few notes into it, she began to cry. Not just silent tears. She heaved big cathartic sobs, her shoulders shaking as she gripped the wheel. A car to the left of her slowed as it passed. She glanced over. The guy behind the wheel looked at her and shrugged, as if offering help. Lilibelle tearfully pressed the pedal and sped forward.

It was going to be a long way to Vegas.

She stopped sooner than she expected, getting off in East Orange, New Jersey, for gas. There was barely an eighth of a tank in the car. This was proof, she realized, of how ill-prepared she was. She hadn't even thought about food for the trip, much less realizing that she hadn't filled up the tank. These were the types of things Adam took care of. He always filled up the cars. He was the one who orchestrated trips. She typically focused on the important things, like what clothes, shoes and furs she was going to take. Which explained why she had three suitcases in the trunk, while the car was practically on empty. Since the divorce, she'd almost run out of gas four times. It was something she never thought about before. There were so many things, simple things, she was going to have to learn to do for herself.

Lilibelle gassed up and bought some bottled water, apple juice and a bag of soy chips. She would get real food later, when she felt genuinely hungry. The chips would do for now. She wanted to get back on the road.

She'd been on I-80 for four hours and still wasn't hungry. She was listening to talk radio. Music stations, she realized, had the potential to make her too emotional. Every song seemed to have some sort of message that she could directly apply to her situation, which was definitely not good. Talk radio made her feel like she had a friend in the car along for the ride. Thoughts of Adam and Robin would still enter her head on occasion, but they began to occur less as the day wore on. There was something about the unlimited miles ahead of her that was exciting, even though she was beginning to hit patches of traffic as cars merged onto the highway. It was Monday, a workday. These were people with jobs and homes to return to. Lilibelle wondered if she was the only wandering spirit among them, with no real sense of home to speak of anymore.

She glanced into the various cars around her. There was a man in the Camry just ahead, vigorously gesturing with his hands. A woman sat beside him, shaking her head. Lilibelle wondered if the man ever got tired of the woman. She wondered if he would tell her if he did.

There was a young woman behind the wheel on the car to her right. A pretty blond girl who was smiling at something, Lilibelle couldn't tell what. There was a nice-size diamond on her ring finger.

Everyone was married.

The woman caught Lili watching. Lili smiled and looked away.

Everyone was going home with someone or to someone. In the past two months since 9/11, during this time of tense national alert, people were coming together, thankful they had each other to lean on should the world crumble around them. Men were proposing to women they had been on the fence about. Babies were being made. Estranged couples were reuniting.

A car passed on her left. Despite the cold November air, a small white dog was leaning out the window. He panted happily, his breath visibly frosting as it met the chill.

Damn, Lilibelle thought. Even the dog was happy. He had somebody. He had his owner to keep him company, which was way more than she could say for herself.

She was lonelier than a dog.

How pathetic was that?

Five hours later, and she still hadn't eaten. She was starving, but was afraid to stop.

She had driven head-on into a winter rainstorm, just outside of Elmira, Ohio. It was coming down in heavy sheets and everything on the highway had slowed down to a crawl. All she could make out clearly were the bright red brake lights of the blurry cars ahead. Maniacal truckers would go flying by every few minutes, driving way too fast for such dangerous weather. Lilibelle was terrified. She'd never had to drive on a highway in weather like this. She'd rarely been on any highway alone, and even then, she wasn't the one behind the wheel. That was Adam's turf.

Fuck it! Everything was Adam's turf!

It was his fault she was even in this situation. What if her car hydroplaned off the road? Or if one of those eighteen-wheelers smashed into her? How would Adam feel then? Would he be sorry? Would he realize that Robin wasn't his *drug?* That maybe his ex-wife was really the big intoxicating love of his life after all?

Lilibelle was breathing heavily, on the verge of panic, almost hyperventilating. The cars and the rain were scaring her silly. The speedometer said she was driving less than twenty miles per hour. The radio was off. There was just the menacing sound of water as big drops splashed hard against the windshield and beat against the car.

She thought she could make out a bright green road sign up ahead for Elmira. An exit. Maybe she could get off and rest for a minute, at least until the rain died down. She could get something to eat, calm her nerves, check the map to see what lay on the road ahead and just how far she'd actually come. Plus, she'd eventually need to find a hotel for the night. May as well stop now. No telling how far away the next exit might be.

The sign said the turnoff was a quarter mile ahead. She began to lighten up. Soon she would be out of this madness.

Just as she allowed her tense shoulders to relax, a big rig came flying past, splashing a sea of water across her windshield. For a moment, Lili couldn't see anything, not even the lights of the cars ahead. She freaked out and swerved to her right, off the road and onto the shoulder. The car skidded and bounced a good distance as the tires tried to grip the slick pebbles beneath them.

Jesus! Help me, Jesus! Oh, God!

Lili's car raced forward about ten feet before she was able to safely bring it to a crunching stop. She dropped her head against the steering wheel, both hands clutching the thing so hard they hurt. Her whole body shook. Her teeth rattled. Her heart was on fire, about to give. The big rig was long gone. The driver never even considered the fact that he'd run someone off the road and left her scared to death in his wake.

She inhaled deeply several times, trying to stop herself from shaking. She looked up. She could once again make out red brake lights ahead through the rainy windshield. Not one car had stopped to see if she was okay. Was this the way they did things on the open road? This was a war zone, every driver for himself.

Lilibelle leaned back against the seat. She pressed her left hand against her heart. The beating was still erratic.

"God," she muttered. "What was I thinking? I have no business being out here. What was I trying to prove?"

She reached for the dregs of apple juice that remained in the bottle. There was only a swallow left, just enough to wet the back of her dry, frightened throat.

She took another series of deep breaths, then cranked the car. It made a churning noise but wouldn't turn over.

Wha...?

Lili tried again. The car made an ugly grinding sound that startled her. She let go of the wheel with both hands.

"What's wrong with you?"

She waited a moment, then reached for the ignition again. She turned the key. This time the car made a very quick *grrr.*

No, no, no, no, no, no, no, no! She pounded the steering wheel, tears welling in her eyes. "You can't do this to me! Why are you doing this to me?"

The rain slammed down heavier as if in answer. Something

hard hit the roof of the car and bounced off. Lilibelle ducked. Another hard thing followed. Then buckets of hard things began to come down. Lili leaned forward, angling her head to get a look through the blurry windshield. The hard white things bounced off the glass.

"Hail?" she said to the sky. "It's hailing! I cannot believe this! God is cursing me! What have I done?"

She sat back, shaking her head. She turned the key in the ignition.

This time all she got was a quarter-crunch, the car turning over even less than it did before.

Lilibelle banged her head against the steering wheel, then suddenly stopped, full of conviction. She was going to make this car work. She'd be damned if yet another thing in her life was going to bail like this.

She lifted her head and turned the key. This time there was nothing. Damn it. The engine was dead. The lights were on, but the car was useless.

She cried. There was no gradual ramp-up to it. She just opened her mouth and bawled.

She didn't turn the hazards on. She was too shaken up to realize that she should. The headlights were still on, but that was it. In all her adult years, Lilibelle Goldman had never been stranded in a car, nor had she ever been in a car that cut off on her and required assistance. She'd never been with someone whose vehicle cut off. The bulk of her life had been spent in the city. There were car services and taxis and Adam behind the wheel. She drove this Mercedes on occasion, but that was mostly when they went out to the country. Adam always drove the car on the way out there and back. She had AAA, but she didn't realize it. It never came to mind. She'd never used AAA for anything before. That was Adam's territory. She had no idea she should use it right now.

Lilibelle realized how ridiculous she had been. Her sole prep-aration for the road trip had been clothes, toiletries, a map and a route to Vegas. That's all she figured she needed. She hadn't checked to see how much gas was in the car. She didn't know what condition the car was in. She assumed she'd just get in it and it would go. That's what cars did, didn't they? She didn't think about the possibility of the vehicle not working. She didn't consider the chance that she would be stranded. Surely someone would stop to help her, she thought. They couldn't just keep ignoring her like this.

She wiped the frost off the driver's-side window so she could look out. It was freezing inside the Mercedes now that the engine was off. It was a wet, cold, hailing November night, and she was stuck in a strange place with no help and no heat.

The cars on the highway kept on going by. Even the ones that were inching along in the heavy rain didn't linger to see if she was in need. Another eighteen-wheeler passed by, soaking her with a ruthless wave.

Lilibelle considered getting out and trying to wave someone down, but it was cold and wet out there. Too cold. Her Juicy velour tracksuit and sneakers would get soaked, and so would her sable coat, which was thrown across the backseat. No, she couldn't get out.

Her stomach growled. She grabbed the balled-up soy chips bag and looked inside. There was nothing, not even any crumbs.

She remembered her cell phone. It was sitting on the armrest area right next to her, plugged into the cigarette lighter. She had it plugged in as a safeguard, but hadn't planned on calling anyone.

Lilibelle immediately picked up the phone and pressed the speed number for Adam. She was about to put the phone up to her ear when she realized what she'd done. She hit the End button just in time. It hadn't started ringing yet.

"Shit. What was I thinking?"

She scrolled through the phone's address book. Sommer, Sam, Jenny. No way could she call her kids. They'd be expecting this. Wasn't Sommer just reminding her earlier of how high maintenance she was?

Lilibelle bit her lip and kept scrolling. There was her hair stylist, her masseuse, the concierge at the Four Seasons... None of these people could do anything for her. She couldn't call them and ask for help. She'd be the crazy divorcée stuck out in the middle of nowhere, doing things on a lark because she couldn't cope with being left by her husband. Her attorney, Bill, had been right when he'd said that people would start looking at her differently. It had already started to happen. No. She couldn't call any of them.

She stopped on a name. Tish Stephens. Tish's husband, Anders, was one of Adam's best friends. Lilibelle and Tish had been friends for years. They lunched together, they shopped together, they raised their kids together. She should call Tish. Tish would know what to do.

Lilibelle stared at the number, but she couldn't bring herself to dial it. Tish would help her, that was true. But she'd tell Anders. She'd have to. He'd want to know who she was talking to at this hour of the night, especially if Tish went into crisis mode. Tish would tell him everything—she and her husband were close like that. And Anders would tell Adam. And Adam would tell Robin. And the two of them would laugh at first, laugh at how stupid she was to go on a stupid road trip without knowing the first thing about taking road trips, and almost getting herself killed as she was run off the road. Yeah, they would laugh at her, and then they'd grow quiet as their laughter turned to pity. And they'd be the ones to come to her aid, not Tish, as originally planned. Because they were all still family. Wasn't that what Adam said?

We're here for you.

Thank you, she thought, but no thank you very much.

Lilibelle put the phone down. There was no one she could call. Oh wait, maybe she could dial 9-1-1.

She was about to reach for the phone again when there was a tap on the passenger window.

"Oh!" She jumped back against her seat.

She could see a large shadowy face pressed against the glass. Eyes, nose, a mouth breathing more frost against the window. Hands were cupped on either side of the face, trying to peer in. The person knocked on the window again.

"Hey," a deep voice called. "Are you all right in there? Do you need any help?"

Lilibelle's heart began to tighten. She desperately needed help, but the reality of the situation suddenly hit her. She was a woman alone on a dark highway in a rainstorm late at night. Her car was broken and she didn't have any means of protecting herself. Whoever this was with the deep voice could be a killer. She was nine hours away from home, several hundred miles away. She'd seen things like this on TV. This could be her final hour. This was how she was going to die. In the rain.

A big hand wiped at the window to clear away the condensation.

"Hey, in there," he called again. "Do you need any help? Is your car okay? I saw you skid off the road a little while ago and you've just been sitting here. I came over to help."

"Who are you?" Lili asked, certain this was the voice of her reaper.

"I'm Chance. Chance Landry. I could see your car from the diner across the way, just off the exit right there. Are you just taking a break from the rain or are you stuck?"

Lili heard a dog bark.

"What's that?" she asked.

"That's Yancy. Do you need help starting your car?"

"Yes," she said. "Yes, I do."

"Is it all right if I come inside?"

Now Lili really began to panic. The man sounded enormous. His voice was booming and the silhouette of his face and head was the size of a soccer ball.

"It's okay," he said. "I'm safe. I'm not going to harm you. I just want to help you get out of this rain. We'll see if we can get you over to the diner."

More barking again.

"Hush, Yance," said the man. "It's not like you haven't been wet before."

A man and his dog were outside her car, standing in the rain, offering to help. She'd be crazy to let them in. She reached for her cell phone. She was going to dial 9-1-1.

"Turn the ignition," he said. "Let me hear how it sounds."

Lilibelle paused.

"Let me hear it," he repeated. "It might just be stalled out."

The dog barked.

Lili put the phone down. It wouldn't hurt to try what he said. Maybe the car would turn over this time.

She turned the key. The car gave a half grunt.

"Pump the brakes," he said.

"Huh?"

"Pump the brakes about five or six times, then try to crank the car up again."

Lilibelle sat there feeling stupid. Pump the brakes? What did that mean?

"Did you do it?" he asked.

"I don't know what that is."

The dog gave a lively yelp.

"Hush," said the man. "Press the pedal like you're riding a bike. Do it five or six times, then try the car again."

Lili pushed against the pedal. She counted the number of pushes in her head. She turned the key. Another half grunt.

"It didn't work," she yelled.

"I heard," said the man. "Do you mind opening the door and letting me in? I could maybe try it and see if I can find out what's wrong."

Lilibelle didn't want to risk it. He could be a killer. Killers were always helpful and friendly. They always managed to materialize when a woman was in a desperate situation by herself.

"I don't think I can do that," she said. "I don't know you. I appreciate your help, but I can't let you in my car."

The dog barked three times in a row.

"Yancy! Stop it!"

What was he doing out there with his dog in the rain like that? They came over from the diner across the way? Yeah, right. It just didn't make sense.

"Listen," he said, his voice still booming but with an understanding tone. "I know you're afraid. You don't know me from Adam..."

From Adam? Of all the things he could have said.

"...I don't expect you to trust me. I'd be just as wary if I were a woman out here alone like you."

The dog barked again.

"I tell you what," the man said. "How about if I push your car up there to the exit. You're pretty close. I'll push it all the way over to the diner. It's well lit over there. It's safe. There's a handful of people in the place—the cook, a couple of waitresses, folks who stopped off to get away from the rain. You'll be all right there. You can get a hot cup of coffee and a solid meal."

Lilibelle could handle that. That meant he didn't have to come inside the car.

"Will that work?" he asked. The man was getting pummeled by the rain, but he acted as though he didn't even notice.

"Okay. I can do that."

"Great. I'll get behind the car and push. You're going to have to guide the way with the steering wheel."

"I can do that, too," she said.

"Okay. I'm going to need you to put the car in neutral."

She did.

"Cool. I'm going to get behind the car." He walked towards the back of the Mercedes. Lilibelle watched him. He stopped halfway there and came back to the window. He pressed his face against the glass.

"Can I just get you to do me a small favor?" he asked.

Here it comes, thought Lili. This was how the killers did it. There was always just one thing, that one little thing.

Lili didn't answer. The man kept talking.

"I have my dog Yancy out here with me. She wouldn't stay behind in the diner when I came over to help. Could you please let her get in the car while I push? I'm afraid she'll be in the way with me out here or maybe get hit by a car. The visibility's not so good out here. People are driving kind of crazy."

Let a *dog* in her car? A *wet* dog? In her *Mercedes?* Lilibelle glanced at her sable on the backseat.

"Please, ma'am. She won't be any trouble, I promise you. And I won't try to do anything tricky. If you unlock the back door, I'll open it just enough for her to get inside, then I'll close it, head around to the back and get to pushing."

Lilibelle's nerves were a jangled knot. She needed help. She desperately wanted to be off the shoulder of this highway in a safer place. The man claimed the diner was just across the way. The exit had been pretty close when she was run off the road. How was she going to let a wet dog in her car? Jeez. This was such a mess, such a pickle she'd gotten herself into. Sommer was so right about her. They all were. She was a high mainte-nance walking disaster. No wonder Adam had left.

The man knocked at the window.

"Is that all right? I'm not going to harm you. I'm just going to let Yancy in, okay? We'll be at the diner in no time. She's a good girl. She won't wreck your car inside, I promise."

Lilibelle looked at the man's silhouette. She couldn't even see the dog, so who knew what kind of beast that was. She closed her eyes and sent up a quick prayer.

Heavenly Father, if I die tonight, please take care of my children. Take care of my soul. She paused. *Take care of Adam.*

She snatched her sable up front and unlocked the door.

The back door opened.

"Get in, Yance."

A big yellow dog jumped inside and the back door closed.

The dog sat obediently, dripping on the seat. She stared at Lili. Lili stared back, certain this creature intended to rip her out of the frame. Suddenly, the dog smiled. A big, wide toothy grin that was unmistakable. Before Lili could respond, the car was moving. It was inching ahead.

"Steer!" the man yelled from the back. "Steer it towards the left, back onto the road!"

Lili turned the wheel to the left.

"Not so sharp," he called. "Just a little, just a little."

Soon they were on the wet highway again and the man was pushing her towards the exit.

Lili glanced over her shoulder at the dog. She was still grinning. She had a big black nose smack in the middle of the yellowest face. Lilibelle found herself smiling back at the dog. Whoever saw a dog grin before?

"Watch the road," the man yelled. "We're gonna be turning off in a sec."

How could he tell she wasn't looking at the road? she wondered. The back window was covered with frosty condensation. She steered the car straight, waiting for his instructions.

In short order, they were at the diner. The man pushed the car toward a parking space near the front door.

"Slow it down," he said. "Keep riding the brakes until it's time to bring it to a stop."

Lilibelle did as he ordered.

"He's pretty good," she said to the dog.

The dog barked.

Lili brought the car to a safe halt. A few people were standing outside the diner watching.

The back door opened. The big yellow dog jumped out.

Lilibelle opened her door and got out of the car. She glanced across the roof of her car. There was the man who had helped her.

He was huge, enormous, a sort of colossus. Six foot three

easy, with broad shoulders, a wide expanse of chest, a scruffy brown face with a rage of stubble across the lower half. A handsome face, yes, but definitely scruffy.

And he was soaked. Every possible inch of the man was wet.

"Get on in here, Chance," a woman in a waitress uniform said. "Before you turn into an icicle right in front of us. You're gonna freeze to death. You, too, Yancy. And you, miss. You three are gonna ketch your death a cold."

The woman held the diner door open. The people who had been watching went back inside. Lilibelle rushed into the warmth of the restaurant. The dog wildly shook herself, then rushed in behind Lili. The big wet man followed. The waitress pushed him inside and closed the door.

"We're gonna all ketch our death, Chance Landry," she said to the man, "foolin' around with the likes of you."

He chuckled, a deep, rich, hearty sound that was just as warm as the diner itself.

The waitress was already back behind the counter, pouring a cup of coffee. She brought one to Lilibelle, who was standing in the middle of the floor, unsure of what to do with herself.

"Why 'on't you have a seat over here at this booth, sweetie." Her hand was pressed in the small of Lili's back, gently guiding her. "Warm yourself up. You must be cold down to the bone, sitting out there on the road in that car all that time like that."

"Thank you," said Lilibelle as she slid into the booth. She sipped the coffee, the steam from the surface of the drink feeling like salvation against her face.

"Yancy! Get over here, girl!"

The big wet dog bounded over to the waitress, who was now standing off to the side with a big towel. She wrapped the dog up in it and rubbed her dry. The dog grinned and wriggled, her tail wagging furiously.

"You mind?"

Lili looked up. The big man, Chance, was standing above

her. He had a towel around his neck. His hand was out, gesturing toward the seat.

"Sure," she said, too surprised by his sudden appearance to say anything but yes. "Of course, sit down."

The waitress was over in seconds with another cup of steaming hot coffee.

"You're the best, Stella," Chance said.

"And don't you forget it," Stella replied as she walked away.

Lilibelle sipped her coffee, trying her best not to examine the man. She kept her eyes downward, feeling awkward and silly. This man had just saved her life. She had thought him a murderer, but he had just pushed her car clear off the highway down to this restaurant, without a thought for the freezing rain barreling down upon him. She owed him a thank-you, but she didn't know how to open her mouth to say it.

"It feels good in here, doesn't it?" he said. "Hot coffee, good food, Stella." He said the waitress's name loudly on purpose.

"What now?" she called back, clearly pleased by the man's teasing words.

He reached for a menu at the back of the table and slid it toward Lilibelle.

"You should eat something," he said. "Get something hot in your body to counter the shock of all that freezing rain and hail."

Lili picked up the menu and looked through it.

"Everything here is pretty good. The chicken-fried steak and gravy. The roast chicken. The soups and the breakfasts are—" he kissed his fingers "—mmmwah! Superb. Nobody slings hash like Señor Chuck."

Lili finally looked up at him, finding it in herself to speak.

"You must eat here a lot."

"Enough," he said. "I've been through this area plenty of times over the years. You get to know the place and the people. Right, Stella?"

"You're damn right you do!"

Yancy came over to the booth and sat at the man's feet.

Lilibelle glanced down at the dog. She was still grinning. She was the happiest, grinningest dog in the world.

"She's funny," Lili said.

"Who, Yancy? Yeah. She's pretty slaphappy as dogs go." He grabbed a menu for himself. "Has the best attitude I've ever seen. On man or beast."

"What about on woman?" she asked.

Chance laughed.

"I've yet to meet the woman who's as happy as Yancy. She's the glad girl, aren't ya?" He chucked the pooch under the chin. Yancy woofed. Chance laughed again.

"So, hey," Lili began, "thanks. Thanks for what you did out there."

"No worries," he said. "That's just what we do."

"We who?" she asked.

"We human beings. People help each other. That's what we're here for in the first place."

Lilibelle smirked.

"What, you don't believe that?" he asked.

"Sure I do. But I don't think the scores of cars that ignored me tonight exactly agree."

Chance drank his coffee.

"People are afraid," he said between sips. "It's a scary world out there. You were frightened when I came up to your car, as well you should have been. I was a stranger banging on your window. I'm a big guy. I could have been dangerous."

"I wasn't frightened," she said, looking down.

"Well, if you were, there's nothing wrong with that. It's human nature. Self-preservation." He continued drinking his coffee as he glanced at the menu.

Lilibelle took the opportunity to examine him closer, now that his eyes were focused elsewhere.

He needed a good shave. That was definite. The stubble around his jawline and chin looked at least four or five days old. It was too tentative. Neither beard nor five o'clock shadow. Everything about it was noncommittal.

There was a cleft in his chin. And dimples in his cheeks. He was a very attractive man, in a rough-hewn kind of way. What was he doing out here, she wondered, pushing cars off of highways in the freezing rain. With a big yellow dog, no less. She checked out his left hand. The ring finger was bare.

I guess everyone's not married after all, she thought. Or maybe he left his wife for another drug of a woman. Someone more intoxicating.

"Twice," he said.

"Excuse me?"

"I've been married twice. Divorced twice, too."

"I—I don't know what you're…"

"You were looking at my ring finger."

Lili blushed.

"No, I wasn't."

"Yeah, you were. Hey, Stella, I'm getting the chicken-fried steak." He turned back to Lilibelle. "What are you gonna have?"

She picked up the menu, flipping through it and feeling exposed, like her dress had just blown up, if she had been wearing a dress.

"Um, ah, maybe some soup…"

"What kind?"

"Oh. Ah, I don't know? Chicken noodle, maybe?"

"Stella," said Chance. "The lady…ah, does the lady have a name?"

"It's Lilibelle. Lilibelle Goldman."

"Lilibelle," he repeated. "That's pretty."

"Thank you," she said.

"Stella, Lilibelle here's gonna have the Big Chuck Bang."

Lili peered closer at the menu, then looked up at him.

"That's not the name of the chicken noodle soup."

Stella hesitated behind the counter, waiting to place the order.

"I know. The Big Chuck Bang is the hash breakfast. It'll be

much more filling than chicken soup. And it's not that canned crap that you get at the store. Chuck makes it from scratch every day. He shreds the meat—" Chance made tearing motions with his hands "—he throws some onion in there, and the potatoes are cooked to perfection. You'll thank me for turning you on to the best hash you've ever had in your life."

"But I don't really..."

He reached across the table and touched her hand.

"Trust me. Seriously. It's the best breakfast in the world."

Lilibelle tried not to glance at his hand on hers. She didn't know this man, even though the warmth of human touch in that moment didn't repulse her.

"You wanna try it?" he asked.

The dog barked at her.

Lili laughed.

"What, do you have her trained to do that on cue?"

"She just knows from know," Chance said with a smile. "Yancy loves the hash breakfast, too."

Lilibelle closed the menu and pushed it aside.

"All right, all right. I'll take the Big Chuck Bang."

"One Big Chuck Bang!" Stella shouted. "How do you like your eggs?"

"Scrambled, right?" Chance was still smiling.

"Scrambled," Lili reluctantly agreed.

"Scrambled on the Big Chuck Bang!" Stella slung orders around as she cleaned the counter and poured coffee. The other waitress wasn't nearly as efficient.

Lili leaned forward, her eyes narrowed at Chance.

"This better be good," she said.

His hand was still on hers.

"It will be," he replied, patting the top of her hand and leaning back.

The hash was delicious.

Lilibelle devoured everything on the plate—the corned beef

hash, the scrambled eggs, the buttered toast and the home fries. She knocked back three more cups of coffee as she ate. As a result, she was pretty wired and chatty. She became much more conversational with Chance, and to her surprise, she enjoyed his company immensely.

"So who are you anyway?" she asked. "Some sort of caped crusader working I-80, saving stranded women from themselves?"

"Hardly," Chance said. He checked on Yancy. She was on the floor at his feet, working over her own big plate of eggs and freshly made hash.

"So?" Lili pressed. "What are you doing here? Do you live in this area?"

"No. I'm from Pittsburgh."

"Oh," she said. "Are you a traveling salesman or something?"

Chance lifted his coffee cup.

"No, not quite."

Lilibelle was leaning back against the booth, sated and at ease. The rain was still coming down outside. The hail had stopped, but large drops of water were still pounding against the building.

"What is this, a guessing game? What's the big mystery about what you do?"

Chance put down the coffee cup. He cleared his throat.

"No mystery at all. I'm about as up-front as they come."

"Well, then?"

Chance placed his elbows on the table and leaned forward.

"My name is Chance Landry."

"I already know that much."

"I'm from Pittsburgh. I often come past Elmira on my way to cities on business. This place has been a favorite stop of mine for years. I own a string of Mercedes-Benz dealerships across the state of Pennsylvania."

Lilibelle pursed her lips together and nodded.

"They're all very successful. Me and my staff have worked our tails off over the years to make sure of that. Besides," he said with a wink, "people love Mercedes-Benz. They're always going to sell very well."

"So what are you doing here? Do you have a dealership in this area?"

"No."

Lili waited for him to answer. When he didn't, she laughed.

"So you want me to pull it out of you, is that it?"

"No. I was just studying your face. Wondering what you're doing around here yourself."

"After you," she said. "You go first."

Over more coffee and two Danishes, Chance told her. His second wife had divorced him four months prior. For cheating. He was the cheater. He was a serial philanderer who had no business being married, especially not to the woman he was married to. She was a one-night stand that he'd tried to turn into a homemaker. The relationship was a disaster from the moment it started, he said. It was a miracle it lasted as long as it did.

"How long was that?" asked Lilibelle.

"Three years," he said. "I don't know why I even bothered. It was just prolonging the inevitable."

"I see."

Yancy stood, stretched and wagged her tail. She walked up to Lilibelle. Lili rubbed her on the head.

"What a sweet dog she is. What's a guy like you—a serial philanderer, as you say—doing with such a wonderful dog?"

"What can I say?" he replied with a smile. "The ladies, they love me. Right, Yance?"

Yancy wagged her tail, but didn't leave the gentle touch of Lili's hand upon her head.

"Anyway, when we divorced, I was ordered to pay her an enormous amount of alimony. A really ridiculous amount. She clearly didn't deserve it, no matter what she believes I did."

"But you said you cheated."

"I know, but that's not what I'm talking about. Kina lived the life of Reilly with me. I never gave her any difficulty whatsoever. She had everything she wanted. There was no emotional abuse, no physical abuse, none of that. If anything, I was the one who took the brunt of the stress. From the moment we married, she began to push me away. She took digs at me at every turn. She stopped being affectionate. I was doing my best to walk straight, but when she began to do all that, I said fuck it, excuse my French. I mean, what's the point of denying myself any pleasure when my wife sees me as nothing but a wallet and a lifestyle?"

Lilibelle was leaning forward now, listening intensely. Yancy was now sitting at her feet.

"Did you tell her all this? Did you try to talk about it with her? Or did you just run into another woman's arms without giving her a chance to turn things around?"

"I didn't run into another woman's arms. Not a specific woman. There were a series of them, none of whom meant anything to me. They were distractions from the hell at home, ways to get human contact. I should have never married Kina. I didn't love her. It was the same situation with my first wife."

"You cheated on her, too?"

"Yes. I didn't love her. I had no business marrying a woman I didn't love. Two times."

"Why do you think you did it?" Lilibelle asked.

Chance ran his hand across his scruffy stubble.

"Because I was following what other people were telling me to do. Saying a guy like me should be married. It'd make me appear more respectable as a business owner if I seemed more stable. It was all a bunch of bullshit in the end. All the wrong reasons. Never do anything for the wrong reasons, Lilibelle. It will always blow up in your face in the end."

"So do you think you just naturally cheat? Is that what it is? Is that what men do?"

"Uh-oh. This is starting to sound like some personal research."

Lili moved back a little.

"Perhaps," she said.

"Do tell."

"I will in a minute. I'm just curious about the whole men-cheating thing."

"What do you want to know?" he asked.

Lili pondered briefly. What was she looking for exactly? A pat answer, she supposed. A guide. Something to put her finger on.

"Do you think that it's just in your blood?"

"What?" he asked.

"Cheating."

"Oh, God, no."

"Then why do you think you do it? Why is it this serial behavior that you keep revisiting?"

Chance laughed.

"That's easy. I just haven't been in love yet. Not really. Not the kind that knocks your socks off and blows your mind and makes it so you can barely get through five minutes without thinking about the other person."

"Do you think that kind of love is out there?" she asked.

"I don't know," he said. "Maybe not for me. I'm a passionate man who feels things very passionately. I'm like that about business, I'm like that about pleasure. If it's in me to feel like that in those areas of my life, I'm sure I have the capacity to feel that romantically. The fact that it hasn't happened yet at my age must mean it's not out there for me, you know what I'm saying?"

"What do you mean, at your age?"

"I'm forty-four," he said. "I'll be forty-five this coming Saturday."

"Happy early birthday," she said.

"Thank you. I appreciate that. Like I was saying, I've known a lot of women in my day, but none of them have brought that kind of feeling out in me. Some of it was my fault. I kept settling for half-assed like, something not even close to what I imagine love would be."

He shifted in his seat, turning his body to the side. Lili got a better look at his profile—the smooth skin, the strong jaw.

"If I loved a woman," he said, "I mean really loved her, and that love was being reciprocated in a healthy, nurturing way…please. There's no way I'd stray from home."

"It'd be your drug," Lili said.

"What's that?"

"The woman you fall in love with would be like your drug."

He rubbed his chin.

"Yeah, I guess so. I never really looked at it that way. But it doesn't matter because that woman's not out there, not from what I can see. Which is why I roll with this lady right here." He pointed at Yancy. She looked up at them and thumped her tail against the floor.

"She loves me no matter what. She's always excited about the presence of my company. She's loyal, she's affectionate. She's the perfect paradigm for the perfect woman."

Lilibelle laughed loudly at this.

"A dog? You want your woman to fawn over you like a dog?"

"I beg your pardon. Yance is not a fawner. Does she act like I run things? She's completely in control of what she wants to do. I'm her pet—it's not the other way around."

They both looked at the dog. Yancy definitely didn't seem to be under anyone's rule.

"So you're divorced and you're paying alimony."

"Big alimony. Huge. Outrageous."

"All right," she laughed. "Then what are you doing out here? Generating more business to keep up with those alimony payments?"

"Nah. Fortunately, I make more than enough to cover those

payments and still be good. That's the problem. Kina knew how much money I made down to the penny, so she knew exactly how to tell her attorney to attack."

Lili listened quietly, thinking of what Bill Archer had wanted her to do to Adam.

"I'm taking a break from work for a while," Chance said. "From the world in general. All the marriages and divorces and businesses and court dates and all that rigid structure was beginning to choke the passion out of me. I want to free-fall for a while. See the country. Let someone else handle things for me. I've got excellent managers at my dealerships. They've got things under control. My financial crew is handling everything else. Now's the perfect time to do it, so I leapt. Me and Yancy jumped in the car and drove away from it all. It's westward ho for us. Two easy riders dropping out from society."

"For how long?" she asked.

"As long as it takes," he said. "I'm not on anybody's clock. It's just a boy and his dog on the open road. An American tradition of the most elemental sort. But I am trying to make it to Vegas by Saturday. I figured it'd be the perfect place for me to ring in my birthday. Maybe it'll take some of the edge off being forty-five."

Lili's chin was resting on both of her hands. Vegas? He was going to Vegas? This was crazy insane. First she discovered that everyone wasn't married after all, and that everyone wasn't headed to a stable home somewhere. She wasn't the only drifter on the road. She was sitting across from her mirror match, except for one major difference, other than the dog—Chance was a cheater. Lilibelle was the cheated upon. She didn't understand his kind, but she wanted to. She wanted to know what motivated a man like him. Maybe that would help her understand Adam's motivations. Perhaps the knowing would somehow make things go down easier. That was her hope, anyway. Adam's departure needed to make sense.

Chance was leaning back against his seat now, his arms at his sides.

"Your turn."

"Huh?"

"I gutted myself to you," he said. "Now it's your turn to do the same in front of me."

Lili smiled and glanced out the window.

"The rain's letting up," she said.

"I know. When it stops, I'll take another look at your car. I can probably fix whatever's wrong with it. The battery's not dead and it did act like it might want to turn over. It might have just needed to sit for a minute. If not, I can get someone out here pronto to look at it."

"I appreciate that," Lili said.

"It's the least I could do," said Chance. "I am pretty well-versed in Mercedes, after all. Mine is parked right outside, not too far from yours."

"Oh, I didn't see it."

"It was raining cats when we pulled up. We could barely see our hands in front of our faces."

"Right," she said.

Chance smiled again.

"I'm waiting," he said. "Unless you're trying to get me to pull it out of you."

"No," she laughed, her voice soft. "Not at all. It's not that much different than your situation. Wait, what am I saying? It is. It's very different. My husband...ex-husband...he wasn't a serial cheater."

"How do you know?" Chance asked.

The comment caught her off guard.

"I... He... No, that's not who Adam is," she said.

"So why did you divorce?"

Lili suddenly felt silly. There was no way she could make what she was about to say sound right.

"Well?" he pressed. "What happened?"

"He left me for another woman."

Her eyes met his directly.

"Did you know her?" he asked after a moment.

"Yes. Sort of. Obviously not as well as he. She worked with him."

"Oh. That. Cheating with a coworker. That's always tricky."

"Tricky? Yes. I guess that's one way to describe it."

"How did you find out?" asked Chance.

"I didn't. He told me."

"Oh, wow. Now that's something. An honest man who came straight with it."

"Not quite. They'd been seeing each other for a while before he finally spoke up. And then, get this—he told me on 9/11, right when everything in the city was falling apart. That's when he decided to announce his exit. During a terrorist attack. How's that for metaphorical?"

"Fuck." He uttered the word quietly, with genuine surprise.

Lili found herself slightly angered at the memory. Her brow creased with displeasure. The corners of her mouth turned down.

Chance reached across the table and touched her hand.

"You all right?" he asked. "We don't have to keep talking about this if you don't want."

"No," she said. "It's okay. I think I needed to say this stuff out loud. I've been living with so much of it bottled inside of me for the past two months. That's one of the reasons I'm taking this trip."

"What's that?"

"To free myself of some of this anger. To let it go and get myself back again. I don't know if I've seen me, you know, the real Lili, in years. I'd like to find that girl again and see what she's about. What she's really looking for in life."

"Where are you headed?" he asked.

Lilibelle laughed.

"You're not going to believe this," she said.

"Tell me."

"I'm going westward ho, just like you."

"No! By yourself?"

Her right eyebrow rose.

"Yes, by myself. What's wrong with that? You're traveling alone."

"No, I'm not."

Yancy barked.

"Yeah, but..." she began.

"Yeah, nothing," said Chance. "Yancy's my road dog, in more ways than one."

Lilibelle reached over and rubbed Yancy's head again.

"You're lucky," she said. "It's just me out there on the big mean highway."

"You headed somewhere specific?" he asked.

"Vegas."

"Really?" he exclaimed. "You're shitting me! No way!"

"Way," she said. She thought that was funny. She'd heard her daughter Sommer respond that way before.

"What's your time frame?"

"I don't have one," said Lili. "I figured I'd work my way there. This is the first real road trip I've ever taken."

Chance leaned back into his seat, then leaned forward again, his hand slapping the table.

"So you know what I'm thinking," he said.

"What's that?"

"C'mon. We're both doing the same thing, headed in the same direction. Neither one of us is on a real schedule, other than me with the Vegas-by-Saturday thing. Why not make this a tag team? That way you won't be out on the road by yourself and you've got help if, God forbid, something goes wrong like it did tonight. And Yance and I'll have some company."

Lili drew back a little.

"No, no," he assured her, "I don't mean like that. I mean like this. Like what we're doing right now. Company for conversation. Good company. Good conversation. Someone to talk to over meals. To explore different towns and cities with and get some perspective. It's worth a try, don't you think? And if you get your fill of us, we can always take the next fork in the road. That's the beauty of it. There's always another fork just ahead."

Lilibelle thought about it. She allowed herself to study him, this time openly, not sidelong like she'd been doing before.

He didn't seem like the type that would harm her, and Stella and Chuck seemed to think he was pretty cool. But they weren't what convinced her.

The closer of the deal was Yancy. That big yellow dog was so sweet, so gentle. An evil man, a mean-spirited person, couldn't raise a dog like that. The dog must have been able to see to the heart of who Chance was. Babies and animals. They were the great discerners of the truth.

"So I can fork off whenever I want?"

"Of course," he said. "We'll just be road dogs. Two people committed to riding together until they no longer want to share the road anymore."

"That almost sounds like a metaphor for your life," she said.

"It wasn't before. Like I said, I stayed in situations way longer than I should have. I'm doing the whole new-leaf thing now. I like women, and I'm sowing my oats. I don't want anything serious with anybody anymore. I'll stay with something for as long as it feels right, and when it feels wrong, then I'll cut it loose. No more lying to women. No more cheating. From now on I'm up-front about who I am. Take it or leave it."

"Is it really that simple?" she asked.

"It can be. Why not?"

Stella was at their table with more coffee. Lilibelle held up her palm.

"None for me. I've already had a hundred cups."

"Me neither, Stella. Thanks."

"How about you, Yancy?" Stella asked the dog.

Yancy thumped her tail.

A hint of pink began to break along the horizon.

"I can't believe we sat here talking all night. It's almost morning. I haven't even gone to bed. I figured I'd check into a hotel room and that would be how I'd spend the evening."

"Are you sleepy?" he asked. "Maybe I should have tried to fix your car already instead of holding you up with all this chatter."

"No, no, it's okay. I'm not sleepy at all. Not in the slightest. It's like I got my fifth wind or something."

"Fifth wind," he said with a chuckle. "That's cute."

Lilibelle rested her back against the seat. She had a road dog. The idea of it was both exciting and scary. Not scary in the sense that she felt in danger. Scary in that who knew what adventures lay before them on the journey ahead. He knew more about this kind of thing than she did, so this would be an opportunity for her to learn. And she'd have a protector, someone to make her feel that she wasn't just out there, all alone.

It was like being with Adam, but different. Adam was always in the car with her. This time the man would be in another car, but he'd still be with her, just a few feet away.

She smiled at Chance. Chance smiled back at her.

"So are we road dogs or what?" he asked.

"*Woof!*" answered Yancy.

"I guess that's a yes," Lili said with a laugh. "You weren't kidding. She does run things."

CHAPTER 4

I'll Be Doggone

Chance wasn't under the hood more than five minutes. He told Lilibelle to get behind the wheel and try the car again. It turned over immediately.

"Oh my goodness, what'd you do?" she asked.

"Nothing," he said, closing the hood. "It probably choked up on you when you skidded off the road. Sometimes all a car needs is a little bit of rest to get itself together. Let it run for a minute. Give it some gas."

Lilibelle gunned the engine.

"Not that much," Chance said.

She lessened the pressure.

It was Tuesday morning, 6:30 a.m.; the weather was crisp, but clear. A few cars had exited off the freeway to stop in at the diner.

Chance and Yancy stood in front of Lilibelle's car, watching to make sure the car kept running. Chance walked over to the driver's side.

"So you ready to hit the road again, or are you tired?"

"No, I'm ready," she said.

"Tell you what...since we had such a night of it, pushing cars off the road and talking for hours on end, how about we make it a short trip today? Since we're not on anybody's schedule."

"How short are you talking about?"

"Can you handle a three, maybe three and a half hour drive?" he asked.

"Yeah. That doesn't sound too bad."

"Good, because that'll put us in Chicago."

"Chicago? Really? It's that close?"

"Yup. We can check into a nice hotel, rest up, have a good meal, see the city…" He stopped himself. "That is, if you're cool with that. We don't have to hang once we get there. You can do your own thing, no pressure. I'll just give you a ring when it's time to hit the road again. But if you're down, I think we could have some fun in the Windy City."

"I'm down," she said. "The whole purpose of this trip was for me to explore and have fun and maybe learn something about myself. I'm ready to do that."

"Good," he said. "The winters can be pretty brutal in Chi-town, but November's a good month. Holiday lights will be up. The Water Tower's beautiful at night. The city's full of magic."

Lili folded her arms tightly. The sable coat was still on the front seat of the car where she'd left it the night before. She didn't want it to get wet in the rain.

"C'mon, let's go back inside," he said, "and get out of this cold air. Hey, before we go in, do you need to grab anything out of your car? They've got decent-size restrooms inside, just in case you want to freshen up. It'll be at least three hours before we can get hot showers and baths."

"That's a good idea," she said.

"All right. I'm going to get some things out of my car and do the same. Once we're finished, let's meet up at the same booth, if it's empty. Then the three of us can hit it."

Yancy brushed up against Lili, her tail wagging. Lilibelle gave her a pat.

"Okay," she said. "I'll grab my stuff and I'll see you back inside."

A half hour later, the two cars were back on I-80, headed west toward Chicago.

Chance and Yancy lead the way in a big black Mercedes-

Benz S500. Yancy was in the backseat, looking out the back window at Lili, who trailed closely behind. She wasn't too close—about two or three car lengths away—but she was near enough to make sure no other cars came between them. She and Chance had exchanged cell phone numbers before getting back on the highway. They were on the phone with each other now.

"This is nice, huh?" Chance said.

"Yeah, it is. It's so much better than having to rely on the radio to keep me company. I couldn't take the music. I was listening to talk radio, but I couldn't always find a good talk station in some areas."

"So what," he said, "you don't like music?"

Lilibelle stared at the back of his head as she spoke.

"Yes, I like music. But it seemed like every song had something to do with me, you know? It didn't matter what it was, somehow it made me feel self-aware."

"Because of the divorce?"

"Exactly. At one point when I had the radio on scan so I could find a talk station, it stopped on its own on the song 'Maniac.' Remember that song? From the movie *Flashdance?*"

Chance chuckled.

"Yeah, I remember 'Maniac.'" He sang a few lines. She could see his shoulders bopping to the beat.

"Yeah, yeah, that's it!" she said.

"And, of course, you thought the song was talking about you."

"I did," she said, laughing. "I thought it was some sort of cosmic message. My husband—my ex-husband—and my kids keep insisting that I'm so high..."

Lilibelle stopped herself. This wasn't a detail she wanted to announce. It wasn't exactly a flattering characteristic.

"You're so high what?"

"Forget it. Change of subject."

"No, no, no." She could see his hand waving as he spoke. "I wanna know. I've been telling you all about me. C'mon now, Lili. No secrets between road dogs. This thing with us is like a Jedi pact."

"Jedi?"

"Don't tell me you don't know what Jedi are."

"Those creatures from *Star Wars?*" she asked. "My son Sam was really into that stuff."

"Those creatures from *Star Wars*, she says. Yes, Ms. Goldman, those creatures from *Star Wars*, although they're not exactly creatures. They're a noble order of protectors, unified by their belief and observance of the Force."

"Huh?"

He laughed. "I read that on the Internet somewhere, on the *Star Wars* site I think. I was really into them, too. Still am. I love big sci-fi and action movies like that."

"Why do you like the Jedi so much?"

"Because," he said, "their training requires this deep commitment and concentration. It's intensely serious. You can't be a Jedi and take life lightly."

"How interesting," said Lili. "That's the opposite of your own philosophy."

There was silence on his end of the line.

"Hello?" she said. "Are you there?"

"I'm here. I was just thinking about what you said. I guess my current philosophy is very anti-Jedi. Ha! And all this time, I considered myself a Jedi apprentice of sorts."

"See that?" she said. "I'm making you see yourself."

He made a waving motion, pointing toward the right.

"Pull over for a second," he said. "I forgot to walk Yancy when we were back at the diner. I'm pretty sure she needs to do her business."

"Okay."

"Talk to you in a minute," he said, and clicked off.

Both cars slowed and pulled onto the shoulder of the road. Chance opened the door and stepped out of the car. Lilibelle was about to do the same when he signaled that she didn't need to get out. He walked back to her car. She let down the window.

"This'll be quick. Stay inside where it's warm."

"All right."

"You doing okay in there?"

She smiled.

"You were just talking to me on the phone. Of course I'm okay."

"Just checking," he said with a wink.

She watched him walk away. He was so tall and solidly built. She wasn't used to being around a man that big. Adam was of average height, five-ten, with a fairly slight frame. This man had the body of a warrior. It was fascinating just to watch him move.

Chance went around to the passenger side and opened the back door. Yancy jumped out. He reached in and took out a leash and hooked it on to her collar. She watched him walk the dog out onto the cold downslope of dead brown grass. Yancy took her time, walking and sniffing everything and nothing. Chance was patient with the big dog, letting her do things on her own terms. Lilibelle knew he had to be freezing. His left hand was plunged into the pocket of his black leather jacket. Frost came from his nose and mouth in gusty puffs.

Yancy kept walking farther and farther back, lingering on certain areas and sniffing. Finally she began to turn around in a circle, her back humping up as she doubled around. Lilibelle turned away when she realized that the dog was about to poop. She counted to ten very slowly, then turned back to see if the dog was finished. She looked just in time to see Chance bending down and picking up the stuff with some kind of paper, then shoving it into a plastic bag. He knotted the bag, then he and Yancy walked back to the car.

Lili was shocked to see that he picked up the dog's poop. He could have just left it out there in the frozen grass. It would have eventually dissolved and fertilized the place. This guy was really attentive and particular about his dog. Yancy got the royal treatment. Maybe, Lili thought, he was serious when he said the dog was his favorite lady.

Chance opened the back door and Yancy jumped in. He leaned in and placed the tied bag of poop on the floor of the backseat. Then he walked back around to the driver's side. He winked at her before he got in.

Lili found herself blushing, although she wasn't sure why. She liked him. It was so hard not to. He had changed into a fresh set of clothes, just as she did, when he had washed up at the diner that morning. He cut quite the striking figure. His outfit—the black leather jacket, a black cable-knit turtleneck sweater, dark jeans and black boots—accentuated his stature. He still had the scruffy stubble, but it didn't detract from him. It added a sort of wild-frontier element.

He started up his car and put on the left blinker. When the road was clear, he merged back onto the road. She was right behind him. They sailed forward on the highway, westward ho for the next hundred and seventy miles.

They spent the whole time talking. Just when Lili was surprised at how long they were talking, the conversation would take another turn and it would fire up again.

He told her about how he tried to fly when he was eight.

"I tied a bath towel around my neck and jumped off my mom's dresser."

"Oh my God," she said. "Did you get hurt?"

"I skinned my knees up real bad and my dad gave me some licks on my backside, but none of it hurt me as much as realizing that I couldn't fly. I was crushed. I just knew I was secretly a superhero. You couldn't tell me that I wasn't."

He was laughing. It was a rich, gutsy sound that made her laugh, too.

"Where's Yancy?" she asked. "I can't see her anymore."

"She's curled up on the backseat sleeping. Sleeping in the car is one of her favorite things. That, and hanging out the window. It's just too cold for that now. That's why she's sleeping."

Lilibelle told him about the princess party her parents threw for her when she was six. She had an actual diamond tiara, a silk dress and a miniature mink coat. Eight hundred people attended the party. There was an orchestra and news reporters. Her sixth birthday celebration was news in all the local papers the following day.

"You're kidding me, right? This must have been a small town."

"It was D.C. Would you consider the nation's capital small?"

"Damn," he said.

"That's how they were with me. I was so spoiled. My dad was a very successful venture capitalist. He had a real eye for the market and business trends. He still does."

"What does your mom do?" he asked.

"She was a stay-at-home wife and mother."

"So you were an only child," he said.

"Yes."

"My, my, my. I'll bet you were a handful for your husband, having come from parents that catered to you like that."

Lilibelle's voice caught.

"What? What do you mean? I wasn't a handful."

"Yeah, you were," Chance said. "I can tell. That's why you changed the subject earlier when you were talking about how your ex-husband and your kids said you were so 'high maintenance.'"

"I never said they said I was high maintenance!"

"That's because you cut your sentence off, like I wouldn't figure it out. Like I couldn't see it."

"Chance Landry," she said. "I am not high maintenance."

"Yeah, right. Everything about you is meticulous and rigidly controlled. The way you wear your hair…"

"What's wrong with my hair?" she asked, glancing at herself in the rearview mirror.

"Nothing. It's beautiful. It looks good pulled back into that tight bun. You've got the kind of face for that. But it's in perfect order, not a hair out of place, not even in the middle of all that rain last night."

"Stop it, Chance. That doesn't mean I'm high maintenance. This is just the way I like to wear my hair."

He ignored her and kept talking.

"That's why I had to push your car in the middle of the night while getting hammered with rain, hail, sleet, people heckling me as they passed by in their cars..."

"Shut up. You need to quit. You offered to push my car."

"Because you wouldn't let me in the car," he exclaimed.

"That's not high maintenance," she retorted. "That's cautious. You even agreed when we talked about it later."

"Aaaaah, I was just trying to be nice."

"What?" she squealed.

Chance exploded with laughter.

"Relax, relax," he sputtered. "I'm just messing with you. Look at how uptight you're getting. See? You *are* high maintenance."

Lilibelle clicked off the phone.

Yancy's head was visible in the backseat again. She was staring out the back window at Lili.

Lili waved at the dog. Yancy barked. Lilibelle's cell phone rang.

"Have you stayed in that new Peninsula Hotel in Chicago?"

His tone was pleasant and easygoing, as though her hanging up on him before never even happened.

"No," she said dryly. "I haven't."

"It just opened this past June, but it's won all kind of awards and stuff as the most luxurious hotel in the city. They've got these gorgeous bathrooms with big bathtubs, and there's a spa and a fitness center and everything's real hi-tech."

"Sounds nice," she said.

"It's mind-blowing. That's where I've stayed the past few times I've come to Chicago. Besides, they always let me sneak Yance in, even though the size limit for pets is thirty pounds."

Lilibelle was quiet.

"You still mad at me, Belle?"

"Belle?" she said. No one ever called her Belle.

"Yeah, Belle. I like that better. Lili's a pretty name, but I really like Belle. It suits you. You're quite the beauty."

"Stop trying to be nice to me," she said. "You called me high maintenance. Now you're trying to make up for it with your bogus compliments."

"They're not bogus."

"Right."

They each waited for the other to speak. Several seconds of silence played between them.

"So does this mean you're ready for that fork in the road?" he asked.

"No," she said, her voice softer this time. "That's not what that means."

"Then what does it mean? Are you seriously mad at me? I was just kidding with you."

Lilibelle felt rather foolish. She was used to sulking to get her way, and here she was, doing the same thing to someone new. This very nice, so-far-very-enjoyable-to-be-around man, and she was about to run him off with her overindulgent, silly ways.

That's what happened with Adam. This was the bull that did it. Okay, she said to herself. The sulking stops. Right. Now.

"Belle? Are you there?"

She chuckled.

"So you're going to keep calling me that, huh?"

"Yeah," said Chance. "I like the fact that no one else does. That makes it special to me."

"Okay," Lili said.

"So are you mad at me or not?"

"I'm not mad at you. I'm enjoying your company immensely."

"Immensely? Wow. Them's fightin' words."

They both laughed.

"So you were just pretending to be mad at me," he pressed. "You were just being—c'mon, Belle, work with me, admission is half the battle. You were just being..."

"High maintenance." She giggled as she said the words. It was like a weight off her back.

"Congratulations! See how easy that was?"

"Stop it," she said.

"So I tell you what. That'll be our thing. We'll call each other on bullshit when we see it. You can call me out the same way I just did you. If it's coming from an honest and good place, we should be able to handle it, right?"

Lili thought about it. Would she be able to take that kind of frankness? She wanted this trip to be about personal discovery, but this might be a little too real.

"Deal?" Chance asked.

"All right," she said. "Deal."

"Cool. Now, about the Peninsula. I was thinking that maybe that's where we could stay. It's expensive, but it's well worth it. I'll cover the cost of the..."

"Oh, no," said Lili. "Hold it right there. We're road dogs. That's it. I'm not expecting you to pick up any expenses for me. I've got all that under control."

"Not even dinner?"

"Dinner's fine, as long as you let me treat you to breakfast or lunch," she said. "Let's keep this thing equitable."

"That's fine with me."

CHAPTER 5

Magnificent Models

Lilibelle was in hot water and bubbles up to her neck as she soaked in the magnificent oversized tub.

Chance had been right. The Peninsula Chicago was exquisite. She was in the Grand Deluxe Suite, a huge space with a sumptuous king-size bed and an elegant living room with a flat-screen TV and a stereo and DVD player. The room had an awesome view of the Water Tower and the Magnificent Mile. Everything was so picturesque, just like Chance had said. Chicago in November was stunning.

There was a picture window above the bathtub. She floated her soap-covered legs over the surface of the water as she thought about Chance and what he was up to in his room. She wondered if he was taking a bath or a shower. That led her to thoughts of what his undressed body must be like. She slid lower into the warm water, smiling. She had no business thinking of him like this, but it seemed so natural. She closed her eyes, remembering the cleft in his chin. She put an imaginary finger in that cleft, playing with the stubble. She wondered if he was in his room showering and thinking of her.

"He's kind of big to be staying in your room, isn't he?"

"Ssssh," Chance whispered to the leggy girl about to go into the room next door.

"Are you sneaking him in?" she asked. "That is *soooo* wrong."

"He's a she, and I'm not sneaking her in. The hotel knows about it. I'm just trying to be quiet."

"Sure you are."

Chance chuckled.

"Trust me, I have no reason to lie."

"Handsome men always lie," the girl responded.

"Oh. Is that right?"

Yancy made a low growling sound.

"Hey, hey," he said. "Cut that out." He pushed his door open. "Go on, get in there."

Yancy slunk inside the room. Chance hung back.

"So what are you doing in Chicago?" he asked.

"I'm here on a modeling shoot," she said.

"A model? Not a surprise."

The girl leaned against her door.

"So, handsome man. Do you like martinis?"

"But it's only one-thirty."

"I'll take that as a yes."

Lilibelle had brushed her hair back into its usual tight bun. She studied her face in the mirror. The bun wasn't that severe, was it? Besides, her hair was so wild when it wasn't pulled back. It was too much to handle. She hadn't worn it loose in years.

She dabbed a few drops of Chanel perfume behind her ears and on her wrists. She slipped into a pair of formfitting jeans and a camel-colored cashmere sweater. She put in her diamond stud earrings and applied a light touch of makeup to her face. The black Gucci boots were last. Her body felt incredibly relaxed. She looked good and smelled good. She wondered what they would do today. It was early afternoon. No definite plans had been made, but Chance seemed eager to get out into the city. They were checking out the next day and getting back on the road, so today was the best day to take advantage of Chicago.

He wasn't answering the phone in his room or his cell phone. Maybe he had dozed off. So much had happened since the night before and neither of them had had any sleep. He could be catching a nap. It'd make sense.

Lili sat on the side of the bed and turned on the TV. She flipped through the channels absently, not really interested in being pent up in the room. She tried Chance again. No answer. She laid the remote on the bed and leaned back. He'd call her when he was ready. No need to press.

Her eyes were on the TV, on some talking head on CNN.

The next minute they were closed as she drifted off into a deep, unexpected sleep.

It was 5:09 p.m.

Lilibelle sat up in the bed, unsure of her surroundings. Her head was spinning, still hovering between wake and sleep. She blinked a few times, then rubbed her eyes. Where was she?

She looked at the telephone beside the bed. The Peninsula. She was at the Peninsula. Right. She and Chance and Yancy.

Chance!

She picked up the phone and dialed his room. He didn't answer. She tried his cell phone again. It went straight to voice mail, like it was turned off.

"Hey," she said, "where are you? Are you napping? You and Yancy didn't take a fork in the road, did you?" She laughed. "It's Belle. Lilibelle. I'm up in my room. Call me."

She hung up the phone. She couldn't believe she'd just called herself Belle.

Lili got up and went into the bathroom. She checked her face. There was an impression down the right side of her face. Must have come from the spread. She brushed her teeth again and freshened her makeup. She decided to go check out the lobby and the spa area. She didn't get to see much when they first checked in. She'd have her cell phone with her. It wouldn't be hard for Chance to find her.

Lilibelle took the elevator up to the top of the hotel to check out the spa. It was huge, taking up two floors. The spa was also connected to the gym. She made an appointment for a massage the following morning. She walked around the magnificent pool. Maybe she'd go for a swim tomorrow before they checked out. Maybe Chance would come with her.

She walked back toward the elevators, considering how much her thoughts seemed to be gravitating to Chance Landry and his big yellow dog. She was attracted to him, that was it. Like he said, there was no point in hiding behind things. It was a curious feeling, being attracted to someone else. For more than half her life, it had only been Adam. All her lust, love and passions were poured into him. Lili had never even flirted with another man before, and she certainly didn't think the ache of being ditched for another woman would diminish anytime soon.

But there was excitement here. Sure, Chance said he didn't want any commitments. What were his exact words? He wanted to free-fall for a while.

Lilibelle understood. Maybe that's what she wanted, too. It would be good to free-fall, to just go with her feelings without worrying about what might come next. She'd just experienced a devastating breakup. She didn't want to jump into another relationship so soon.

But it might feel good to free-fall into Chance. Just for a little bit.

Just until the next fork in the road.

Lilibelle stepped off the elevator, pushing past the small crowd of people rushing to get on.

She wandered around the sprawling lobby, with its table and chairs occupied with people who seemed to have so much to say. The whole place felt alive with chatter. Lilibelle smiled as she walked across the room.

She passed by The Bar and doubled back. She could use a good drink. Something light. An amaretto sour. She stepped inside.

The place was busy with people and even more chatter. There was the faint scent of cigar smoke. As Lili walked toward the chairs at the bar, she glanced to her left for no particular reason and happened to notice Chance with a cigar in his hand. He was sitting in a corner with a beautiful young woman with golden-brown skin and cascades of curly hair. Chance was leaning in close to her. He whispered something. She tossed her head back and laughed, a musical sound that rose above the din of the other patrons. Chance nuzzled his face into the young woman's neck. She angled her face so he could come in closer. Lilibelle watched as Chance kissed the span of her neck—making his way up to her chin, and then her mouth. The kiss lingered. Lilibelle didn't.

She turned on her Gucci heel and fled the bar. She rushed across the lobby with long-legged strides, unable to get to the elevators quick enough.

There was a crowd of people waiting for the lift. Lili's heartbeat was rapid. She just wanted to be inside her room.

Lili sat on the edge of the bed, her breath coming fast.

She unzipped her boots and tugged them off. She peeled off the jeans. She felt like she was choking, strangling, desperate for air. She rushed into the bathroom and splashed water on her face. Why the hell, she wondered, was she acting like this?

Lili stood at the sink, gazing up at her reflection.

"Who are you?" she asked the face staring back at her. "What's wrong with you? Why don't I even know you anymore?"

She rested both hands against the sink, her head hanging down. She couldn't get the picture of Chance kissing the woman's neck and mouth out of her head.

He was single. He made that very clear.

She wasn't looking for anyone. She barely even knew him.

Then why was she in here now, practically having a stroke? She'd known Chance Landry for less than twenty-four hours, and already her cap was twisted.

"This just doesn't make any sense."

Lili found herself worried about the dog.

Where was Yancy in all this? Locked up in the room?

Perhaps Chance and the young woman were up there with Yancy, and Yancy was watching the two of them get it on.

Lili pressed her hands to her face, freaking from the images that wouldn't stop racing through her head.

"Shake it off," she said. "Shake it off."

She was acting high maintenance.

She definitely needed to shake this stuff off.

Lili was in Saks Fifth Avenue.

There was no way she was going to stay in that hotel room and fret over a situation that wasn't even real. There was nothing between her and Chance. He was her road dog, nothing more. Both of them were newly divorced. He was a serial philanderer. What the hell would she even want with someone like that? Shopping would fix this.

A few pairs of shoes and a couple of new outfits later, and her manic jitters were under control.

She went for a swim in the pool at the hotel.

No point in waiting until tomorrow morning to do it, she thought. The swim would help her destress, and she'd be able to get in a good night of sleep.

At 10:38 p.m., she was under the covers watching *The Sopranos*. A half-eaten dinner from room service was on the floor beside the bed. Lili was dozing off. Neither the phone in her room nor her cell phone had rung all night. She fell asleep still worried about Yancy. She seriously hoped the sweet dog wasn't in the hotel room alone.

Lilibelle was awakened by the ringing phone. She snatched it up.

"Yes," she said, her voice not quite there.

"Good morning, Ms. Goldman. I'm calling to remind you about your 8 a.m. massage."

"Yes, right. What time is it?"

"It's at 8 a.m., ma'am, the first appointment of the morning."

"No," Lili said, glancing around, "what time is it now?"

"It's seven o'clock."

Lili sat all the way up. She scratched the back of her head.

"All right, thanks. I'll be there at eight."

"Thank you, Ms. Goldman."

Lili hung up the phone.

She stretched her arms skyward and yawned. It was Wednesday. She'd been asleep for almost ten hours.

She reached for her cell phone on the nightstand. There were no messages.

Chance Landry wasn't about anything, she decided.

He didn't even have the courtesy to call and check on her.

She was at the Gucci store in the Bloomingdale's building, contemplating a pair of burgundy boots, when her cell phone rang. It was 10:17 a.m. They were going to be checking out of the Peninsula in a couple of hours and getting back on the road.

Perhaps it was finally Chance, calling to remind her of that. She reached in her purse and took out the phone. It was her daughter Sommer.

"Hey, pumpkin."

"Mom?"

"Who else? Is everything okay?"

"Everything's great, Mom," said Sommer. "I just wanted to

see how you were doing out there on the road all by yourself. Aren't you proud of me? I waited a whole day to call you."

Lili held up the boot and gestured to the sales associate. *These, size seven,* she mouthed to the man.

"Yes, pumpkin," she said to her daughter. "I'm very proud of you."

"So how's it going? Anything fun happen yet? Where are you?"

"I'm in Chicago."

"Oh my gosh, already? Wow! You must have been flying."

"Actually, no," Lili said, sitting down to wait for the boots. "It's been a pretty leisurely trip."

"Oh, yeah?"

"Oh, yeah."

"Cool," Sommer said.

Lilibelle's phone beeped. She pulled it away from her ear and looked at the number.

It was Chance.

"Sommer, I need to take this other call. I love you, pumpkin."

"Will you call me later?"

The phone beeped again.

"This is supposed to be time for me, remember?"

"Oh, all right. Whatever. I love you, Mom. Be safe."

"I will," Lilibelle said. She clicked over to the other line. "Hello?"

"Hey, Belle. Whatcha been up to?"

Lili couldn't believe it. He was acting as though he'd just spoken to her minutes ago. And he'd called her Belle. The nerve.

"I've been out in the city."

"I figured," Chance said with a yawn. "I called your room and you were gone. I'll bet you're on Magnificent Mile shopping, aren't you?" He mumbled something that she couldn't quite hear, then said, "Get off me. Back up."

"Excuse me," Lili said.

"It's Yancy. She's trying to take up the whole bed."

"Oh."

"What's wrong with you?" Chance asked. "You don't sound the same."

"Nothing," Lili said.

"You sound like you did yesterday when you were mad at me for calling you high maintenance."

Lilibelle couldn't believe it. He was taunting her, wasn't he? He knew she was mad. He was just going to wait for her to say it so she'd come across as difficult again.

The sales associate returned with the boots.

"Size seven, right?"

"Aha! You are shopping," Chance said.

"I never denied it," Lili said as she took the boots.

Chance was quiet. Lili fumbled with the boots. She took off the shoes she was wearing.

"All right," he finally said. "Are you going to tell me what's wrong or am I going to have to play detective again?"

"I'm just trying on some shoes, Chance. No big deal."

"You're mad about yesterday, right? You're mad because we didn't hang out."

"We never said we were going to hang out," she said as she pulled on the boots, "so why would I be mad?"

Chance laughed.

"Because that's just how you are."

Lili was heated now. She definitely wasn't up to this.

"I met this little tasty," he said. "A model. Her room was next door to mine and she was flirting pretty heavy. What was I supposed to do? I'm a man in free fall. I was momentarily distracted."

"Spare me the details," Lilibelle said.

She stood up in the boots, checking them out in the mirror. They looked good. At nine hundred eighty-four dollars, they'd better. She sat down and took the boots off. She signaled to the salesman that she was going to take them.

"So you mad at me or not?"

"That's become your favorite refrain with me," Lili said.

"That's because you keep giving me heat."

Lilibelle walked over to the counter to pay for the boots.

"Right?" Chance said.

"Right, what?"

"All right, listen," he said. "How about if me and Yancy swing by and pick you up. We can go somewhere and grab something to eat."

"I ate already."

"Uh-oh, Yance," Chance said away from the phone. "She's mad at us. She's about to make that fork in the road."

"Stop saying that," she said. "It's almost like a threat now. Are you sure it's not you who's ready to fork off?"

Chance let out a deep sigh.

"I'm coming to get you, crazy woman. Where are you?"

"You don't have to…"

"Ah, ah, ah! Hush with that already. Where are you?"

"I'm at the Gucci store," said Lili, her voice flat.

"In the mall with the Bloomingdale's?"

"Yes," she said, still sounding dry.

Chance chuckled.

"All right, spoiled brat. Give me a few minutes. Yance and I'll be right over. I'll call you when we're pulling up. Just keep shopping till we get there. Take the edge off."

"Fine," she said.

"Fine," he replied, mocking her tone.

She flipped her phone closed.

Chance was thinking about the sexy model.

At first she seemed like she might be some fun, but his interest in her waned pretty quickly. The more she talked, the less sexy she became. She'd rambled on about this photographer and that designer, things he didn't give a damn about, and she kept coming back to the same inane fashion world subjects no matter how much he tried to divert the conversation to something else.

Things had gotten off to a great start with the promise of a hot and heavy night. By the third martini, his head was hurting. He attempted a few amorous moves, but didn't feel motivated enough to want to follow through. After he smoked his cigar, he made his excuses and went up to the room.

He'd been so tired from the night before, when he had pushed Belle's car off the road. He'd been able to keep his body running on fumes, but after the drinks, the cigar and the incessant hooting of the increasingly-less-attractive model, his body finally crashed on him. He fell across the bed and didn't wake up until this morning. The first thing on his mind when his eyes opened was Belle. Lilibelle. No, just Belle.

Their conversation had been so easy, hours of it on end. It had energized him. He'd been able to keep going because it was so exciting talking to her. Being on the phone with her as they trailed each other to Chicago was great. It made the trip an altogether wonderful experience. If only she didn't get mad so quickly. The slightest thing, and her feathers were up.

Yancy was sitting in the backseat with her nose close to the window.

"Don't you touch that glass," he said, looking back. "It's too cold, Yance. I'm not gonna open it."

Yancy made a whining noise.

"What'd I just say?"

She made the sound again.

Chance looked at the dog. Yancy gave him a under-eyed glance.

"All right, damn it!" he said. "Five minutes. Hurry up."

He cracked the back window. Yancy raised her snout up to the opening, happily sniffing the brisk air. Chance turned up the heat.

"We don't want it to be cold when she gets in the car."

The Bloomingdale's building was up ahead. He picked up his cell phone and hit redial.

"Yes," she said.

"Come on out, Belle. We're about to pull up."

"All right," she said, and hung up.

There were several cars alongside the curb. Chance negotiated his way over. A horn suddenly honked in his left ear, startling him so that he jumped in his seat. Yancy pulled her snout from the window and barked.

"What the f…"

It was a cabbie, trying to cut in front of him.

"He's gonna get somebody killed," Chance said.

He turned his attention back to pulling up at the curb. Chance saw her immediately. She was standing there holding three bags.

Her hair was down, falling around her face and over her shoulders.

She was extraordinary. He couldn't catch his breath.

He almost hoped she didn't see him yet. He needed another moment to drink her in.

She noticed them. She began walking toward the car.

Something in Chance's stomach began to hurt. Not his stomach itself. Something inside it. It didn't make sense.

She was at the door now, reaching for the handle. Yancy was barking and wagging her tail.

Chance jumped out of the car and went around to her side. He took the bags from her hands. His eyes met hers. Now the sensation in his belly felt like a knife stab.

"Let's put these in the back," he said. He opened the back door on the passenger side. "Slide, Yance." The dog moved over.

Lili got inside the car while Chance dealt with her purchases. What was that perfume she was wearing? he wondered. She smelled delicious. Something stabbed him in the belly again.

Chance shut the door and walked back around to the driver's side.

Fuck, he thought, as he neared the door. *This can't be happening. Not now. Not now.*

He opened the door and slid behind the wheel. He looked over his left shoulder, checking for cars as he pulled away from the curb. Once he was safely in traffic, he turned to her.

Her face was luminous, even though he could tell she was pissed about something.

The sharp pains in his stomach increased, coming like contractions.

"How you doing, lady?" he said with a smile.

"Fine." She was curt. She didn't attempt to say more.

Normally something like that would piss him off. He was turned on instead, suddenly completely unnerved by the woman sitting beside him.

This couldn't be happening.

He was falling for Belle.

CHAPTER 6

The Jedi Pact

They went back to the Peninsula and checked out. They were on the road by 12:45 p.m.

"So do you think you can handle an eight-hour haul today?" Chance was on his cell phone talking to Lili.

"I did nine hours the day you met me," she said. "I think I can handle eight."

"All right, missy. Although it'll be more like eight and a half. We're going to drive as far as Lincoln, Nebraska. Then we'll sock it in for the night."

"Okay."

Chance felt tense. He wanted to find a way to break through to her, but she wasn't letting her guard down so easy this time.

"How's it going back there with you?" he pressed. "She giving you any trouble?"

"No," Lili said, her voice gentler. "She's lying down in the backseat. She's not sleeping, though. She's just kind of looking at me."

"You know that's the first time she's ever rode with anyone other than me. Yancy being in your car is a really big deal. For both of us."

"Both of who?" she asked.

"Me and Yancy."

Lilibelle made a smirking sound.

Chance's nerves were on edge. This was not in the plans. Vegas was going to be all about tits and ass, tits and ass, and now this. He glanced in the rearview mirror to see if he could catch a glimpse of her. All he could see was her full head of hair. Damn, she looked so freaking beautiful today!

"Belle," he began, "let me ask you something."

"What's that?" She was still aloof.

"Remember yesterday, when we were driving to Chicago. Remember our Jedi pact?"

She made a sound that he couldn't make out.

"Was that a 'yes?'" he asked.

"I remember the pact."

"No secrets between road dogs, right? We said that'd be our thing. We'll call each other on bull, and as long as it's coming from an honest and good place…"

"Yeah, yeah, yeah, I remember," Lili said.

"Good. All right then. So, Belle, I'm about to call you out. It's coming from an honest and good place."

"So go, already," she said with irritation.

"Now you're mad. Damn it, I'm going anyway."

He breathed in deeply, then exhaled.

"You're mad because I didn't call you yesterday once we got settled in the room. The rest of the afternoon and the night went by and I didn't call or check on you or anything, right?"

"I'm not mad, Chance."

"Girl, quit lying and be honest! Just tell me how you feel. Be real with me."

"I'm not mad."

"Belle, don't do this. You and I have a real opportunity in front of us right now. I said I wanted to be more straightforward with people. No doing what I don't want to do because it's what other people expect of me. You talked about how much it hurt you that you had no warning from your ex-husband about what was going on. You didn't have a chance to talk about it. Here's your chance to talk about this. Here's my chance to answer honestly."

He couldn't believe how nervous he was as he said all this. She could probably see right through him. And if she did, what if she pushed him away?

"Chance, the situations you're talking about were marriages," Lili said. "You saw that you needed to give more honesty in yours. I needed to get more honesty in mine. You and I are just road dogs, isn't that what you said? It's not that deep. You keep talking about how we could fork off at any time. Why does it matter to you to get to the truth of what I'm feeling?"

"Because we made the Jedi pact."

He heard what he was sure was a hint of a giggle.

"You're so stupid," she muttered.

"I'm serious, Belle. We've got to honor the pact."

She sighed on her end of the phone. He waited, letting her find the voice to hopefully tell the truth.

They drove in silence for at least two miles. He didn't pressure her. Just knowing she was on the other side of the dead air was strangely comforting.

"I'm glad I got the extended minutes," Chance said.

"See? I was just about to tell you," said Lili, "and now you're cracking jokes."

"My bad. Speak, girl. Speak your mind."

Lili giggled.

"All right, yes, I was pissed yesterday."

"And today."

"Whatever," she said. "Don't cut me off, or I won't be able to say it."

He remained quiet.

"I was looking forward to spending some time with you once we both got situated," Lili said. "I enjoyed our conversation at the diner when my car broke down. I enjoyed our conversation on the drive to Chicago. It was nice. It was fun. It was funny. It was refreshing. It was something I needed after all the shit I've just been through with my ex. So yeah, it kind of messed with my head when we checked in and I didn't hear from you at all. I felt like maybe what I felt was one-sided. That you weren't as into the conversations as much as I was. Maybe."

"What? I wasn't as into them? I sat in that diner all friggin' night with you. I'm the one who suggested we become road dogs. You're crazy. I wasn't as into the conversations? I was totally into them. Having you to talk to is making the whole trip a richer experience for me."

There was silence from her side of the line. He wished they were in the same car together. He wished he could look into her eyes as he said what he did.

"I got distracted, Belle. As soon as I went up to my room, right when I was putting my key in the door, this chick started messing with me about Yancy being too big to be in the hotel. She thought I was trying to sneak her in. That jumped off the whole thing, and then she just started kicking it to me, asking me if…"

"Chance. Stop it. You don't have to tell me this. I'm not your girl. I'm your road dog. You do what you've got to do, what you want to do. I have no right to get upset about it."

The words *I'm not your girl* slammed him in the face. He wasn't looking for a girl, rather, a woman, but damn if one hadn't shown up. He didn't even know what to do about it, let alone know what to tell her. He sat behind the wheel feeling helpless, like a stranger inside of his own destiny, not knowing exactly how he wanted it to go.

"I know you're not my girl, Belle," he said, "but I do want to show you a level of respect. I don't want you to think I just ditched you for the first piece of ass I saw when we got to Chicago. That's not what happened. I couldn't even deal with her for long. Once I realized she…"

"Don't tell me," Lili said. "*Lalalalalalalalala…*"

"What are you *doing?*"

"I don't want to hear what you did with that girl."

"But that's just it...I didn't do anything with her. I couldn't even talk to her right. After spending all that time talking to you, I was spoiled for conversation. That chick just couldn't stack up."

"But I saw you kissing her," Lili whispered.

Chance's pulse quickened.

"Kissing her? Kissing her? Ohhhhhh," he said, remembering the moment. "In the bar. I kissed her in the bar. I was trying to get her to shut up."

"Oh, please. Really now, Chance. That's just absurd for you to even say."

"It's true. And I was trying to see if I could still get turned on by her, even though I didn't give a shit about what she had to say. As it turns out, I couldn't. So I drank another martini and went up to the room. I fell asleep in my clothes, stretched across the bed. That's how I woke up this morning."

"Oh," said Lili.

"And since we're being real honest," Chance dared to add, "when I woke up this morning, the first thing I thought about was you."

They were both quiet again. Chance stared at the road ahead and watched broken white lines go by.

"So what am I supposed to do with that?" Lili asked, her voice barely a whisper. "What does it mean?"

"Fuck if I know," he said. "I was just getting settled into my new skin."

Damn, he thought. Now it's out there. Even though she hadn't admitted anything to him. She'd only said she was pissed because he didn't call her to hang out. He didn't know if it meant she was attracted to him and therefore kind of jealous when she saw the model. He didn't know anything. He wondered if he'd said too much. He didn't want to be wrong. What if he saw some sweet ass at the next stop and everything he thought he was feeling just—poof!—disap-

Page 190 of 320

peared. Then he'd be an asshole. There would definitely be a fork in the road.

"This is kind of heavy," she said. "This Jedi pact thing may be a bit too intense."

"But it's coming from a place of honesty and good," said Chance. "You can't knock that, can you?"

"Perhaps. Chance, why don't we take a phone breather for a minute. We've both had our chance to vent. A little silent reflection might not be a bad thing right now."

"Oh," he said. "Um, ah, yeah, ah, okay…well, if you need me, I'm right in front of you. Just press redial or flash your high beams. I got you in my sights."

They didn't speak again until Lili called two hours later to ask Chance what it meant when Yancy made a certain whiny sound.

"She's gotta pee," he said, "or more. Let's pull over."

They did. Chance hitched Yancy to the leash and took her for a quick spin. Lili got out of the car and stretched her legs.

"Do you want me to put her back in my car?" he asked when they were finished.

"No," said Lili. "I like her with me. I like the company."

Chance led Yancy back to Lili's car. Yancy jumped inside the open door. Chance closed it and walked up to Lilibelle.

"So what made you take your hair down?" he asked.

"I don't know," she replied. "I guess I thought about what you said about it being so controlled and severe. I didn't want to be that. Not anymore."

Chance reached out hesitantly and touched it.

"It looks incredible. You look incredible."

Lili gazed up at him. He let himself gaze back at her, uninterrupted.

A hint of frost came from both of their mouths as they stood in front of each other on the shoulder of the road.

Chance knew one thing—he wanted to kiss her, but he was

so afraid to cross that line, so afraid of what it would mean if it was just a passing feeling on his part.

He couldn't read her anyway. Her eyes were fastened on him so intensely. It could have been interpreted as passion or judgment. He was glad she spoke when she did. It broke the awkward spell.

"We'd better get going," Lili said. "It's cold out here, and we've got 'miles to go before we sleep.'"

"Right," said Chance. "Robert Frost. How appropriate."

He opened the driver's-side door for her and closed it when she got in. He walked back up to his own car and got behind the wheel. They pulled onto the road and plunged headlong into the next few hours.

They didn't talk again until they were in Lincoln, Nebraska's city limits and Chance called to suggest a hotel.

They checked in, said their good-nights and went to their separate rooms. It was still fairly early, only about 9:30 p.m., but they were both tired and planned on ordering room service instead of doing dinner together. They would be driving for six hours the next day, Thursday, from Lincoln, Nebraska, to Denver, Colorado. They needed to make good use of their time in order to get to Vegas on Saturday as planned.

Chance sat in his bed eating a hamburger. Yancy was eating a hamburger, too. And fries.

He was sitting there trying to figure out how he and Belle had gone so quickly from excellent conversation to strained, courteous remarks about which hotel to stay in and what time they planned on leaving.

It was because feelings had come into play. She'd had expectations of him in Chicago, and when he didn't meet those expectations, she felt bad.

And, for his part, he wanted her, couldn't stop thinking about her. She'd let her hair down and knocked down his heart at the same time. It wasn't just about the hair. It was the whole of her. He might not have even noticed these things as profoundly if it had not been for the ditzy model. The contrast between the two women was stark.

This was the model's fault.

No, it was Belle's fault. If her car had never broken down that night on the road, he and Yancy would have rolled on with their lives just fine.

Lilibelle had been asleep for half an hour when she was awakened by a knock at her door. She thought she was dreaming. She slipped back into sleep.

The knock came again.

She threw the covers back and padded over to the door in her thick winter socks. She looked through the peephole. It was Chance.

"What's up?" she said through the door.

"Can I talk to you for a second?" he asked.

"About what?"

"Open the door, Belle. I'll wake people up if I have to talk to you from the hallway."

Lili slid the chain out of its slot and turned the bolt. She opened the door. Chance walked past her.

When she turned around, he was right in front of her. He pulled her into his arms and kissed her. Lili's arms encircled his waist. They kissed like that for five long minutes, standing right there in the middle of the floor.

Then Chance lifted her and carried her to the bed. He laid her down on the pillow, then climbed in behind her. As much as he wanted to make love to her, he didn't. But he did want to hold her. All night.

He refused to deny himself that.

When Lili awoke the next morning, she was in bed alone.

She sat up, looking around for Chance. There was nothing to indicate he'd ever been there. Had she been dreaming?

She turned in the bed and noticed the deep indentation in the sheets. There it was. He *had* been with her.

Her phone rang.

"Hello?"

"Hey. How you doing?"

"I'm fine," said Lili. "How are you doing?"

"I'm good," Chance said, his tone vague and practical. "I was thinking maybe we could be outta here in the next hour. Can you swing that?"

"Sure," she said.

"Great. We can grab some breakfast at that diner across the way before we get back on the road. Are you hungry?"

"Yes. I didn't eat much last night. I was so sleepy."

Lili figured that would be a lead-in to him saying something about having been in bed with her.

"All right," he said. "How about we meet at the cars in an hour? After checkout and everything. Cool?"

"Cool."

Hadn't this man just spent the night spooning her? Hadn't he literally swept her off her feet when he came into her room? What was his deal?

This was definitely *not* cool. Chance was acting so strangely, especially after the bold step he had taken the night before.

It was time to effect the Jedi pact. Now it was her turn to do the questioning...from a place of honesty and good.

CHAPTER 7

Rocky Mountain Highs

They were sitting across from each other in silence, big plates filled with eggs, grits, bacon and hash between them. Yancy couldn't come inside. She was inside the big black Mercedes, bundled under a thick winter blanket to combat the cold. Chance had ordered a take-out breakfast for her.

"We won't be long," he had reassured the dog.

Lili was picking at her plate now, taking small, half-hearted bites.

"I thought you were hungry," Chance said. He was plowing through his food.

"I thought I was, too."

"The hash can't touch the Big Chuck Bang."

"Huh?"

"The Big Chuck Bang. Chuck's hash back in Ohio. The one you had the night we met?"

"Oh," she said, perking up, seeing her opening. "So you remember that?"

"What, the hash? I'm the one who told you about it."

"No," said Lili. "I mean you remember the night we met. You know, a mere three nights ago. Those hours of conversation, nonstop, both of us spilling everything to each other."

Chance smirked and shoveled his fork into his eggs.

"Jedi pact?" she asked.

Chance looked up.

"Jedi pact?" she repeated.

He exhaled, his shoulders slumping.

"Fine," he said. "Go ahead."

Lili reached for her orange juice and took a long sip. She leaned back against her seat, contemplating him. Then she put the glass down and leaned forward again.

"What happened last night? What was that all about?"

Chance smiled awkwardly, his eyes cast at the table as he shook his head.

"I knew that was going to come back to haunt me," he said.

"Come back?" Lilibelle said, trying to keep her voice from shrieking. "It never left. It just happened. It's still here."

Chance drank some juice.

"Yeah," he said.

"Yeah? That's all you've got to say?"

He shrugged.

"Jedi pact, Chance. You made me do it. Jedi pact. Come on."

Chance put down his juice. He reached for a napkin and wiped his mouth. He did everything but look at her.

"Come on," Lili said.

He sat back, finally looking at her.

"All right, fine. Last night was about me being caught up with these feelings for you. Crazy feelings, okay? Feelings I don't know what to do with."

"So you couldn't talk to me about that? You just get up in the middle of the night, or whenever you left, and leave me thinking that it never even happened? If it weren't for your giant print in the bed..."

"Look, Belle, I'm not ready for this. This is supposed to be my free fall time. I've got Kina breathing down my back for alimony, and Jacie..."

"Who's Jacie?"

"Jacie's my first wife. Every time I think she's gone away, she keeps turning up like a bad penny, trying to stake some ridiculous claim."

"On you?"

"No. Hell, no. On my businesses. Stupid stuff. Shakedown shit. Small-time hustles. Jacie's a small-time, small-minded kind of girl."

"You didn't tell me about Jacie," Lili said.

"I'm telling you about her now," Chance replied with a frown. "That's what I'm trying to explain to you. I've still got those women hanging off me like ticks that refuse to let go. I can't handle another one. I can't keep piling up ticks on my back."

"*What?!!*"

She was shrieking now. She didn't bother to try to contain herself. It was enough to have Adam walk out on her the way he did. Now another man, a man she was developing strong feelings for, had just called her...a tick?

"No, Belle, I wasn't applying that to you. You totally took it the wrong way."

"There aren't too many ways I can take it, Chance. You were just describing your ex-wives and the way they suck off your life, and you segued to them after trying—unsuccessfully, I might add—to explain why you're tripping about what's going on with you and me."

"I told you I don't do this well."

"Do what well, talk?"

"Relationships. I screw them up. If I let myself get with you..."

"Let yourself get with me? I'm in this equation, too. You act like this is your sole consideration."

He pushed his plate away.

"See, this is what happens when feelings come in. Things get complicated. They get ugly. Everything was so beautiful between us at first, and now, what, it's just three days later and we've completely derailed."

"Have we?" she said. "I didn't see it that way."

To Lili's dismay, her eyes began to well up.

"Aw, damn. Belle. See. This is exactly what I didn't want."

Lili stood up from the table. She opened her purse and took out a twenty. She placed it on the table.

"I think it's time for our fork in the road."

"Belle...no. What are you doing?"

Lilibelle was already walking out the door.

She stopped at the black Mercedes and looked in on Yancy. The big dog came to the back window, her nose pressed against the glass. Her tail was wagging with vigor. A tearful gasp escaped from Lili's mouth. She clasped her hand over her lips to keep herself from audibly crying. She pressed her other hand against the glass. Yancy tried to lick it through the material separating them.

"Love you, Yance," Lilibelle whispered.

She did love the dog. That sweet, sweet, big yellow dog.

Chance was standing inside the door of the diner, watching her and Yancy bonding through the window of his car.

He was so damn stupid. He'd said the most ridiculous things. This was why men couldn't be totally honest. His new approach might be great in theory, but it sucked in practical application. He didn't want to hurt Belle. Not Belle. He wanted the opposite of that. He just didn't want her to get in the way of his life.

She was walking over to her car now. She was opening the door.

He shoved the door of the diner open and raced over to her, grabbing her in his arms and pulling her tightly into his chest.

"I'm an asshole," he said. "I'm an idiot. I'm a fool."

Lilibelle was crying into his sweater.

"Don't leave, Belle. Don't leave like this. I don't want you to take the fork in the road."

"You don't know what you want with me," she said, pushing back from him, wiping her face.

"I know. I'm sorry. This is...it's unexpected, okay?"

"Like I was expecting it?" she snapped. "I got on the road to get away from heartache, not run into a bigger dose of it."

"Let's talk about this," he said. "Both of us are emotional right now. Can we do that? Can we stay together for now? Please, Belle. Just don't take the fork in the road."

She looked up at him. He wiped her tears.

"Besides," he said. "Yancy would be devastated. Look at her over there."

The dog was at the window watching them. Her nose prints were all over the frosted glass.

"So you'll stay?" he asked. "For now? I'll feel better knowing we're on the road together."

He knew that wasn't telling her much, but he didn't know how much to tell. He wasn't sure of anything. This was fucked up all around.

"All right," she said. She squared her shoulders back. "All right. Fine. We're road dogs. No complications. This is too much as it is. I sort of feel like you. I don't know if I can take on any more."

Chance felt that pain in his stomach again.

A waitress came rushing out of the diner with a bag.

"You forgot your to-go order," she said.

"Thanks," said Chance.

"Look at that," Lilibelle said. "Poor Yancy would have probably starved."

Chance looked down at her. She had a tiny hint of a smile, even through the pools of her tears.

They were talking again, six hours, all the way to Denver.

"Our phone bills are going to be astronomical," Lili said. "How many minutes do you have in your plan?"

"Ten thousand," he said. "I upped it right before Yance and I hit the road. I must have been psychic, huh?"

"I wish I had been. I've got three thousand minutes."

"Oh, you're still good," Chance said.

"Yeah, but we've still got a ways to go. Ah, who cares. It's worth it."

"Is it?"

"Yeah. It's worth it just to be talking like this again."

"I know," he said. "It's just like it was in the beginning."

She laughed.

"You're so silly. You make the beginning seem like it was years ago."

"It kind of feels like it."

"What?"

"Wait now. I mean that in a good way. I feel like I've known you for a long time. Not just since Monday. I'm more open with you than I think I've ever been with anybody."

"Even your wives?" she asked.

"Especially my wives."

"I can't even begin to tell you how jacked up that is."

They both laughed.

"Okay," he said, "let's play favorites."

"Huh?"

"Favorite food."

"Huh?"

"What's your favorite food, fool."

"Oh," she giggled. "Alaskan king crab. What's yours."

"Chicken," he said. "Fried."

"You're so cliché."

"Favorite number."

"Six," she said.

"Why six?"

"The birthday party?"

"Oh, yes. The diamond tiara. The eight hundred people."

"You remember that?" she said.

"Remember it? How could I forget. That's the visual of a lifetime."

Lilibelle laughed, light and at ease.

She loved this feeling. It was almost like being able to fly.

"So what do you think about us staying at the Loews in Denver?"

"I like Loews hotels," she said.

"Good. Yancy and I have stayed at this one several times. They don't care how big she is. She gets a special bowl and all kinds of goodies. They've got a pet menu and pet room service. She gets better treatment than I do there."

"As she should," Lili said.

There were just approaching Denver's city limits. The snow-capped Rocky Mountains were picture-postcard perfect.

"It's so beautiful here," she said.

"Yeah. You can see really see God's handiwork in a place like this."

Yancy was pressing her nose against the window, making a whining sound.

"No, Yance. It's too cold. I'm not letting it down."

"Poor Yancy," Lili said. "All she wants is to feel the wind on her face."

"And give me Bell's palsy in the process," Chance said. "The wind out there cuts to the bone. It's really cold here today. Things might be warmer as we get closer to Vegas. I'll let her have her open window then."

They checked into the Loews Denver Hotel around 4:20 p.m. and headed up to their respective suites, which were on different floors.

"I'm gonna get it right this time," Chance said as they rode up on the elevator.

"What's that?"

"I'm gonna make a plan. *We're* gonna make a plan. That way there's no question about expectations."

"That'd be great," Lili said. "But I don't want you to feel obligated to hang out with me."

"Yes, you do, so shut up."

"You're so stupid," she said.

"I know that already. So listen…how about we give ourselves a chance to get cleaned up and rested, maybe take a nap and I'll give you a call around seven, seven-thirty. We can have some dinner, if you want. I'll get a sitter for Yance."

"They've got dogsitters here?" she said.

"This hotel has everything."

A few hours later, they were dining downstairs in the Tuscany Restaurant. Chance said it was one of the best restaurants in the city. There was a roaring fireplace and the food was exquisite. Lili was beautiful in a simple black dress that conformed to her body. Her hair was still loose, falling all around her shoulders and face. Chance couldn't stop looking at her. Lili couldn't stop looking at him. Her mouth fell open when they met up in the lobby before they headed to the restaurant.

"Oh my God, you *shaved!* Look at that." She reached out and touched his skin. It was silky smooth. "Why were you hiding a face like that?" She stuck her finger inside his cleft. It felt just as she imagined it would, minus the stubble.

"That's nice," he said about her finger on his face. "No one's ever stuck their finger in my cleft."

"I'm not nobody," she said.

"You're not kidding."

They were on their second bottle of wine. They were laughing and singing silly songs from *The Flintstones.*

"My favorite was the Ann Margrock lullaby that she sings

to Pebbles. *The last little lamb was the littlest lamb. Too little for such a big leap...*"

"No, no, that's not the best Ann Margrock song. It was the one they did at the end of the episode where Fred and Barney are onstage performing with her, doing the twist. *I ain't gonna be a fool no more...*" Chance did the twist in his chair. "*I cried and cried until my eyes were sore...*" He twisted again.

A couple at a nearby table laughed.

"Stop dancing," Lili whispered. "You're drawing attention."

"Oh, like singing cartoon songs isn't."

Lili giggled.

"This is nice, Chance," she said. "Thank you for showing me such a good time."

"You're my road dog," he smiled. "If you can't be good to your road dog, who can you be good to?"

"Certainly not your ex-wives," she joked.

"Don't start. We're doing good here."

"I know. My bad."

She leaned back in her chair, her lids feeling heavy.

"You're tired, huh?"

"A little. But it's a good tired."

"Good," he said. "We don't like the bad kind of tired."

"Would you be mad if I went up? I think the wine's kind of gotten to me. My head's beginning to spin a little."

"No, not at all. Let me walk you up."

"No, no, no," she said. "I don't want to ruin the rest of the evening for you. It's early yet."

"It's ten o'clock."

"What time are we planning to get back on the road tomorrow? We've got to make it to Vegas in enough time for your birthday on Saturday."

She yawned.

"It's almost eleven hours from here. I was thinking maybe we could leave around one in the afternoon so we'll be scheduled to hit the Vegas city limits right when my birthday's coming in."

"Ooh, that would nice! Yeah. Let's do that." Lilibelle yawned again.

Chance stood and walked around to her chair. He clasped her by the hand, pulling her up.

"C'mon," he said. "Let's get you to your room."

He stood beside her as she put the card key in the door.

"Thanks for bringing me up, Chance," she said.

He looked down at her, so small and beautiful. Even tipsy and sleepy, she didn't lose her appeal.

"No problem, Belle. I really enjoyed your company tonight."

They lingered.

Lilibelle stared at the floor.

He wanted to do it. He wanted so badly to take her in his arms and kiss her. He wanted to carry her over that threshold, into the room and do what he didn't do the night before, even though he had been aching to do it.

He leaned down and pecked her on the cheek.

"Good night, road dog," he said.

Lili looked up at him with a hint of disappointment.

"Good night, Chance. Kiss Yancy for me."

She pushed the door open and went inside. The door closed slowly at first, then slammed shut, as heavy hotel doors were wont to do.

Chance stood outside the door for a long minute.

"Shit."

He wasn't ready to go back to his room. He went back down to the lobby for one last drink.

He was sitting by himself in the T-Bar, staring at the various frescoes that adorned the walls. He sipped his cognac very slowly, savoring the taste. He wished he had a Montecristo to go with it.

"I like that one best," said a lovely blonde with a soft voice. She slid into the empty seat beside him. "Do you mind?"

Chance waved his hand, offering the seat.

"I'm Katya," she said, offering her free hand. The other was holding a glass of wine.

"Nice to meet you, Katya. I'm Chance."

"Now that's a frontiersman's name, if I ever heard one. It suits you."

Chance smiled, drinking in the woman as he sipped more of his drink.

She was gorgeous, with flaxen hair and sky-blue eyes. And she smelled wonderful, like some sort of exotic garden. The tops of her breasts swelled out of her formfitting dress.

"You here on business, Chance?"

"No. This is a pleasure trip."

Katya leaned forward, purring.

"Ooh. We like pleasure trips." She put her hand on his knee. "I'm on one, too. This is the first vacation I've had all year. You have no idea how much I need to wind down."

Katya's cues were unmistakable. Chance had seen them a thousand times before. He could have her right now if he wanted. Katya, with her flaxen hair and sky-blue eyes and bubbling breasts and exotic-garden smell. He could take Katya to his room—or better yet, go to hers and hit it and quit it. He thought about it.

"That cleft in your chin is amazing," she said. "You've got such a strong face. So sexy."

Katya's hand was still on his knee. She sipped her wine, her eyes still on his.

Chance smiled. He was going to do it.

He turned up the glass of cognac, finishing it off. He patted her hand, the one that was on his knee.

"A pleasure meeting you, Katya. I've got something I need to go do."

She pulled her hand back with surprise as he stood.

"Enjoy your stay here," he said. "Denver's one of the most beautiful cities in the country. I'm sure you'll find plenty of ways to help you wind down."

* * *

He stood outside her door for a solid minute, breathing in, breathing out, bracing himself for what he realized was the real free fall.

He knocked on the door.

He waited just a few seconds, then knocked again.

He could hear her stumbling around the room, finally making it to the door.

"Yes?"

"It's me, Belle. Open up."

"Chance?" She sounded groggy.

"Yeah, it's Chance. Open the door."

He heard the chain come off and the bolt turn, and then the door was open, darkness beckoning him in.

He stepped inside.

"Is this a repeat of last night?" she asked. "Because I don't think we should…"

He flipped on the light.

"Ssssh. Don't speak. Let me talk for a minute."

She was standing in front of him, her face so sweet, clear and innocent, her hair all over her head. She didn't look forty-three, not that there was anything wrong with that. But his Belle was a true belle, a timeless beauty who had taken him over. She was in a big T-shirt and socks, but in that moment, she was the sexiest woman he'd ever seen.

"I've been thinking about all the things I said to you. My new philosophy. All that crap about no attachments and forks in the road."

She gazed up at him. The way she was looking at him made him want to fall at her feet.

"Both of us have had some shitty experiences," he said. "I brought a lot of mine on myself. In your case, you didn't deserve what happened to you."

She lowered her head. He put a finger under her chin and lifted it back up.

"I didn't think the love thing would ever hit me, you know? I've escaped it for so long, and there's so many bogus women out there. Maybe it was because I was a bogus man."

Lili's lips parted. He put his finger over them.

"Let me finish," he said.

She closed her mouth.

"So I was thinking…" He inhaled deeply, then exhaled the same way. "All right, let me try this again." He reached for her hands, clasping them in his. His eyes were fixed on hers.

"I was thinking that, you know, if you're open to it, if I'm someone you think you could see yourself being with…" He swung her hands nervously as he held them. "I was thinking… No, I've decided—" another breath "—that I don't just want you to be my road dog anymore."

Lilibelle's eyes were full of water. Fat with tears that didn't drop, they just held on to her eyeballs as if for dear life.

"I'd like for you to be my woman, Belle. No, no, not like that. I'd love for you to be my woman. I love you. Just downstairs, just now, I knew for a fact that I loved you. I knew it that day when I picked you up from the curb at Bloomingdale's, but that was just a hunch. I know it for real now."

He was swinging her arms so hard he was yanking her. He caught himself and slowed them down.

She was still looking up at him with big, wet eyes. He'd messed it up, he realized. He'd rushed all the way up on the elevator to tell her, but had screwed up the whole thing.

"Shit. Look how you're looking at me. I understand. That whole thing I just said, it sounded corny, didn't it? I don't even know what to say or how to say it or even know if I'm saying it right. This is all fucked up," he stammered. "I've faked it so long with so many people, I don't even know how to do it when it's the real thing."

"You do it like this," she whispered, standing on her tiptoes to kiss him.

He leaned down, his lips meeting hers.

"You love me, Belle?" he asked, pulling away. "Is it possible you can love me back the way that I love you?"

"Yes," she said. It was the smallest, surest sound either of them had ever heard.

The tears in her eyes finally fell as he lifted her in his arms and carried her to the bed, this time getting it right, doing what he hadn't done the night before.

This time they made love.

CHAPTER 8

Wet Noses Double Down

They were driving through the desert.

"So what are we going to do now?" Lilibelle asked as she let the passenger window down. For the very first time, they were traveling on the open road in the same vehicle, no more tag-teaming from place to place.

They'd left her car at the Loews Hotel, having made arrangements with the concierge for them to pick it up on their return. Or not. They'd discussed her having it shipped back to New York while they remained on the road once they'd done Vegas.

Chance was behind the wheel. She was a passive rider in his car. *Their* car. They were a "they" now. Deep inside herself she wanted to scream. A good scream. A hysterically ecstatic one. Something inside her had finally let go.

The strong cool breeze of the desert night assailed her face. She quickly let the window back up. It was cooler than she thought. Not freezing, but uncomfortably cool.

Yancy whined from the backseat.

"All right, girl, you can finally have it."

Chance let Yancy's window down. The big dog thrust her head directly into the intense wind, her black nose wet, her ears flying back.

"See how she loves it? Sometimes you've just gotta plunge headlong into the breeze."

"So suddenly you're an expert at plunging headlong," she said.

"Yeah. I'm free fall man, remember? When I fall, I fall hard."

"Right."

"Seriously. Look at Yancy. Look at how she just sticks her head in the wind and rolls with it."

Lilibelle turned in her seat and glanced back at the dog. Her mouth was curled up into a most magnificent smile. The fast cool air to Yancy was nirvana. Was it really that easy? Could happiness be as simple as hanging one's head out of an open window in a speeding car?

"What are we gonna do?" she asked again.

"First," he said, "you're going to let your window down."

"No, Chance. It's too much. Yours is down and so is Yancy's. If I let mine down, it'll be like a windstorm in here."

"And what's wrong with a little windstorm? Don't you think that pretty much sums us up? Embrace it."

"But my hair will get messed up," she whined. "It'll be too cold."

"No whining. Just do it. I'll turn the heat on and it'll balance the temperature so you won't get cold. Let your hair down, Lili. C'mon. All three of us are going to let go together."

The old, resistant Lilibelle—the control freak, the hysterical hyperventilating drama queen who had been getting her way the majority of her life because the people closest to her had indulged her way too much—was still hanging on, even if it was to a ledge with just one fingertip that refused to let go. She'd been a lion for so long, roaring for attention. The thought of going out like a beaten-down lamb just didn't seem possible.

But she wasn't beaten down, was she? She'd been liberated from a world of doubt and abandonment. She had found herself during all of this, and, along the way, had found someone—*someones*—who had been happy to find her in return.

She opened her mouth to protest. Chance placed the palm

of his right hand over her parted lips, breaking the sound before it could break the spell.

"It won't kill us," he said. "Just consider it an experiment."

He removed his hand from her mouth. Lilibelle was quiet.

"You trust me, Belle?" he asked.

Her eyes met his. They'd been across the country together. He'd had her back for everything. Either one of them could have taken the fork in the road at any moment. But he never left her. He'd stayed close, respectful, considerate, always within reach, never more than two car lengths away.

Her ex-husband Adam had chosen the fork when it was most convenient, not even allowing himself to be stopped by one of the most horrific crises in American history. After twenty-five years of marriage, he had simply merged off the road without warning, abandoned his ride and jumped inside another car. Not Chance. Chance was a long-distance man. He had proven himself up for the journey.

"Do you trust me, Belle?"

"Of course I do."

"Do you trust Yancy?"

Lili smiled. She'd never been a dog person. Now she couldn't imagine life without that big yellow beast in the backseat.

"I love Yancy."

Yancy barked, her head still thrust into the wind.

Chance now had both hands on the wheel, at ten and two, as he stared at the road ahead.

"Do you love me?" he asked, his normally big voice suddenly small.

She reached out her hand. He grasped it.

"Yes. I do."

"Better than Yancy?"

"Well, I don't know about all that..."

Chance laughed.

"Then let your window down," he said.

"And then what? What happens next?"

"Life happens next," he said. "We leave it to chance."

"Life isn't like that," she said.

"Of course it is. It's exactly like that. Life is a gamble. You gambled on me that night your car broke down. You played your hand big letting me into your life, and Yancy and I did the same."

"I can't keep gambling. My whole life can't just be one big risk after another."

"Why not? Hasn't it been already?"

Lilibelle stared at the road. He was right. She'd bet on Adam, and had completely crapped out.

"So…" she said.

"So let your window down. Let's keep playing this hand. Let's put all our chips in, go all out. Let's double down, baby."

"And then what?"

"We let it ride. We tag-team the world."

Lilibelle looked at Chance. He was as serious as she'd ever seen him, yet as unencumbered as a soul could be.

"I'll be right by your side," he assured her. "No matter what, you got me, Belle, and I got you. Yancy's got you. You won't be gambling alone. The three of us are in this, all or nothing."

Lilibelle considered his words. Why not step into the unknown? Hadn't she done that anyway, this entire trip? What was the worse that could happen? She'd already seen the worst. Adam leaving her. People jumping out of the windows of two burning towers.

It was just letting her window down. Every window of her life.

She placed her finger on the button for the window. She slowly lowered the glass. The breeze tore into the car, blowing random toll receipts and errant napkins around. Lilibelle began to laugh. She pulled the pins out of the back of her hair and the wind whipped it into her face. She let her hair blow into a tangle around her head. Chance began to laugh along with her.

Lili noticed the time on the stereo.

"It's midnight, baby!" she yelled over the breeze. "Happy forty-fifth birthday, Chance!"

She leaned over and kissed him. The lights of Vegas loomed as the city grew closer on the horizon.

Yancy pulled her head inside the car and stood with her forepaws on the armrest between the two of them. The cross-breeze whipped over her, her ears flapping around her head. She barked four times at nothing, at happiness, at freedom, at the road. Lilibelle stuck her head out of the car, headlong into the wind. The cool breeze immediately made her nose run a little. She sniffled, but kept her head outside.

Her mouth curled up into a most magnificent smile.

To all of my sisters who have found love
the second time around.

THIS TIME AROUND

Anita Bunkley

CHAPTER 1

Danika Redmond tilted her chin toward the ceiling, removed her gold-rimmed glasses and deftly squeezed two drops of Clear View into each of her weary brown eyes. *Thank God tomorrow is Saturday,* she thought, looking forward to a rare weekend with no paperwork to deal with at home.

Sighing, Danika replaced her glasses and turned her attention to the single floor-to-ceiling window on one wall of her office, letting her gaze drift over the stunning downtown Houston skyline. At night, the city's soaring modern buildings lit the blue-black sky like tiny squares of sparkling ice, creating an indelible display of the power, wealth and space-age progress for which the city was well-known. The sight always took Danika's breath away and never failed to remind her of the day, twenty-two years ago, when she launched her career in the oil-driven economy of her hometown.

Lifting her straight brown hair off her neck, she removed her gold button clip-on earrings, and then rubbed the tight spot at the top of her spine, rotating her head from side to side while mentally picturing herself in an executive office on the thirty-fifth floor of the Cranstar building with the title Southwest Division Manager—SDM—behind her name.

"Very possible," she decided with conviction, returning to the document that would determine the direction of her career.

The whir of a vacuum cleaner outside her door distracted Danika from her musings—the cleaning crew was steadily making its way toward her office and she knew she had better hurry to get out of Lupe Cruz's way. A recently circulated memo had requested that all Cranstar staff vacate their offices by 7 p.m. on Fridays in order to accommodate the cleaning crew, and here Danika was, once again, still at her desk two hours after the curfew.

With a jerk, Danika leaned forward and refocused on her computer screen, her fingers flying over the keyboard as she made the necessary adjustments to her document. Finished, she pushed Print just as the busy cleaning women descended on her office in a flurry of feather dusters, Windex, paper towels and vacuums. Danika glanced up, smiled sheepishly and then pulled on her navy blazer, stuck her feet back into her low-heeled navy pumps, and grabbed the two copies of her document that the printer had spit out. Snatching her purse from her bottom desk drawer, she lifted one hand in a short wave. "Just leaving. It's all yours."

"Thank you," Lupe stated in a toneless, no-nonsense manner as she moved into the room, her vacuum cleaner blaring.

Pausing outside her door, Danika stuck one copy of her proposal into her briefcase and the other into a large manila envelope, which she carefully sealed. Hurrying down the deserted, shadowy corridors of Cranstar International, she made her way to the elevators, thinking that she enjoyed being in the building after hours, all alone, without the ever-present sea of men in conservative suits, white shirts, understated neckties and dark shoes.

In order to conform to the company's dress policy, Danika also wore clothing that was similar in color and style—tailored navy or gray suits, white silk blouses, very little makeup and small gold button earrings or an occasional pearl drop necklace. Simple, classic and businesslike—those were her guidelines for her wardrobe, hairstyle and makeup, creating an easy approach to her workday appearance.

When the shiny steel elevator doors opened, Danika got in, pressed "thirty-five," and zoomed upward to the area where no females, other than a handful of executive secretaries, resided.

Outside of Jim Planker's sumptuous office, Danika slipped the sealed copy of her document into the IN-tray of her boss's secretary's desk, and quickly saw that two other sealed envelopes were already there—one from Todd Poston and the other from Mike Andrews—her two competitors for the Southwest Division Manager position.

Out of curiosity, Danika gingerly lifted one of the packets, calculating its weight, trying to visualize the pages, wondering how this proposal differed in comparison to hers.

"What do you think you're doing?" A stern, yet puzzled, voice came to Danika from the shadows at the end of the hallway.

Danika whirled around, eyes wide, and stared in surprise as Todd Poston walked slowly toward her, his blue eyes narrowed in suspicion, his pink, fleshy lips tight with accusation.

"Oh, Todd. It's you," Danika called back, releasing a long breath. "I was just leaving my report for Jim…."

"Really? Well, that's *my* report you're holding. Are you tampering with confidential documents? Snooping around in matters that are none of your business, perhaps?" he probed, stopping at a distance to lean casually against the wall as he continued to watch her.

Embarrassed, Danika quickly dropped the sealed envelope back into the IN-tray, cleared her throat and rushed to explain. "Ah, I wasn't tampering, Todd. I was simply…straightening things out." Feeling stupid and annoyed with herself for having been caught checking out the competition, she began to back away from the secretary's desk.

"I doubt that Jim would be pleased to know that you've been sneaking around up here after hours." Todd sneered, stepping closer to wag a long finger in Danika's face. "He might even decide to disqualify you as a candidate for the SDM position."

Narrowing her eyes, Danika digested his threat as anger

gathered in her chest. "You can stop right there!" she suddenly shot back, not about to let this white boy admonish her as if she were a naughty child. She was tired, eager to get home and not in the mood to listen to this crap. He might be able to talk this way to his submissive administrative assistant, to whom he barked orders in an intimidating manner, but not with her.

I have more tenure with the company and seniority within our division than Todd, she thought, silently fuming. *I don't have to take this bull from him.*

"Don't try to make this little scene into something that it isn't," Danika finally told him. "I was *not* sneaking around. I was delivering my proposal." She snapped back her head in disgust and leveled a hard stare at her too-smug coworker.

"Looked like you were doing some pretty shady maneuvering to me," Todd replied, pushing both of his hands deep into his pants pockets.

"Well, you got it all wrong…but you know what? Go ahead and run to Jim and tell him anything you want, if you have to. He knows me… He's been my boss for six years, and he wouldn't believe your childish accusations."

"You sound pretty sure of yourself," Todd tossed back, propping his lanky frame against the side of the desk as he brushed a handful of blond hair off his forehead. Folding his arms across his chest, he went on. "Just because you've been at Cranstar for twenty-two years and I arrived only eighteen months ago, don't think you are a shoo-in for the SDM. I've got the credentials, the drive and the vision to pull this project off. As a matter of fact, I was tossing around some ideas with Jim the other night…while we were working out. We both belong to the Downtown Power Place, you know? He loved my approach. He was very enthusiastic."

"Bully for you," Danika muttered, feeling her face begin to warm under Todd's insistent smirk.

"We also play racquetball together every Saturday morning, and go to Starbucks quite often for coffee afterward," Todd added. "Jim appreciates my aggressive marketing strategies, and trusts me to pull them off."

"Isn't that nice," Danika threw back, barely moving her lips, attempting to keep annoyance from her voice. Well, here it was at last, that good-old-boy connection thrown in her face, making sure she understood her place.

Danika studied Todd's casual stance, his assured expression, the satisfied gleam in his ice-blue eyes, infuriated that he dared to look so entitled. So damn overconfident.

"Sucking up and getting close to the boss outside of the office is not my style, Todd," she stated, forcing a smile. "I prefer to keep my personal life separate from my professional life and let my work speak for itself. I have no need to cultivate an out-of-the-workplace friendship with Jim in order to get ahead."

"Suit yourself, Danika. But that's the way things work. It's all about *who* you know and how well you know them, not *what* you can do or what you have done. I'd have thought you understood that by now. Cranstar is moving ahead quickly. It needs people like me—new blood, younger blood, more energetic blood...that's what Jim Planker is looking for in a division manager."

"Jim will be fair, and that's all that matters," Danika said with conviction. "He'll make his selection based on the best marketing project, and you can bet he's going to take more into consideration than who he plays racquetball and drinks coffee with on a Saturday morning." Giving Todd a curt nod, she turned, preparing to walk away.

"You know, Danika, at your age, you ought to be seriously thinking about retiring, not going head-to-head with me and Mike Andrews. We're on a fast track to move up, while you need to be moving out...to make room for fresh ideas and new faces. Your time is past. Accept it."

Danika spun around, biting her bottom lip to keep from screaming at him and telling him how much she resented his very presence at the company, as well as his nasty remarks. On the day of his arrival eighteen months ago, when she had shaken his hand and welcomed him to Cranstar, she had noticed his superior attitude at once and had been hit by a strange premonition that one day, a conversation like the one they were having now, was going to take place. He had not proven her wrong.

Everything about Todd Poston's demeanor had set off warning bells in her head. He strutted around the office in a self-satisfied manner, often became pushy and overly aggressive when he did not get his way and was forever revealing intimate details about his marriage, betraying his male chauvinist attitude toward women. Danika had forced herself to ignore his irritating character in order to maintain a good working relationship, but now, his true colors were definitely showing. She was not his administrative assistant, nor his wife.

I am not going anywhere, anytime soon, so you will just have to deal with me! she wanted to scream, but held her tongue. What good would it do to get into a verbal sparring match with Todd? Clearly, he was baiting her, hoping to force her to say or do something that he could twist into an ugly encounter to circulate around the office on Monday morning. Well, she was not going to fall into that trap.

Gritting her teeth, Danika drew in a deep breath and forced a fake smile. "Sorry you feel that way, Todd. However, I don't want to discuss any of this with you. I've gotta go."

"Really? Go where?" Todd taunted, lifting both hands in an empty expression. "Home to your television?" He chuckled sarcastically. "Everyone around here knows you have no life other than Cranstar. No husband, no children and from what I've been told, you don't even date."

"My personal life is none of your business," Danika replied with conviction. She clutched her briefcase to her chest and glared at Todd. "You are way out of line, and I advise you to stop before you say something that you'll regret." She turned on her heel, dismissing her colleague with a shake of her head. "See you Monday," she called over her shoulder, not waiting for his reply as she entered the elevator and pressed the button to descend to the lower level.

In the underground garage, she got into her car and sat stunned behind the wheel, staring straight ahead. *Forty-nine is not old,* she told herself, struggling to stop shaking and keep from tearing up. *And I do date...not a lot, but I go out often enough to truthfully say I have a social life. So what if I decided to dedicate my life to this company? It was what I wanted to do, and Jim knows I am much more qualified to become a division manager than Todd Poston. The prick! The lousy prick! I can run circles around that shallow pretty boy and everyone at Cranstar knows it...don't they?*

With an unsteady grip Danika stuck her key into the ignition, wishing she *did* have something else to do other than go home to her empty apartment.

CHAPTER 2

The plant-filled balcony facing the wooded area behind her apartment building was Danika's favorite spot to sit and read the paper while drinking a leisurely cup of coffee on Saturday mornings, though it had been a long time since she had afforded herself such luxury. However, now that her marketing analysis report and her bid for the SDM position were behind her, the rare work-free Saturday stretched before her like a clean sheet of paper.

Danika opened her copy of the *Houston Chronicle* to the classifieds and began casually scanning the used vehicles section, giving in to feelings of confidence about the promotion. If Jim selected her as the new division manager, the salary increase would be significant—significant enough to trade in her 1999 Honda Civic for a 2005 BMW, maybe even a Lexus. Cranstar executives were given private parking spots in the company garage where they parked their Mercedes, Porsches, Cadillacs and monstrous SUVs, and though Danika rarely concerned herself with appearances, a new car was going to be her only real indulgence.

She circled a few ads for used luxury cars that sounded interesting, making a mental note to check them out on the Internet and compare prices. A cautious spender, she never made a major purchase without doing substantial research, and approached every transaction over fifty dollars as a serious negotiation.

Closing the paper, she sat back in her chair, hoping she was not getting too far ahead of herself, and praying she had not underestimated Todd Poston, whose smirking expression of entitlement and sarcastic remarks remained vividly clear in her mind. Was Todd playing racquetball with Jim Planker right now? Had Todd told Jim about catching her in the act of looking through the folders in his secretary's IN-box? Was she being naive to think that her tenure, loyalty and experience with the company would carry more weight than the close personal relationship that Todd was obviously cultivating with their boss?

She thought back to the day she had started working at Cranstar, a male-dominated company that focused on the development of products related to energy conservation. She had been twenty-seven years old, pencil-thin, recently divorced and determined to make it at the international oil and gas giant. She had started out as a field supervisor's assistant, earning little more than the minimum wage, and over the years had worked her way up to senior marketing analyst, becoming one of two female supervisors, and the only African-American in a midlevel management position. If things went her way, she might very soon reach the next goal she had set for herself— to become the first African-American executive in the history of the seventy-five-year-old company.

Todd had been right about one thing: She *had* sacrificed a significant part of her personal life in order to go above and beyond what had been expected of her and rise slowly, but steadily within the company. But her dedication was going to pay off, she was certain.

Her name remained on the short list of candidates, and her boss, Jim Planker, was going to base his selection for the promotion on the most effective proposal for the domestic launch of *Eco Quick-Valve Cleaner,* Cranstar's new, environment-friendly silicone motor lubricant.

The competitive nature of this promotion was exactly the kind of challenge that Danika embraced. However, she was well aware of the strength of her competitors—two white males who were at least fifteen years younger than she was and who had more personal connections with her boss.

With a silent groan, Danika pushed her worries aside, determined not to ruin her weekend with runaway speculations that had no foundation.

"Good morning, Danika. Beautiful day," her next door neighbor called out, stepping onto the adjoining balcony and breaking into Danika's worries.

Danika looked over and smiled at her neighbor, Ming Tran, who waved back as she crossed the balcony that separated the two apartments. The gentle April morning breeze billowed the young woman's loose-fitting white silk robe, exposing the skimpy yellow shorts and matching tank top she was wearing underneath. Ming Tran's jet-black hair was pulled up into a spiky ponytail that seemed to erupt from the top of her head. Her oversized sunglasses covered half of her diminutive face.

"Well, hello, stranger," Danika called back.

"Stranger for real!" Ming laughed. "Glad to see you finally outside. You've been missing some great sunshine." Ming peeled off her robe and plopped down in a deck chair, then stretched out her legs and leaned back, absorbing the late-spring sun.

"Been too busy at the office to think about catching some rays, and it's not like I need any more color," Danika laughed, lifting a burnished brown arm in jest. She set her newspaper aside and gave Ming her full attention. "Remember the District Manager position I told you about a few weeks ago?"

Ming nodded as she slathered sunscreen over her arms and shoulders. "And I hope you took my advice and went after it."

"I did. Turned in my marketing plan last night."

"Good for you. What's the competition look like?"

"Two other candidates, but neither has the experience with the company nor knowledge of the product that I have. Todd Poston talks a good game, but never follows through. He's young, good-looking and has an MBA in marketing from Stanford. He and Jim, my boss, are pretty close—outside the office and all that—so he thinks his personal relationship will give him an advantage. The other guy—Mike Andrews—quiet, studious, even younger than Todd, I think. He has a background in science...one of those nice guys who may be *too* nice, you know? I don't think he has the charisma and drive that Jim is looking for."

"Sounds like you've got the job, Danika. Count on it. When's the decision?"

"Sometime next week, I hope."

"Well, until then, put Cranstar completely out of your mind. Relax, read a good book, watch TV. Do nothing for a change, Danika. You work too damn much."

"Have to," Danika quickly responded. "A sister has to go way beyond the extra mile. Every day. Besides, I really like my job," she added with sincerity. "And launching a new product is so exciting. A lot of work, but...once it's out there, in the stores, in people's homes, I feel proud of having had a hand in it. You must know what it's like...you design clothes, people buy them, and don't you feel buzzed when you see someone walking around in a dress or blouse that you created?"

"Absolutely," Ming agreed. "But launching an eco-friendly valve cleaner can't be nearly as exciting as putting together a fashion collection. But if it turns you on..."

Danika laughed. "Ming. I didn't say it turned me on, only that I get a lot of satisfaction out of the process...and I understand it better than Todd Poston or Mike Andrews, neither of whom have the background to successfully position a new product."

"The guys. Both white?" Ming probed, squinting one eye nearly closed.

"Of course."

"Yeah, girl, you're going to be Cranstar's first female *and* African-American Division Manager. Count on it. In this day and age, getting a female minority into an executive position is almost mandatory. Cranstar knows that, and you are definitely qualified, so how can they pass you up? And with your background, they won't be accused of pulling off some affirmative action promotion, either, you know?"

Danika chuckled, nodding. "You called that one right."

Ming finished with the sunblock, recapped the bottle and set it down beside her chair. "And if you do get the job, please let me pick out your new executive wardrobe. You gotta dress the part, girlfriend. Get some color going on, some feminine style, some ruffles, anything to lighten up a bit, please!" Ming took a sip from the bottle of water she had brought out to the patio, and then changed the subject. "*A New You* was the bomb last night. Did you record it?"

"Yeah, I knew I'd be working late so I set the DVR. What was going on?" Danika asked, looking forward to viewing the latest installment in her favorite television program—a reality series that showcased two women each week, giving them extreme makeovers that often resulted in dramatic changes in their personal and professional lives.

"Well, they made over this woman from California who had been homeless for five years. Face-lift, liposuction, haircut, porcelain caps on her teeth. The works! They even found her a job at a day care center. God, what a change in that woman. The poor soul went hysterical when she saw herself in the mirror. I even cried right along with her. It was so emotional...the best segment yet. And...I thought about you when they announced their summer contest."

"Yeah? What's that about?" Danika asked with interest.

"The network is giving away twenty thousand dollars worth of dental work, cosmetic surgery, professional makeup and designer clothing for a complete makeover for two women who work in male-dominated environments. You ought to enter, Danika."

"You're saying I need an extreme makeover?" Danika

prompted, trying to joke, while Todd Poston's comments about her age still echoed in her ears.

Ming waved a hand, the colorful gemstone rings she wore on each finger sparkling in the sunlight. "Every woman over twenty-one can use a bit of sprucing up… Don't get me wrong. You've got great skin and a beautiful smile, Danika, but you play down your femininity way too much. You could change your entire look if you cut and lightened your hair, got Lasik surgery and tossed the glasses, stopped wearing so much navy and gray. And a bit of lipo here and there wouldn't hurt, either."

"Gee, thanks a lot," Danika groaned, impulsively running a hand across her midsection, which had expanded a few inches each year after thirty.

When she joined Cranstar Oil and Gas and began working among the dark-suited men on a day-to-day basis, she had stopped thinking much about fashion trends, hair styles and makeup—areas that now, it seemed, might carry more weight than she had thought.

"The deadline to enter the contest is midnight tonight," Ming continued, recapping her bottle of water. "So watch the show and think about it. You can submit everything online at their Web site. All you have to do is e-mail a recent photo and few paragraphs explaining why you deserve the makeover. Go for it, Danika. Think of it as twenty-thousand dollars' worth of preventative maintenance that will carry you nicely into old age. I'd go for it…if I thought I needed it."

Danika scowled, and then broke into a hearty laugh, shaking her head. "Right, Ming. Like you will ever need a makeover. You're genetically programmed to look twenty-five forever, and I guarantee you will never weigh more than…" Danika paused, scrutinizing her tiny neighbor. "What do you weigh now? One hundred pounds?"

"One hundred five," Ming corrected.

"Exactly," Danika said, folding her newspaper. "I can barely remember those days." She picked up her coffee cup and stood.

"You've got me curious now. I have some errands to run, but when I get back, I'll catch *A New You*. I'll let you know what I decide after I watch the show." She waved to Ming and went inside, where she pulled on a pair of jeans, a loose-fitting T-shirt, and her walking shoes. She fastened a tortoise clip into her hair to hold it back from her face, pulled on her sunglasses and left the apartment.

Traffic around her neighborhood was awful for a Saturday and Danika crawled her way through the streets to pick up her dry cleaning, buy groceries and gas up her Honda that had been hovering near empty for two days. She ended her morning outing with a quick three-mile power walk along the path that encircled the woods behind her apartment, realizing that it had been weeks since she had taken the time to get out and simply enjoy the fresh air, clearing her mind of worries at work. However, with every step she took, the more she thought about Todd's remarks about her age and Ming's comments about a makeover. Though it was a bit tough to admit, Danika knew both her coworker and her neighbor had touched a chord.

Maybe a cosmetic overhaul would be a good idea, she considered as she drove back to her apartment through heavy traffic. *Would it give me an edge at work? Boost my chances for moving up? Perhaps even rejuvenate my social life?*

After putting her groceries away, Danika showered, grabbed a Diet Coke and immediately sat down to watch *A New You*.

At the conclusion of the program, which had been as emotionally uplifting as Ming had reported, Danika jotted down the contest entry Web site and opened her laptop.

Why not enter and see what happens? she thought, doodling with her pen on the pad of paper as she waited for the Web site to pop in. *Time is not standing still and though appearance and age are not supposed to matter when promotions are at stake, everyone, at least every woman, knows that her looks are important in the workplace. Todd Poston is already trying to use this age-gap issue to his advantage, and if he can find a way, he'll press the subject until he discredits my credentials. If I plan to outwit him and stay in the game, I'd better take steps to get prepared.*

Danika read through the contest entry rules and began to compose her pitch.

In Houston, Texas, the word *oil* is synonymous with wealth, power and the unshakable industry dominance of white males. As an African-American woman, I find myself a double minority surrounded by male coworkers at Cranstar Oil and Gas International, where I have worked for twenty-two years. Early in my career, I learned that I had to downplay my femininity, keep a low fashion profile and place little importance on my appearance if I wanted to be taken seriously by the engineers and scientists with whom I worked. When I entered the workforce, I was a self-conscious twenty-seven-year-old divorcée whose marriage to a dominating, power-hungry male chauvinist had just collapsed. My work became my salvation, and over the years as I moved from an entry level job in advertising to senior marketing analyst, I have paid less and less attention to the way I look. I guess I've wanted the men to think of me as one of the guys—but as we all know, that never really happens. All I have been doing is denying myself the opportunity to showcase my feminine attributes while settling into a dull fashion rut in which I am now stuck. I am currently one of three candidates under consideration for an executive level position. I am forty-nine years old and have a Bachelor of Science degree in marketing. My white male competitors both have Masters degrees in Engineering and have not yet hit thirty. If I were to be selected, I would make history as the first African-American—male or female—to attain such a level of responsibility at this seventy-five-year-old, male-dominated company. I'd like to see it happen.

Would an extreme makeover help me win the promotion I feel I deserve, or better perform my responsibilities if I am selected? Probably not. However, I do believe that an overhaul of my outward appearance would rejuvenate my fighting spirit, strengthen my self-confidence and hopefully allow me to anticipate the remainder of my working years at this company with the excitement, curiosity and creativity that have carried me this far.

Respectively submitted,
Danika Redmond

Danika went into another file and located a JPEG photo of herself, taken at the last company annual meeting, and after linking the photo to her text, pressed Send and relayed her submission directly to the television producer.

Well, it's done, Danika thought as she got up and walked into the kitchen to take a handful of grapes from the refrigerator. A giddy sense of adventure crept over her as she popped a grape into her mouth. She had not felt so deliciously spontaneous in a long, long time.

CHAPTER 3

Fifteen minutes after Danika entered her office on Monday morning, she received a call from Gina York, Jim Planker's efficient secretary.

"Danika, can you come up to Mr. Planker's office right away?" Gina queried in her crisp, always-rushed tone.

"Yes. Sure, right away," Danika quickly replied, stifling her excitement. Had Jim worked through the weekend in order to announce his selection for the SDM position today? Had he seen how much more extensive her report had been than either Todd's or Mike's? By this time tomorrow would she be clearing out her desk and preparing to move to the thirty-fifth floor? The prospect gave her pause, while initiating a great sense of relief. To have been summoned to her boss's office so early in the day must mean that he had selected her and wanted to let her know right away. At last, the waiting was over. Her hard work was paying off.

Danika hurried into the elevator, her heart pounding in anticipation as she glided upward, and when the elevator doors opened, she smiled at Gina, who greeted Danika and immediately escorted her to the small conference room at the end of the hallway.

Upon entering the room, Danika was surprised to see both Todd Poston and Mike Andrews already seated at the conference table, arms folded, looking completely at ease. She cautiously nodded at the two men and slipped into a chair next to Todd, across the table from Gina, who remained standing, holding the three sealed envelopes that contained the *Eco Quick-Valve Cleaners* marketing projects in her pale, blue-veined hands.

"Thanks for coming up so quickly," Gina started, an expression of concern suddenly coming over her usually placid face. "Mr. Planker asked me to meet with the three of you first thing this morning to tell you what he has decided to do."

Danika arched a brow, wondering where her boss was and why he would leave his secretary in charge of such an important matter.

"When I spoke with him this morning," Gina started, but paused when Danika lifted a hand in question.

"Excuse me," Danika stated. "I hate to interrupt you, Gina, but where *is* Jim?"

Widening her eyes, Gina blinked, one hand to her chin. "Oh. You haven't heard, then?"

"Heard what?" Danika tossed back, turning her gaze from Gina to study her two colleagues. "What's going on?"

Todd leaned toward Danika, shifting so close to her that his nose nearly touched her shoulder. In a breathy voice he informed her, "Jim had a little accident over the weekend. Well, I guess you'd call it a big accident, really. Broke his leg. In two places. I thought you would have heard."

Danika found Todd's tone to be too smugly self-important, clearly inferring that he was privy to personal information about their boss, while she remained an outsider.

"Broke his leg?" she repeated, ignoring Todd to turn her attention back to Gina. "How'd that happen?"

"He fell from a ladder Saturday afternoon while attempting to repair a loose shingle on his house." Gina shrugged. "Very unfortunate."

"Is he in the hospital?" Danika asked.

"Not now," Mike Andrews broke in, entering the conversation with the same *I know-more-than-you-do* tone that Todd had already used, indicating to Danika that he, too, was closer to their boss than she was. "He's at home, but in pretty bad shape. I spoke to him Sunday night. He'll be laid up for a few weeks," Mike finished.

Gina nodded solemnly. "Right. Mr. Planker will be out of the office for at least two weeks, so he asked me to tell you that the selection for the Southwest Division Manager position has to be put on hold for now."

"So he hasn't even read our reports?" Danika stated, slightly disappointed.

"Not yet," Gina confirmed, placing the three envelopes side by side on the table. "He asked me to put them in his safe until he is up to reviewing them."

"When do you think that might be?" Mike asked.

"Hopefully by the end of the next week at the latest. He's in a lot of pain and taking medication every four hours. He needs a few days to simply rest, and then he'll try to start doing some work at home. When he's ready to deal with the SDM matter, he'll contact each of you individually. So, your reports will remain unopened and in his safe."

"What about the TriVale case?" Todd interjected. "I'm in the middle of closing that deal. Who's gonna sign off on it?"

"Take it, and any other emergency matters, to Howard Rich in legal," Gina answered.

"What about cards? Flowers?" Danika prompted.

"I know Mr. Planker doesn't really want visits or phone calls, but if you or any of the employees in your section want to send him a card or flowers, I know he'd appreciate hearing from you. For now, just go about your regular duties and I'll keep you posted on his progress." With that, Gina picked up the envelopes and left the room.

Todd and Mike got up at the same time, gave Danika a short, parting nod and walked out of the conference room together.

The news initiated an immediate sense of panic in Danika, who had to use a great deal of restraint to keep her imagination from running wild with thoughts of what this turn of events meant. She knew that Gina's statement about Jim not wanting telephone calls had been lost on Todd, who was most likely already at his desk and on the phone, talking with Jim. The wait was going to be unbearable, especially in light of the fact that Todd Poston would definitely find a way to use this extra time to his advantage.

Maybe I ought to do the same, she decided, wondering how, as she settled in to begin another routine day at the office.

The hours flew by in a blur of consultations with her staff on the section's advertising budget, telephone conversations with outside consultants who were working with her on a slick promotional piece and the endless e-mails that had to be answered and processed. At least Todd stayed away from her, and at the end of the day she left the building feeling relieved not to have had another encounter with him. Until Jim returned, she planned to mind her own business, stay in her area of the building and give Todd a wide berth. The last thing she wanted to hear was more of his crappy criticism. From now on, she was only going to think positive thoughts.

Danika's strategy paid off. The week flew by without another nasty confrontation with Todd, and by Friday afternoon she was feeling exceptionally relaxed and optimistic about the promotion. Even the staff members under her supervision had become vocal in their support of her, slyly criticizing Todd for thinking that Jim Planker would choose him, a relative newcomer, over Danika, with whom many of them had worked for years.

Hopefully, it will all be over soon enough, Danika sighed as she entered her apartment on Friday, looking forward to a quiet weekend without thinking about Todd Poston, Mike Andrews or Cranstar International at all.

As soon as she shut the door, the phone rang, but she did not rush to answer it, calculating that it was most likely her widowed mother, Judith, on the phone. Judith Redmond lived in Hillview, Texas, one hundred fifty miles north of Houston, and she telephoned Danika every Friday evening to recap her entire week with her only daughter. Danika knew that her mother, who had lost her husband four years ago, was lonely for conversation, so she visited her mother at least once a month and faithfully spent several hours a week speaking with her on the phone. However, tonight, all Danika wanted to do was kick back with a glass of wine, listen to some CDs and wind down.

Going over to the answering machine, Danika looked down at the caller ID window and gasped. The area code was 212— New York! Immediately, she snatched up the receiver and was greeted by a perky, fast-talking woman who identified herself as Bella Davis, a producer for *A New You.*

"Oh, my God. You're really calling me...from New York?" Danika asked, struggling to keep from screaming at the woman.

"I most certainly am, Danika. You're a winner!" Bella announced in a smoky, sophisticated voice that reminded Danika of Lauren Bacall's. "You have been chosen as one of two contestants who will receive a makeover package equal to no less than twenty thousand dollars."

"For real?" Danika croaked, swallowing her excitement.

Bella laughed, a deep throaty chuckle that resonated through the phone line. "For real. You are on your way to becoming A New You! Just answer a few questions for me, and then start packing your bags. We will announce your name on tonight's show, and you must be in New York by eight o'clock Monday morning."

"This coming Monday?" Danika asked.

"Yep. Eight a.m. sharp. We've got a tight schedule to work with. We'll e-mail your flight information to you and make reservations at the Ritz-Carlton for your fourteen-day stay. A car will pick you up at the airport. The first thing we need to do is have our in-house physician give you a complete physical examination, and then—"

"Ah...you really mean *this* coming Monday?" Danika interrupted, wanting to make certain that she understood what the woman was asking of her.

Bella sighed, her exasperation evident. "Yes. This Monday. That won't be a problem will it? If so, you'll have to bow out now. If you recall, the contest rules stated that the winner would have to be available to fly to New York on short notice. And you have to remain here for two weeks, then be able to recuperate at home for another two. Maybe three."

"Right, right," Danika quickly agreed, recalling having read the requirements, never truly believing that they would ever apply to her! "I just didn't think..."

"That you'd win?" Bella finished. "Ha. They all say that. So, will we see you at our studios on Monday morning or not?"

"Absolutely. I'll be there," Danika hurriedly assured Bella, now beginning to feel excited.

CHAPTER 4

Even though she was about to be showered with a bounty of new clothes, makeup and personal attention, Danika allowed Ming to drag her into the mall on Saturday morning as soon as the stores opened.

"You can't get on that plane looking like a nun in one of those dreadful navy suits that you wear to work," Ming admonished as they moved from shop to shop. "I'm going to hook you up, girl. When you leave Houston, your transformation will have already begun."

"I'm still numb," Danika confessed, following Ming into a trendy boutique where her tiny neighbor began flitting from rack to rack. "Bella said there were eighty thousand entries," Danika went on, scurrying behind Ming. "Eighty thousand. And I got selected. I'm stunned."

"I'm not," Ming confessed, deftly removing coordinated pieces to a pale peach pantsuit from several hanging racks. "I knew you'd win. Something in my gut just told me that it was your time. So stop feeling stunned and start feeling glamorous, Danika. If you want, I could come to New York with you. I have enough frequent flier miles to get a ticket and I can always do some scouting for new design inspirations while you are getting made over."

"Oh, Ming. That's really nice of you to offer, but I think this is something I'd better do alone."

"Sure," Ming agreed. "You're right, but I *had* to offer anyway. And since this is all about you, I hope you will have some fun!" Ming shoved the pantsuit with three matching shirts, two belts, a purse and a handful of oversized, multicolored scarves at Danika. "Go into the dressing room and try these on while I scout out the perfect jewelry." Then she was gone.

Inside the dressing room, Danika did as ordered and tried on the delicate suit with several different shirts and scarves. The look was soft, feminine and quite unlike anything she would have picked out for herself. Ming's personal fashion style was over-the-top, and Danika rarely went shopping with her ultra-stylish friend, but now she could see that Ming's understanding of fashion went far beyond what she favored for herself.

Studying her new outfit Danika thought about what lay ahead. When she returned, she would be different—but in what way? How would the makeover change her? And what if something went wrong? She had seen television shows about plastic surgery gone bad and terrible haircuts or color treatments that turned out disastrously. What if she did not like the results?

With a shudder, Danika pushed the thoughts aside and scrutinized her image in the mirror. The prospect of surrendering herself totally to strangers while in a strange city, was both exciting and frightening, but she was definitely not going to back out.

A big relief had come when she had telephoned Jim at home this morning, not only to inquire about his broken leg, but also to request the required vacation time to go through with the makeover. She had been shocked when he told her that he had been expecting her call—his wife, who was a devoted fan of *A New You*, had recognized Danika's name when the contest winners had been announced.

"It's all very exciting, Danika," Jim had told her. "I hope you know that everybody at Cranstar thinks you're perfect just the way you are, so we don't want to lose the real you," Jim had joked, after congratulating her on her win. "But if this makeover is important to you, you certainly have my blessings.

Your staff can handle your section until you return, so go. Enjoy yourself. We'll all be eager to see the new you."

Now, as Danika modeled the peach-colored pantsuit in front of the big mirror, she grinned, totally ready to go.

Danika's flight to New York was a breeze. She arrived late Sunday night at JFK Airport, where a driver met her at the baggage claim area, whisked her into the longest black limousine that she had ever seen and drove her to the Ritz-Carlton hotel. The next morning, he picked her up at seven o'clock and headed straight to CBS studios, where Bella Davis, a plump, raven-haired woman with flashing black eyes, a creamy smooth complexion and a husky voice greeted her with a fast hug.

"Thank God, you look like your photograph," Bella tossed out, not waiting for a reply as she directed the driver to return for Danika at 6:00 p.m. Turning back to Danika once the driver had taken off, she went on. "Can't tell you how many contestants send in photos that were taken ten or fifteen years ago, then when they show up, it's an entirely new game."

"Well, what I sent in is what you see," Danika replied lightly, hurrying to fall into step with Bella as they rushed down a dimly lit corridor lined with portraits of the station's well-known newscasters, talk-show hosts and on-air personalities.

The carpet was deep red, plush and soft. The attractively lit alcoves in the gray suede walls exuded class, taste and high style. The people who passed by in the hallway appeared professional, important and too perfectly gorgeous to be real.

Danika suddenly realized that she, too, was about to become somewhat of a TV personality. When her new look was revealed on A New You, she would become semifamous, even though her fame might not reach the fifteen-minute level. "This is so exciting," she murmured, more to herself than to Bella, who was obviously consumed with sticking to her make-no-exceptions schedule.

Bella pulled a Sharpie from the bundle of dark hair piled on top of her head, handed Danika a sheaf of papers stapled together and then tapped the papers with her pen as they continued to make their way deeper into the studio. "That is your itinerary for the first week, which will be your roughest," she remarked.

Danika flinched involuntarily at that remark. In her rush to get out of Houston, she had pushed aside the fact that she would have to undergo several serious surgical procedures as part of this experience.

"Read the schedule, memorize it and please don't lose it," Bella was saying. "Every minute of this makeover session has been carefully scripted and there can be no variations. My cell phone number is at the top of page one...in bold print. You do have a cell with you, don't you?"

"Yes," Danika replied, now listening carefully to Bella's rushed instructions.

"Good. Call me if you have a problem or can't figure out what your next step is...but it's all clearly explained in those papers. As I told you—first thing is a quick physical exam." She stopped in front of an elevator door and pressed the up button. "I'm gonna drop you off at the medical suite on the fifteenth floor. Up there are the offices of all of our doctors— plastic surgeons, opthamologists, dentists, dietitians, dermatologists. Dr. Gargelis, our lead physician, will give you your physical, then he will hand you over to the others. Each one will make an assessment of what needs to be done and prepare you for their recommended procedures."

"Today?" Danika queried, beginning to feel a bit queasy and overwhelmed. "I may have surgery today?"

"Most likely. You're having your eyes done, aren't you? And you're gonna go for lipo?"

"Ah...I hope so," Danika replied, running a hand over her stomach and hips. "A few inches off here and there would be nice."

"Right," Bella tossed back in a snappy voice. "Lasik is a

breeze and liposuction is not a big deal. After the lipo, you will feel bruised and woozy and you will look like Puff Mommy for a while, but in a few days your body will begin to adjust and the swelling will go down. Be prepared to leak a ton of fluid from the incisions…and you'll have to wear a supportive undergarment afterward, but that's not so bad when you think about the payoff. I know, from experience. I had my entire lower body done last year."

Danika ground her teeth together. Leaks? Holes? She had not thought seriously about the fact that having holes punched in her body meant yucky stuff was going to drain out. The idea of lying in bed wearing a padded suit while fluid seeped from her wounds made her shudder.

"Don't worry," Bella tossed out, placing a calming hand on Danika's shoulder. "You will have all the necessary pain medication to get through this with as little discomfort as possible." Bella stepped into the elevator. "We like to get through with the surgeries as quickly as possible, so you'll have plenty of time to heal…and while we're waiting for all that swelling to go down, we start planning your wardrobe, hair and makeup, leading up to the grand finale, which we'll tape at the end of next week."

"It all seems so…rushed," Danika began. "Are you sure—"

"Don't worry," Bella cut in. "We've done this hundreds of times. You'll be pleasantly surprised by how quickly your body will heal and your new look will emerge." She checked the paper on her clipboard, then entered the elevator.

At the fifteenth floor, Danika stepped out, but Bella remained behind. "Go to the end of the hall," Bella instructed, leaning out to point to a door with a frosted-glass inset. "Doctor Gargelis is ready to give you your physical. He's a dear. You're gonna love him. After that, you'll see Dr. Marick, who will evaluate your candidacy for Lasik surgery, and then, Dr. Amanda Hollis, the plastic surgeon. Ready to toss your glasses?"

"That would be fantastic. I did some research on Lasik surgery when it first came out, but never had the guts to do it."

"Well, Marick is a very good ophthalmologist. He's performed Lasik on hundreds of patients. He'll answer all of your questions. As you can see, you're gonna be a very busy lady! Well, I gotta go." She waved a plump hand, then pressed a button and disappeared behind closed doors.

Danika stared at the door at the end of the corridor as if it might lead straight into purgatory. She hesitated for a few long moments, then took a deep breath and started off toward the beginning of her bold, but scary adventure.

Bella was right. Dr. Gargelis was a soft-spoken, polite physician, who moved her quickly, yet thoroughly, through a routine exam that revealed no problems that would prevent her from participating in the makeover. Next, Danika was escorted into an adjoining room that resembled a regular eye doctor's office where she sat on a black leather couch and waited for Dr. Marick, who arrived shortly and gave her a reassuring smile before seating her in the examination chair.

"I am going to map the topology of your eyes," he told Danika, who nodded as if she understood what that meant. "It's like mapping mountains in a geologically based map," he explained as he slipped a large lens over one eye, then the other. After a few minutes, he pulled the lenses away and focused on Danika. "You have a very slight astigmatism… that's an uneven curve on the cornea."

"Is that a problem?" Danika asked.

"No, not a problem at all," he said with certainty. "We can get started on the Lasik right away."

With a sigh, Danika straightened her shoulders and sat back, ready for whatever was coming next.

His nurse came in and placed colored paper dots on Danika's forehead above each eye, then put in several drops. Danika could feel a sudden numbness begin to spread as soon as the drops settled in.

"Sit back and relax, Danika," the nurse advised. "I need to put four drops in each eye, ten minutes apart."

Again Danika did as she was told, almost afraid to talk as the nurse went about her business.

After the last set of drops had been administered, the nurse tilted the examination chair back until Danika was lying nearly flat on her back. When Dr. Marick returned, he placed two plastic eye-openers in each eye to keep her from blinking and asked her to focus on the bright white light above her while a circular piece of equipment swung down before one eye, then the other. The whirring sound was calming, almost as soft as a whisper, and when it stopped, the doctor swiveled her beneath another piece of strange looking equipment, and said, "Keep your eye on the red dot."

Tick. Tick. Tick. A blinking red light. Danika felt no pain at all. Tick. Tick. Tick. Again she felt nothing at all.

"That's it," Dr. Marick announced. "But we must shield your eyes for protection."

Danika blinked up at the ceiling. "It's blurry, but I can see." She sat up and looked around, shocked that without her glasses, everything was nearly crystal clear.

"That's to be expected," the doctor remarked with satisfaction as he handed her a pair of black goggles and warned her to expect mild discomfort for a few days and a bit of eye watering, but nothing more. With that, she was shuffled, goggles and all, into Dr. Amanda Hollis's office.

Dr. Amanda Hollis, a plastic surgeon who looked more like a supermodel than a skilled doctor with a worldwide reputation for making over movie stars, was tall, willowy and very blond, with flinty blue-green eyes and a wide smile that split her delicate square jaw in half with a show of perfect white teeth.

Dr. Hollis greeted Danika and then summoned her nurse into the room. "Shirley," Dr. Hollis told her assistant, "please prepare Danika for her assessment. We've got a lot to do."

"Follow me, please," Shirley told Danika, pausing at the doorway.

Within minutes, Danika had removed her clothes and put on the paper string bikini and bra that Shirley handed to her. Then she went to stand in front of a screen under white-hot lamps while Dr. Hollis began her rapid-fire diagnosis, accompanied by detailed drawings that flashed immediately onto the huge computer screen, recording her surgical plans.

"You have beautiful skin, no real problems there," Dr. Hollis started right in, making quick notes on Danika's chart. "You'll have to have a tummy tuck, lipo on the outer hips and bit of a breast lift, too. Bioplasty on both the upper and lower eyelids will rejuvenate your face and accentuate the sharpness of your already lovely cheekbones. We'll definitely whiten your teeth, and a small amount of BOTOX on your upper lip will improve your smile. I'm going to schedule your procedures for two o'clock this afternoon."

Too overwhelmed to reply, Danika simply nodded, amazed at the process. She watched the computer screen as the projected slimmer, tighter and more youthful-looking Danika emerged, the sight buoying her determination not to panic, but to surrender herself to the experience while anticipating a positive outcome.

"This is what you will look like when it's all over. Tell me what you like most about your new appearance," Dr. Hollis asked, referring to the computer module as she drew on Danika's body with large red and green markers, outlining the areas of fat that were to be removed.

Danika studied the computer screen. "My eyes, my flat stomach, my slimmer hips, whiter teeth and no glasses," Danika confessed. "I am amazed at this profile. Will I really look like that?"

Dr. Hollis chuckled as she continued to make her squiggly markings. "You will. You have no major problems to correct. We will do your eyes first, uppers and lowers, then lipo your stomach and hips. You will have tumescent liposuction, and that means you will be pumped full of quite a bit of liquid."

"That's what Bella mentioned." Danika tried to sound confident, but there was a definite quiver in her voice.

"I'll inject about eight thousand ccs of tumescent fluid into the defined areas on your stomach and hips, and I expect to extract about seventy-five hundred ccs of fat. Once the fluid drains away, your new shape emerges. But you have to be patient. Results may not be evident for at least ten days, maybe two weeks. I'll also tuck your breasts. You are going to look fabulous. Trust me, Danika."

Once Dr. Hollis was finished with her pre-op work, Shirley directed Danika into a hospital-like operating room, where she climbed onto an operating table, prepared for her first operation.

Excruciating was not the best way to describe the pain that gripped Danika when she awakened from surgery. Agonizing, relentless and white-hot, was more like it. Bandages covered her face, with slits at her eyes and holes around her nose and mouth. Her head throbbed, her chest, stomach and hips were on fire, and her entire lower body was wrapped in heavy padding that had been pierced to insert draining tubes. Her whole being seemed to pulse with intermittent spasms of pain. Easing her head to the side, she remained flat on her back in her darkened cubicle and stared at the window on the other side of the room, afraid to move.

It was pitch-black outside, but bright lights twinkled in the windows of the tall buildings and on the colorful advertising signs that rose high above the traffic-clogged streets of Manhattan. The room was very cool and so quiet that Danika could hear the whir of the monitoring equipment to which she was attached. The oppressive sensation of being entombed came over her, and she suddenly started to panic.

What had she gotten herself into? Not one of the doctors

with whom she had spoken had led her to believe that she would be in this much pain. And here she was...alone, in a strange hospital room, far away from everything safe and familiar with her entire body aflame.

Well, it's done, she thought, forcing her attention away from her fears and onto the fact that the most difficult part of the makeover must certainly be behind her. From now on, she'd concern herself with the fun stuff—picking out clothes, creating a new hairstyle and putting the finishing touches on her new image.

Gazing at the blazing city lights, she thought about Ming, and suddenly wished her neighbor had come along to keep her company. Only once before had Danika felt so totally and miserably alone, and that had been when her husband abandoned her, leaving her for a woman he hoped to mold into the wife she could not be. He had wanted a woman who would agree with him, cater to him and hand him control over her life. The breakup had devastated Danika, who had been too proud to beg him to stay, and she had fallen into a crushing depression for weeks afterward, living in total isolation for months. In the midst of her despair she had blamed herself for the failure of her marriage, thinking she might have done more to hold on to her husband.

I've managed just fine on my own for twenty-two years, she thought, studying the dazzling Manhattan cityscape. *I'll get through this and I'll emerge stronger for it, too.*

With a sigh, Danika went limp, releasing the tension that had been gathering inside her for the past twenty-four hours as she slipped into the welcome embrace of a deep, black sleep.

Day one—sore all over and leaking like crazy. When Shirley came in to change Danika's soaked padded undergarment and told her to get up and walk, Danika simply glared at the woman as if she had lost her mind.

Get up? Walk? Who is this woman talking to? Surely not me,

Danika thought, barely able to open her eyes. However, after much coaxing, Danika did manage to stand, but nearly passed out from dizziness. Shirley patiently helped Danika into the bathroom where she managed to give herself a semblance of a sponge bath, and then it was back into the padded suit and back to bed.

Pain medication every four hours was the only way Danika got through the rest of the day and the next night. However, by morning, she did feel strong enough to actually put on a comfortable sweat suit and sit up in her bed and read. As the days passed, each one brought another surprise, and each one was more tolerable than the last. Danika's face and body began to heal and the pain eventually subsided. However, by day four the swelling set in, and as Bella had warned, she did indeed feel and look like Puff Mommy all right, with a bloated face, swollen chest and huge hips the size of a big screen TV. And in addition to the awful swelling, bruises suddenly appeared all over her body, and when Danika saw the ugly black splotches that covered her torso and hips, she sat down on the toilet and sobbed, wishing she had never entered the contest, certain that she had made the biggest mistake of her life.

In spite of the swelling and the bruises, she forced herself to remain optimistic, and on day five the padding finally came off. Shirley placed regular Band-Aids over Danika's incisions and allowed her to take a bath. With delight, Danika sat for one hour in a tub of warm water laced with baby oil, and when she got out and examined her body in the mirror, she finally smiled. Her stomach was flat. Her bust was very perky. Her saddlebag hips, which she had had forever, were astonishingly gone. Grinning, she popped another round of pain pills into her mouth and got dressed in real clothes, which sagged from her newly slim form. At last, she was on the downhill side of this painful, beautiful journey.

By the end of the first week, Danika was talking haircuts and color with the hair stylist and had undergone laser whitening on her teeth, from which she emerged with a brilliant, beautiful smile. The second week began with waxing, plucking, buffing skin and polishing her finger and toenails. With her liposuction wraps off, she fingered the small lump above her navel with concern, though Dr. Hollis assured her it would disappear in time.

The removal of the bandages on her face was last, and beyond the bruising and the swollen flesh were her newly chiseled features—wide-open eyes, sexy, plump lips and a tight, yet youthful profile.

Danika sucked in a deep breath and stared at her reflection, too stunned to make a comment. It was as if she had literally turned back the clock fifteen years, to those carefree days when she had known she looked good with no makeup, her hair uncombed and wearing tight jeans and a skimpy halter top. And it wasn't so much the youthful glow that took her breath away, it was the realization that her mature character had not been masked in a too tight, plastic little-girl face. She looked like a real woman—a healthy, well-preserved one who had a lot of miles left to go.

"I can't believe it," she finally murmured to Dr. Hollis and Bella, who had come in for the unveiling.

"Like what you see?" Bella asked, one eyebrow arched.

"Like? I love it!" Danika gushed, a sudden rush of tears filling her eyes. Holding a hand mirror, she examined every visible inch of skin.

"Didn't I tell you that the pain would be worth it?" Bella went on.

Nodding vigorously, Danika agreed. "You did. And you were right. This came at exactly the right time in my life."

When Dr. Hollis and Bella opened their arms and offered Danika a warm group hug, she giggled and fell into their embrace, keenly aware of how much she owed them for this miracle come true.

Shopping day finally arrived at the end of the second week,

and Danika, accompanied by a studio stylist, went by limo from one pricey store to another, where, clad in tight black leotards, a loose-fitting black shirt and oversized sunglasses she tried on a minimum of six outfits in each store. She selected four pricey business suits in vivid summer colors, seven daytime dresses, four very expensive cocktail dresses and five pairs of the tightest jeans she could stand to get into, all two sizes smaller than what she had been wearing when she arrived in New York. And this was only her first round of shopping! With an assortment of shirts, blouses, handbags, shoes and jewelry to match each outfit stuffed into the trunk of the limo, the driver finally deposited her back at her hotel, where a valet had to use a luggage cart to transport her packages up to her suite.

When the following Monday rolled around, Danika entered the studio makeup room at 6:00 a.m. where a makeup artist camouflaged her remaining bruises and transformed her into a vision of perfection.

By ten o'clock the taping of the finale began and she met the other contest winner, a petite redheaded mother of four from Wisconsin who had been stashed at the Marriott Marquis during her makeover. The two women chatted excitedly about their shared experiences, exclaiming over their new images.

Taping ran until six that evening, and after that, the two women were whisked from the studio and taken to the airport, to return to their normal lives, which would most likely never be normal again.

CHAPTER 5

During Danika's four-week absence from work, her boss had recovered fully from his broken leg and returned to the office. Via daily e-mails during her continued recovery at home, she had kept up with what was going on at the company and knew that Jim was postponing his announcement about the promotion until she returned.

Her arrival back at work caused quite a stir. Coworkers came out of their cubicles to congratulate her, stare at her and make comments of praise for the new and improved Danika.

"Welcome back, Miss Celebrity," Jim Planker, the first to greet her, said, still struggling with a single crutch under one arm. "You really do look fabulous. What a change!"

"You're beautiful!" a young engineer added, coming up to stare at Danika, his mouth hanging open in surprise. "I never knew you could look like that!"

"You've sure been hiding yourself from all of us," another coworker, a mature man with a nearly white head of hair accused, as he sauntered over to add his comments. "It's amazing!"

"I'll never get any work done now," said a tall dark-haired colleague whose office faced Danika's. He placed his hands on his hips and openly assessed her. "I'll be looking at you all day."

"Gordon, I doubt that." Danika laughed, truly enjoying the attention, yet concerned that her looks were going to become a real distraction. The few female employees who worked on her floor stuck their heads into her office one by one to give her a big thumbs up. "You go, Danika. You look fabulous, girl," each one said in turn.

The results of the makeover had surpassed Danika's expectations, and she was secretly thrilled with the reaction of her coworkers. They seemed to be curiously in awe of her, as if she were a new hire, and not a twenty-two year veteran at Cranstar with whom most of them had worked at one time or another.

She knew she looked at least ten years younger, twenty pounds slimmer and carried herself with a jaunty air of confidence that she had never felt before. Her once-longish brown hair was now cut into a short carefree tousled bob lit with deep blond highlights. Without glasses, her newly sculpted eyes zapped years off her face, and her white teeth added to her dazzling smile. And except for occasionally feeling tired, she was suffering no lingering effects from her procedures at all.

For her return to work, Danika had ditched her uniform of navy and gray to wear a light tan two-piece jacket dress that showed off her recently trimmed stomach and hips. Her accessories, real turquoise and silver jewelry, added a touch of glamour to her outfit. Danika felt beautiful, energized, optimistic and focused.

"Thank you guys for the compliments," Danika began, lifting a hand as if pleading for them to stop. "I have to admit I'm flattered. It was a crazy, wonderful—and at times, quite painful—experience. However, I'm thrilled to have won the contest and I couldn't be happier with the results. But I am still the same old Danika Redmond, and we have work to do." With that, she waved her manicured fingers and shooed everyone out of her office, ready to get down to work.

Danika stayed in her office most of the morning, only venturing out to the copy machine twice, where she felt every eye in the room on her as she crossed the open area leading to the bank of machines.

I'll just have to get used to being stared at, she thought, realizing that it was a new experience for her, and definitely enjoyable. On her way back to her office, she actually swung her hips a bit, as if to let the guys who were staring at her backside know she had it going on.

By late afternoon, her celebrity status had worn off and she was once again deep into the planning stages of the next ad campaign assigned to her group. Her three o'clock meeting with her staff lasted until six, and when the team finally broke up, she was exhausted, ready to head home. Just as she was about to turn off her lights, Jim Planker arrived, leaning heavily on his crutch.

"Hi," he said, limping into her office. "Got a minute, Miss Celebrity?"

Danika laughed. "Of course, Jim. Sit down. Just wrapping up the first draft of the Pearce Management campaign."

"Good to have you back on the project," Jim stated, shifting around to find a comfortable way to stretch out his bulky, plaster cast encased leg.

"Well, I know the Pearce advertising launch is coming up soon, so I made the campaign today's priority," Danika said. "I put Gordon in charge of all the graphics. He's such a dream to work with. Always comes through with exactly what I, and the company, need."

Jim nodded, then took a deep breath. "So do you, Danika. You are a hard worker with a great attitude and I wanted to talk to you about the proposals for the *Eco Quick-Valve Cleaner* launch. I've already spoken with Todd and Mike about their proposals. Just wanted to go over a few things with you."

"Sure," Danika said, holding her breath, as if making any comment would cut into Jim's space and she definitely wanted to give him plenty of room to say whatever he had come to tell her, good or bad.

"I had a lot of time to review the three proposals while you were out and I was recovering. The extra time came in handy. Really allowed me to take my time deciding which way to go. Each proposal was excellent. Todd took a very serious, strategic approach, focusing on the high-end consumer market. Mike's report was heavy on statistics and driven by our demographic studies of the Western region, where we will launch first."

Danika nodded, forcing a smile, wondering if Todd had dared to tell Jim about her handling of the competition's proposals that night in his office. If so, she was prepared to defend herself against his accusations. No way was he going to trash her without a fight. However, if Jim decided to give the promotion to Todd or to Mike, Danika knew she'd have no problem living with his choice. After all, she was a team player and she would be gracious if the selection turned out to be one of her younger male competitors.

"Now, about your proposal..." Jim started, shaking his head, and then pausing to make eye contact with Danika. "I don't exactly know what to say about it."

Danika raised a brow, her newly sculpted brown eyes fastened on Jim. Out of habit she reached to adjust her glasses, then realized she no longer wore them. Nervously, she clasped both hands together, and then told Jim. "Too much background on the demographics, huh? Yeah, well, I thought maybe I was putting in too many..."

"No. It was exactly what I was looking for," Jim interrupted.

An audible sigh escaped Danika's lips and she tensed her fingers into two balls. "Really?" she breathed out, the sinking feeling in her stomach instantly vanishing. "Then I'm glad I spent the extra time to dig deeper on this one."

"You hit it exactly right, Danika. Great job. However, there is one problem."

"Oh?" she replied, thinking, here comes the I-hate-to-say this-but...bit that he was leading up to. "A problem? What's that?"

"You won't be around to implement your proposal."

Danika's stomach turned over. "I won't?"

"No," Jim shot back, lowering his head to peer at Danika over the top of his glasses. "You're going on a special assignment. To West Texas…as the new Southwest Division Manager."

"The new SDM? Me? For real?" Danika grinned, leaning forward to zero in on Jim's face. "*I* got the promotion?"

"You certainly did, and I am pleased to have played a part in the selection of Cranstar's first female executive—"

"And first African-American," Danika interrupted, smiling.

"Yes, that is important, too, Danika. Cranstar has been slow in rectifying that void in management and I am so pleased that you have broken that not-so-pleasant record." He reached over to extend his hand. "Welcome to the thirty-fifth floor."

"Thanks. I'm looking forward to the move," she tossed back releasing Jim's hand to slump back in her chair. "You can't imagine what this means. This is what I have been working for so long." She glanced around, thinking that it would not take her long to pack up and vacate her office. Swiveling from side to side, she let the news sink in.

How would the other executives react to her promotion? Would she be watched, monitored, scrutinized, tested and perhaps even resented? She was sure that most of her peers would applaud Jim's choice, while others might accuse her of using her race, or her vastly improved femininity, to influence the boss and get the job. It would be disappointing—but not surprising—if some of her coworkers felt that way. But Danika knew in her heart that neither her race, gender or her recent makeover had had anything to do with her success. She had simply been the best-qualified candidate for the job.

"Thank you, Jim, for all your support," she managed to say. "I won't let you down."

"I know you won't," he replied with ease, folding both arms onto the edge of her desk to study her for a moment. "Your first assignment as Southwest Division Manager," he began, "is to lead the transition team and bring R&P Manufacturing into the Cranstar family."

"R&P Manufacturing? Don't think I've ever had any dealings with them," Danika stated, grabbing her pen to begin taking notes.

"It's a midsize metal equipment manufacturing company near Abilene in West Texas. They make oil containers, oversized cans, specialized tubing, things like that. A few months ago, Cranstar sealed the deal to buy R&P. We're going to use the plant to manufacture the *Eco Quick-Valve Cleaner* containers domestically."

"Sounds good," Danika commented, busy taking notes.

"However, the plant is overstaffed, and the CEO is balking at trimming personnel. We need a fifty percent staff reduction and it needs to be done yesterday."

"Why is the CEO stalling?"

"He has a lot of loyal old-timers on staff, entire families, it seems. Most have been with him for years, and he is resistant to letting anyone go. Says he needs time to prepare them, but we don't have it."

"Do the employees know about the takeover?"

No," Jim replied, with a shake of his head. "That's another problem. The owner refuses to tell them until *he's* ready."

"Can't you send out a memo about the new ownership, and go ahead and make the staff cuts from this end since Cranstar now owns the company?" Danika asked.

"We could, but it would be better if the current owner worked with us. Keeps Cranstar from coming off as the heavy, and prevents unnecessary ill feelings against us among those who will remain after the transition."

"What can I do?" Danika asked.

"Your role as SDM is to go to R&P, assess the situation, communicate our intentions to the employees and get the numbers down in the least intrusive way possible. You will have all the severance information when you go, and full authority to recommend staffing cuts. If the CEO interferes, you have the authority to fire him, too, but I don't really want to see that happen. He has been offered the option of staying on as general manager, which he has agreed to do, and I'd like to keep him around. He can be extremely valuable to us in the long run."

"Got it," Danika assured Jim. "In other words, you want me to ease in between the CEO and his staff, communicate the news about the merger and get the cuts done."

"Exactly," Jim agreed, rising to go. He braced his body against his crutch. "We've got to move fast. You only have one week to get this done, and I know you can do it. I trust your judgment."

"Thanks."

"Travel arrangements have already been made. You'll fly into Abilene on Wednesday, rent a car and head to Bolan... thirty miles to the west in a fairly isolated area. But for now, go home. Celebrate your promotion. We can talk more about your assignment in the morning."

"Right," Danika replied, standing. "And I'll get started on researching the company right away. Oh, and what is the CEO's name?"

"Raymond Pruitt," Jim answered, pausing at the door. "I'll give you my folder on him and the company tomorrow."

As soon as Jim left her office, Danika quickly sat down and pressed her fingers to her lips. *It can't be,* she thought. *Raymond Pruitt is the CEO of R&P Manufacturing? Raymond Pruitt? My ex-husband, whom I have not seen nor heard from in twenty-five years? God, I hope not.*

CHAPTER 6

It took only seconds to locate the Internet Web site for R&P Manufacturing and confirm Danika's suspicion—Raymond Pruitt, CEO, was indeed, her ex-husband.

Should I tell Jim that I was once married to the man he wants me to whip into shape...or fire? she wondered, staring at the photograph of Raymond Pruitt that was posted on the R&P Web site. Quickly, she mentally calculated that he must be fifty-two years old now, as he was three years older than she. He looked just as handsome as ever, she thought, even with flecks of gray in his short wavy hair and a few crinkles at the corners of his deep brown eyes. His chin was still strong, almost arrogant in its lift and his facial expression was one that she remembered—steely, determined, void of emotion and difficult to read.

I've got the promotion, Danika rationalized. *I am Cranstar's new SDM and I already have agreed to the assignment. It's too late to claim a conflict of interest. I'll keep quiet about my past involvement with Raymond Pruitt and do the best job I can.* Having settled that matter, she picked up her purse, shut down her computer and headed home.

Before entering her apartment, Danika tapped on Ming's door, anxious to tell her about the promotion. Ming opened the door with a flourish. "Enter, my Royal Highness," Ming laughed, bowing in an exaggerated salute.

"Girl, please," Danika tossed back, entering Ming's calm, cool living room. She sat down on the green suede sofa and dropped her purse to the floor. "I need your opinion on something very important." Danika filled Ming in on her promotion and her first assignment.

"Didn't I tell you that you'd be the first African-American executive at Cranstar? Great news!" Ming squealed, giving Danika a big hug. "And as for your ex—forget about him. Keep your mouth shut, do the job and be done with it. No one needs to know you two had a relationship. Why jeopardize your assignment? Jim might have second thoughts about sending you out there...might think you cannot be objective in your dealings with R&P. The last thing you need is to have him pull you from your first assignment."

"Right, and besides, that would give Todd Poston too much satisfaction. Ming, I'm worried. Things could get ugly if I have to fire Raymond Pruitt from his own company. Very Ugly. He's not the kind of man who would accept being canned, especially by a woman, without a fight. You don't know him. He will fight me and Cranstar to the end, and probably accuse me of firing him out of revenge."

"After all these years?" Ming queried, flopping down on the floor at Danika's feet, pulling her caftan around her. "The man would think that you still hold some kind of a grudge against him for walking out?"

"Probably," Danika answered. "That's the kind of person he is...and that's why I am better off without him. He dumped me, but if he hadn't, in time I'm sure I would have left him. We just weren't meant to be."

"What happened between you two, anyway?"

"We met in college...at Rice University. I was studying advertising, and he was studying engineering. We fell in love, got married and struggled to make ends meet while we both finished our degrees. Raymond went to work for an engineering firm in Dallas right away—a good job that paid well. From the beginning, Raymond knew I wanted to start an advertising agency, but I guess he thought I was just talking. However, once we settled in Dallas and I began moving forward with my plans, he was suddenly against it. We had our first real blowout argument when I hired a young man who had great graphic skills. Raymond got jealous over the amount of time I spent with the guy and insisted I fire him. I refused. After that, things were never the same. I ignored Raymond's objections to everything I did and went ahead with my business plan, so he began ignoring me and gave me no emotional or financial support. I did manage to launch my company anyway, and snagged one pretty good client at the beginning, but the business never really took off. I guess my heart was not in it, with Raymond so dead set against my succeeding. He had a unpredictable temperament...used to sulk a lot and give me the silent treatment, especially whenever I came home late after spending time with a client. He wanted my full attention."

"Sounds like what he really wanted was a stay-at home wife," Ming interjected, pushing back a lock of black hair that escaped her spiky ponytail.

"Exactly," Danika agreed.

"A true throwback to a caveman mentality, huh?" Ming added.

"You might say so," Danika replied. "The final insult came when, behind my back, Raymond began making contacts to find financial backing to start his engineering company. When I found out that he planned on leaving Thompson to start a company...after giving me absolutely no support, I blew up. We argued. He admitted that he did not want a wife who was a busy entrepreneur, and he hated the fact that I was away from home so much. Things deteriorated. One day he simply walked out. Eventually he took up with a woman named Julie, whom I guess he thought would be the perfect wife. After that, Raymond and I separated. I moved to Houston, filed for divorce, took back my maiden name and went to work for Cranstar."

Ming let out a loud sigh. "It seems to me that the wheel has turned in your favor. Girl, it's time to go on out there and do your thing. Show Mr. Raymond Pruitt exactly what a mistake he made when he tossed you aside."

CHAPTER 7

The temperature gauge on the dashboard of Danika's rental car flashed one hundred six degrees. After adjusting her new designer sunglasses and punching the radio's scan button for the tenth time, she gave up on trying to find an English language station and refocused her attention on the dusty two-lane highway that was bordered by bristly, stunted mesquite trees, huge clumps of prickly cactus and mile after mile of gunmetal gray chain link fencing. The rugged countryside, which was flat, arid and empty, slipped by in a haze of shimmering heat and blinding sunshine.

"Enough of that," Danika muttered in frustration, switching off the Mexican music that was blaring from her car radio, wishing she had thought to bring along her MP3 player. Some Vanessa, Whitney, Mariah or Luther would sure sound good right now.

After her arrival at the Abilene airport, she had rented the only available car—a two-year-old Ford Escort with a slightly dented hood—and headed west. The road to Bolan had been virtually empty for miles, though an eighteen-wheeler did whiz by, stirring up clouds of dust, and a pickup truck filled with farm workers pulled into her lane without warning and nearly ran her off the road. The occasional ranch style house, set far back from the road, and usually under a canopy of trees, was the only indication that the area was inhabited. The isolation of the desertlike landscape made Danika glad that this assignment was not going to be permanent. She'd go nuts living in a place like this.

Why in the world did Raymond place his business here? she wondered, remembering her sophisticated ex-husband as a man who enjoyed the hustle and bustle of the city life. After graduating from college in Houston, he would only consider job offers from firms in big cities, and eventually had settled on Dallas. Whatever had drawn him to Bolan, Texas, must have been pretty darn special to make him forego access to the sports arenas, shopping malls and upscale lifestyle that big-city life offered, that much Danika knew.

Curiosity about seeing her ex-husband took hold once more, and for a few moments Danika let her mind go back to those early days with Raymond, when they had only been concerned with being in love—before the complicated issues of living together had surfaced and forced them apart.

Raymond Pruitt had been Danika's first serious boyfriend and first lover, and for that reason she had been devastated when the marriage fell apart. She believed that a woman never really got over her first love, and though she had put Raymond totally out of her mind for years, she had never really forgotten him. How could she? Early in their relationship, he had been tender, thoughtful and appreciative of her independent personality and energetic spirit, winning her over with flowers, small unexpected gifts and funny cards. He had effectively hidden his compulsively controlling personality until months after they were married. His change in attitude had been gradual, starting with insignificant decisions, which she had gladly let him make, and then escalating into interference and outright dominance. When he had tried to squash her dream of starting her business, she had balked at his demand for control, and from that moment on, Raymond had resented every move she made toward independence, expressing disappointment when she refused to consult with him or involve him in her plans.

After the divorce, Danika had had to undergo counseling to get her life back on track. During her counseling sessions she had come to the conclusion that Raymond's personal sense of insecurity, not his lack of love for her, was what had driven them apart. *His father left him when he was six years old,* Danika recalled. *His only brother ran away when he was ten. His mother died when he was twenty, and shortly after that he met and married me. He never had a chance to feel really secure,* she mused, swinging off the highway and into a gravel driveway where signs indicated that R&P Manufacturing was five miles ahead. *It's what happened in Raymond's life before I met him that made him try to hold on to me so tightly that he forced me away.*

Pursing her lips, Danika scanned the structures beyond the ever-present chain link fence—an assortment of large one-story concrete block buildings arranged in a horseshoe design. "R & P Manufacturing," she murmured, arriving at the entrance gate.

She gave her name to the guard and was directed to a white stucco building with tinted glass windows across the front. She pulled into a visitors parking spot, got out of the car and tried to smooth out the wrinkles in her white linen suit.

"I could have worn blue jeans, cowboy boots and a denim shirt," she muttered, distressed that the deep creases across the front of her skirt were definitely not going to go away. She had brought along many pieces from the new wardrobe she had won in the makeover contest—classic designer suits, stylish shoes with matching handbags and accessories to go with each outfit. Now, she wondered if it might be better to make a quick run to the local Wal-Mart, if such a place existed in the area, and purchase several pairs of slacks and sleeveless shirts.

The blazing heat burned down on the top of her head, melting her perfectly applied makeup, wilting her freshly curled hair and bringing a ring of perspiration under each arm. The professional image she had carefully put together that morning, in a desire to meet Raymond in a cool businesslike manner, was ruined. Feeling frustrated, anxious and off balance, she slammed the car door and strode purposefully toward the building entrance, ready to get on with the job she had come to do.

Inside, the office was dim and cool, easing Danika's irritation. She gave her name to a cheerful, heavily freckled woman with red hair who seemed genuinely glad to have someone to welcome to the complex, and then took a seat by the water cooler. She smoothed her skirt again and fluffed her hair, anxious to see Raymond's reaction when he realized that D.A. Redmond, the person with whom he had been communicating via e-mail to arrange this appointment, was his ex-wife, Danika Anne Redmond.

"Miss Redmond?" the woman said, interrupting Danika's thoughts. "Mr. Pruitt will see you now. Follow me, please."

Rising, Danika followed the woman, suddenly nervous about coming face-to-face with the man she had once loved more than anything else in life—the man to whom she had given her heart, her soul, her virginity! God, how lovestruck and naive she had been back then!

After ushering Danika into a spacious office that was decorated with Native American artifacts and accessories of a rugged western theme, the woman smiled cheerfully at her visitor and left.

Danika instantly locked eyes with Raymond, who was sitting behind his rustic wooden desk staring back at her, his confusion obvious. He was wearing a light blue dress shirt, a navy-and-gold silk tie and seemed to have changed very little during the years they had been apart. His cocoa brown skin was still even and smooth, his slightly wavy jet black hair was still longish at the back and traces of gray shimmered at his temples. His chin remained as firm and proud as it had always been, retaining his familiar air of self-importance.

"Hello," she said, breaking the tension, praying her voice would not betray her nervousness.

"Ah...hello." Raymond replied, rising, then leaning forward to extend his hand across his desk. "I'm Raymond Pruitt. I...well. Excuse me." He pulled his hand back, clearly puzzled. "For a minute...I thought. Well, you remind me of someone."

"Danika Redmond, perhaps?" Danika prompted, now offering her hand in greeting, looking up at her ex-husband who, at six feet three inches, towered over her.

"Well!" he stuttered, now coming around his desk, as if to get a better look at her. "Danika? Is that really you?"

"It's me all right," she managed, controlling the growing quiver in her voice while secretly enjoying the expression of surprise that creased Raymond's still-unlined face. He was as heart-stopping handsome as she remembered. "Hello, Raymond. Looks like you and I are going to be working together...after all these years."

Stunned, Raymond studied his ex-wife as he shook her hand. "So, *you're* D.A. Redmond?" His statement was more of an acknowledgment than a question.

"The same. I hope that my being here won't be a problem," she replied sincerely, having already decided not to make this encounter any more complicated than it had to be. They ought to be able to work together in a professional manner to complete the staffing matters without any complications or unnecessary confrontations. The last thing she wanted was a messy situation that might bring her boss into the mix.

"No, not a problem at all. So, you're the new Southwest Division Manager for Cranstar?" He looked at her in wonder. "My God, I never would have connected D.A. Redmond with *you!*"

"Quite a surprise, huh?" she answered, letting her words drift off, watching him squirm.

"A big shock," he stated, moving closer to Danika. He blinked, and then impulsively extended his hand once more, shaking Danika's firmly. "But, it's good to see you."

Danika simply nodded. "Thanks, Raymond. Quite a turn of events, huh?"

"Damn straight. And you look great, too," he remarked, now giving her a pointed once-over, clearly checking Danika out. "I hate to stare, but you don't look a day over thirty...and you know, I know how old you are."

Danika felt a sudden wave of heat flush into her face. Was she embarrassed to be complimented by her ex-husband, or simply experiencing a hot flash? Either way, the sensation was disconcerting.

"Just holding it together as best as I can," she said and laughed, not about to mention anything about her recent makeover. This was the new Danika, and the only Danika that Raymond needed to know about. The gleam of surprise and appreciation in his startled brown eyes was exactly the reaction she had hoped for.

"Have a seat. Please," he rushed on, going back behind his desk to sit down. "I have to admit that I was a bit concerned about this meeting. The buyout happened so quickly, and I was expecting Cranstar to send Jim Planker out to work through the details of the merger. Is he your boss?"

"He used to be. Now, he's my...peer," Danika answered with pride.

"Oh. I see. Well, Planker drove a hard bargain and we butted heads a few times, but I'm glad the deal is done. And now this! What an unexpected sight you are." He leaned back in his chair, grinning. "This makes things so much easier." He blew out a long breath, as if relieved that Danika had come and not Jim. "We're going to get along just fine."

"I'm sure we will," Danika agreed in an even tone, crossing her legs, hiding her sudden annoyance. She recognized that familiar, self-satisfied ring to his words—the one he had used so many times with her, especially when having things go his way had been extremely important. Easier? She doubted he had any idea of how firm a negotiator she could be.

"How have you been? What have you been up to all this time?" Raymond pressed ahead, unable to take his eyes off Danika. "Never married, I assume, since you are using your maiden name?"

"Nope. Never gave it a second try," she answered, trying to make light of their disastrous past. "My work is all I need. What about you? Did you and Julie marry?"

Raymond shifted in his chair as he nodded, his grin quickly fading. "Yes. I married Julie, and we moved to Abilene to be near Julie's parents...that's why I located my business out here. Cheap land, low taxes. Good place for a business start-up."

"Any kids?" Danika asked.

"Two boys, Carl and Eddie...fifteen and seventeen. Real teenagers, now. And avid cyclists, too. They drag me along on their bike rides." He patted his waist, encircled by a thin black leather belt. "I guess keeping up with them keeps me in shape, too, so I go riding with them whenever I can."

"That's nice," Danika murmured, a surprising jolt of envy suddenly striking. Early in their marriage Raymond had often mentioned how much he wanted *her* to have his children—a boy and a girl, he had always said. He had wanted to start a family right away, but she had wanted to wait until after she launched her business. Too bad they had not been able to compromise. Cycling with his sons was certainly keeping him in top shape, and Danika could tell from the way that his dress shirt hugged his torso that firm, well-defined muscles lay beneath it.

"Well, it took me and Julie several years to start our family," Raymond went on. "But by the time our second child, Carl, was born, Julie had been diagnosed with breast cancer. She died five years ago, when Carl was ten years old."

"Oh. I'm sorry, Raymond. That's very sad. And you remained in Abilene?"

"No, I live here in Bolan. Not far from the plant. Got me a little place that suits me fine. During the school year the boys live with their grandparents in Abilene and go to school there, but they come home on most weekends and we spend holidays and summers together."

"That's great...that you are close to your sons," Danika remarked, genuinely saddened to learn that Julie had died and left Raymond a widower. She suddenly felt sorry for him, knowing how much he had wanted that perfect little family unit, the one that she had not been able to give him. It seemed that his luck with women was no better than hers had been with men, and neither had been able to hold on to the persons they had thought would be their lifelong mates. After a short pause, she leaned forward and placed one hand on the corner of Raymond's desk. "I know that losing your wife must have been difficult."

"It was," Raymond acknowledged, his eyes flickering shut for a brief moment. "Especially for the boys...but we're managing. And they're good kids, you know? They study hard, get good grades. Never give me serious problems. I can't complain." He paused and then glanced toward the window, as if drifting off in thought.

Feeling uncomfortable to have slipped into such a personal discussion, Danika coughed lightly, and broke into Raymond's reverie. "Well, we've got a lot to do and I have to report back to Cranstar this evening, so why don't we just jump right in and get started. Okay?"

"Sure," Raymond replied, swiveling around in his chair. "The first thing I want to do is take you on a tour of the plant. You've got to see it. State-of-the-art equipment. Nothing but the best. Once we get into production..."

Danika raised one hand, palm up, anxious to interrupt him. "Raymond. Thanks, but maybe later. I'm a bit tired and it's so hot! Why don't we stay inside where it's cool and start on a plan to deal with the Human Resources issues. I'd be happy to take the tour tomorrow."

"Fine. However, I won't be at the plant until late afternoon tomorrow. An appointment I can't break...but I can arrange for one of my staff members to take you around early in the day."

"That would be wonderful," Danika replied, secretly relieved not to have to spend any more time than necessary outside in the heat...or alone with Raymond. Though she was trying hard to remain detached and efficiently professional, seeing him again had impacted her in a way she could not define. Being near him now was initiating so many memories—good ones as well as bad ones, and she didn't want to go there. With a shake of her head, she cleared them away and refocused on the task at hand. "Have the employees been informed of the sale of the company yet?" she asked, tunneling her attention to the present.

"Not officially," Raymond answered. "Though the rumor mill is grinding out all kinds of stories."

"I understand what you are saying. We'll put them to rest. I've brought along answers to many of your questions. We'll get everything out in the open tomorrow."

"That's good, but I want to be very careful in how I release the news," Raymond told her. "If I tell everyone at once a panic might erupt...a frightening possibility. My longtime employees will want to stay, no matter what, so I'd like to meet with them individually over the next few weeks, assure them that I am not going to force anyone out."

Tensing, Danika sat up straighter. "Sorry. We don't have time for that, Raymond. The staff reduction needs to be done right away, and Cranstar is offering very generous separation packages, you know," Danika clarified, wondering why Raymond was dragging his heels. Most CEOs viewed a merger as an opportunity to clean house, get rid of nonproducers and bring in new blood to pump up the operation. It seemed that Raymond just wanted to hold on to the past. No wonder Jim Planker had sent her to get this done.

"You don't understand," Raymond began. "My people don't want separation packages. They want jobs. Many have been with me for twenty years or more, and they love their jobs. They look forward to coming to work every day. I can't simply make a grand announcement that fifty percent of my employees have to go."

"I know that, but we have to start somewhere. My job is to make sure the numbers are reduced," Danika told him, opening her briefcase to remove a stack of papers, which she spread over Raymond's desk. "I'd like to begin by setting up a general staff meeting for tomorrow…"

"*You?* You plan on holding a meeting with *my* staff?" Raymond prompted, eyes wide in question.

"Yes, since you haven't," Danika finished in an efficient manner.

Raymond tapped his fingernails on the arm of his chair, his eyes suddenly becoming hooded as he focused on Danika. "I thought there would not be any interference from Cranstar. I told Jim Planker as much, the last time we talked. We had a verbal agreement to let me handle my staff."

"Well, I am not aware of any verbal agreement, Raymond. All I know is what I have to do." Danika took her time letting Raymond digest her message. She was prepared to meet any challenge he might make to her authority.

"Obviously, you misunderstood the way this is going to work," he replied. "I won't be forced to follow Cranstar's schedule. I'm still in charge here and I'll handle things at my own pace. Is that clear?" His voice had become hard and steady.

Danika sighed, realizing that this was not going to be easy after all. "Sorry, Raymond, but right now, I'm in charge, and I will be making the decisions. Is *that* clear?"

The dark scowl that appeared on Raymond's face confirmed Danika's suspicion: He had assumed that she was simply a figurehead with little decision making power.

"Do you think that I would let you…a total stranger to my employees, decide who stays and who goes?" he finally managed to ask.

"*Let me?*" Danika's words flew out as her brow creased into a deep frown. "R&P belongs to Cranstar International. I have every right to hold such a meeting, and even terminate whomever I want."

Raymond scoffed loudly. "We'll see about that."

It is not your role to decide what you will or will not comply with during this merger, Danika thought, her body becoming rigid as she listened to Raymond describe, in detail, the value of each employee and the role of every outside supplier working with his company. His frustration, his anger and his demanding tone brought back painful memories of the heated arguments they had had during the final stages of their marriage. Patiently, she let him ramble on, knowing it would do no good to interrupt. When he finished, she started right in.

"Raymond, if you can't...or won't...cooperate with me, then...I hate to say it, but—*you* might be the first to go."

CHAPTER 8

When Raymond pulled into the driveway of his sprawling Texas-size estate, the first thing he saw were his two golden retrievers, Willy and Nilly, racing through the water sprinklers that were soaking the thick green lawn, yapping as they ran to greet him. The familiar sight of his faithful pets welcoming him home temporarily took his mind off Danika, whose arrival at the plant had initiated too many disparate emotions to describe.

After parking his cherry red Cadillac Escalade in the three-car garage, he got out, absently rubbed each dog behind the ears, and then headed down the vine-covered walkway that led to the main house—a four-thousand-square-foot, one-story red brick ranch with a pool and a professionally landscaped yard.

Inside, he grabbed an ice-cold beer from the double-door refrigerator and popped the cap, then took a long swig before sitting down at the polished black marble bar, glad to be home, glad to be alone and as frustrated as hell over Danika's parting threat.

"Fire me? I don't think so. She might be an executive with Cranstar Oil and Gas International, but she is not in charge of my future," he muttered under his breath. "Who the hell does she think she is dealing with? How dare she try to boss *me* around?" Shaking his head, he finished off his beer, slid off the bar stool and went into his study—a wood-paneled room done in dark reds and browns at the rear of the house that afforded a view of the pool.

Standing at the window, he watched his dogs playing tug-of-war with an old piece of rope, his mind fastened on Danika and the task that lay ahead.

Why did she have to come out here and complicate things? he fretted, rationalizing that he planned to take care of the staffing issues, eventually. And as *he* saw fit. Now he had a fight on his hands that he was not about to lose.

Danika was definitely tougher, brasher and more difficult than he remembered her being when they had been married, but he'd find a way to put her in her place. "She is not gonna push me around," he vowed aloud, suddenly wondering if Jim Planker knew that he was Danika's ex-husband. "Probably not," Raymond murmured. "He needs to know that she is threatening to fire me in order to punish me for walking out on her twenty-some years ago. She will use this assignment to pursue a personal vendetta—I know she will, and that's going to be a real conflict of interest for Cranstar. Maybe even grounds for a lawsuit. Let her try to fire me. Hell, *she* might be the one to lose her job."

Turning from the window, Raymond went into the kitchen where he had left his briefcase, opened it and took out his PDA. Quickly he searched for Jim Planker's phone number, and then pushed in the numbers in his cell phone. "I'll be damned if I am going to let Danika call a meeting with my staff and make me look like the bad guy. I'll do things my way or I'll make sure she goes back to Houston, with a lot of explaining to do."

Danika pushed Send, forwarding her first e-mail update to Jim Planker, promising that the staff meeting to announce the buyout would be held no later than Friday. After signing off, she closed her laptop and slumped back against the headboard of her motel room bed, listening to the aging air conditioner that was working hard as it knocked and whirred and blasted streams of moderately cool air into the room. She fanned her face with her hand, exhausted, frustrated and much too warm.

Her boss was counting on her to bring R&P Manufacturing and its CEO into line as soon as possible. If only she could make Raymond see that his coddling and overprotective approach to his employees was neither appropriate nor fair, she might be able to make progress and get out of there as quickly as possible.

The tension between Danika and Raymond had been so heavy she could still feel the weight of it on her chest as she lay in bed thinking about tomorrow. Tomorrow. He *would* sit down with her to plan the staff meeting or she would find someone else to help her. *He'd better cooperate,* she mentally grumbled, wondering what kind of a boss he really was. Though he talked of genuinely caring about his employees, in her opinion, he was still the same old control freak. Keeping his staff in the dark about something as important as a buyout was cruel. *If he balks at cooperating with me, I'll fire him on the spot,* she decided, knowing that Raymond most likely thought she had been bluffing. *I'll be happy to show Mr. Pruitt that I have the balls to follow through on my threat, and I certainly am not afraid of him.*

Frustrated, she reached up and snapped off the lamp at her bedside, then lay awake for a long while, staring at the blinking Desert Flower Motel sign flashing over the parking lot, thinking about Raymond.

He had said that he lived in Bolan. Where? she wondered. He had never been overly concerned with appearances, so she suspected his home must be a very simple place. What was his life like now? He had said his two sons lived with their grandparents in Abilene. Was Raymond a loner? A lonely, bitter man whose life revolved around his work? Or did he have an active social life? Did he have a steady girlfriend?

Danika shivered despite the stifling heat in the modest motel room as she visualized him in bed, making love to an attractive woman. The image initiated a surprising ripple of regret. She had to admit that he was even more good-looking than he had been when he was younger. He had a mature solidness about him that was definitely appealing, and since he was obviously a financially successful businessman, he must be considered an extremely eligible bachelor in the area.

But who would want to marry an insecure control freak like him? she dismissed, curious about how he was coping with her unexpected arrival. Did he view her as simply an unwelcome ghost from his past, or a threat to his future? she wondered.

CHAPTER 9

Carlos Golan walked fast, talked fast and did not leave out a single detail about the history of the company as he explained R&P Manufacturing to Danika. His heavily accented voice crackled with energy as he whisked her from one section of the sprawling plant to another in his shiny blue golf cart, which had a fringed canopy top, a two-way radio and a CD player that blasted Latin music all along the way.

A young man who looked to be in his early thirties, he had jet black hair, Antonio Banderas eyes, a sexy bronze tan and the deepest dimples on both cheeks that Danika had ever seen. He had met her at the front gate on her arrival, informing her that Raymond had instructed him to give her the grand tour of the plant, but not to let her talk to any of the employees.

"Not let me talk? Why?" Danika had asked, shocked at what she felt was a stupid, childish directive.

"He didn't say, and I didn't ask," Carlos had replied with a shrug. "However, I do know about the merger, so I guess he wants to be the one to tell the rest of the employees who you are and why you are here, and that Cranstar now owns R&P."

And because he is afraid I will one-up him, Danika thought, extremely irritated to have been drawn into his power play. *I'll go along with Raymond, for now,* she'd decided, not wanting to upset things too much.

"I can tell that a lot of skill and hard work goes into the manufacture of each product," Danika remarked at the end of the tour, after moving into and out of numerous huge warehouses and observing the efficient assembly lines that had been especially designed to process the raw materials required to manufacture the company's products.

"Exactly," Carlos replied, swinging himself back into the golf cart next to Danika, then starting the engine. "Mr. Pruitt runs a damn fine operation and we are lucky to have him as our boss. Everyone loves him, and most everyone actually looks forward to getting started each day. Mr. Pruitt has never let anybody go. Ever. That's a good boss, don't you think?"

"Yes, I guess so," Danika vaguely agreed, holding her comments to herself. She grabbed the strap next to her seat and held on tightly when Carlos sped away from the warehouse and zipped around a corner, nearly on two wheels.

"I know cuts will have to be made in some areas, but I sure hope the pink slips will be minimal," Carlos went on, braking suddenly to come to a jolted stop at the entrance to the plant. Jumping out, he rushed around the front of the cart to help Danika out, then checked his watch and grinned. "Exactly eleven thirty. I timed our tour just right. If we leave now, we can beat the lunch hour rush at Dos Amigos—best Tex-Mex food in the state. You hungry?"

Danika blinked into the blinding sun that was beating down from above, feeling wilted and faint, not sure if the empty feeling in the pit of her stomach was from hunger, the heat or Carlos's attempt to impress her. A chatty escort, he had openly flirted with her all morning, and she had found his attention both disturbing and pleasantly amusing.

Today, she had had the foresight to wear a light cotton blouse, a loose-fitting skirt, flat shoes and a wide brimmed hat. And minimal makeup, too, which she could get away with after having had skin resurfacing and dermabrasion peels during her makeover. With her highlighted hair held back from her face by two silver barrettes, she looked more youthful and felt much more comfortable than she had on her arrival yesterday.

"The truth is, I am more thirsty than hungry," she finally decided, not having the heart to tell Carlos that food was the last thing on her mind.

"Thirsty? No problem," Carlos tossed back, reaching past Danika to get to a small plastic cooler he had stowed in the rear of the golf cart. Hesitating, he let his upper body rest against her shoulder for a second too long, then held up an ice-cold bottle of water. "Anything for a pretty lady," he finished with a flourish, wiping the wetness off the bottle with a handkerchief that he pulled from his shirt pocket. He deliberately let his fingers graze Danika's as he handed her the drink, a sly smile touching his full, sensual lips. "Never go anywhere without water around here. That's an order."

Chuckling, Danika accepted the bottle of water and took a long, much-needed swallow, aware that Carols was intently watching her. He was an outrageous flirt, and a very charismatic guy. Extremely loyal to Raymond, too.

"Whew! I needed that!" she laughed, giving Carlos a genuine smile, thinking that the guy was a handsome fireball of energy, and a very entertaining tour guide.

He had told her his life story, and the life stories of most of his coworkers, while showing her around the complex. A graduate of the University of Texas, he had grown up in the area and come to work at R&P Manufacturing ten years ago with a degree in engineering and a passion for inventing. Working with Raymond, he had come up with several innovative improvements in much of the company's machinery, including a protective covering for plastic tubing to insulate it from extreme temperatures. He was thirty-three years old, a bachelor who loved to hike in the nearby mountains and his passion was collecting baseball memorabilia—preferably over eBay. He was fit, trim, muscular and attractive, with an exuberant personality to match his good looks. He had an outgoing chattiness about him that made him easy to talk to, and boy, did he love to talk.

If I were only a few years younger… Danika began to fantasize, barely listening to Carlos as he described his favorite dish at Dos Amigos.

"So do you?" Carlos finished.

Startled from her mental wandering, Danika squinted and shrugged. "Sorry. Do I what?"

"Want to go over to Abilene for lunch at Dos Amigos or grab a sandwich in town?"

"Oh. Dos Amigos is in Abilene?"

"Yeah. Only thirty miles up the road. Around here, that's pretty close."

"Well, then sure. Abilene it is," Danika agreed, deciding to enjoy the attention that Carlos was clearly giving her.

Raymond was glad that Danika was not around when he arrived at his office later that afternoon. He needed time to plan his next move. With a sigh, he opened the personnel flow chart and began going over the names. As he read through the documents, a sinking feeling came into his stomach. Every person on the chart belonged at R&P, was important to the company and deserved to remain on staff. No way could he bring himself to let anyone go, nor was he going to allow Danika to do so. Somehow, he would have to get her out of his way so he could handle things as he saw fit. He knew what was best for his company, and himself. No way in hell was he going to let her call the shots.

The enchiladas verdes at Dos Amigos were the best that Danika had ever tasted. After completing a steamy platter of the cheesy creations, half a pitcher of margaritas and too many tortilla chips to count, Danika pushed back from the table and groaned.

"Absolutely, the best," she told Carlos, placing a hand at her waist. "However, this can never happen again. I must have gained five pounds while sitting here."

Carlos clucked his tongue. "Surely you don't worry about what you eat. Not with a schoolgirl figure like yours." He winked, and then gave her a dazzling smile.

If you only knew what I went through to get this school-girl figure, Danika thought, flashes of her liposuction recovery flitting into her mind. She was finally a solid size eight once more, and had no desire to pack the pounds back on and go through that struggle with weight loss again. "Can't be too careful," was all she told Carlos as he paid the check and stood. Joining him, they made their way back to his car.

"Where to now?" he asked before starting the engine, his hand poised to turn the key.

Danika looked over at his profile, so sharp and youthful and strong, it made her heart begin to pound. She widened her eyes in question. "What do you mean, where to? Back to the plant, of course."

Without glancing over at her, Carlos spoke in a steady voice, his words directed toward the windshield. "You don't have to go back right now. I could take you to the Mercado Plaza. Great shopping. Or out to Great Mountain Park, at the foot of the mountains. It's much cooler there. I'd love to show you around and give you a real feel for what West Texas is all about." Now, he did look at her, and his joking expression had been replaced by a serious gaze that gave Danika pause.

"Oh, I don't think so," she began, clearly getting his message. This was certainly neither the time nor the place to get personally involved with one of Raymond's employees, but truthfully, she would much rather go sightseeing with this handsome young man than return to the office and fight with her ex-husband. However, she had work to do, and knew she had to maintain her professional demeanor. "Better take me back to the plant," she told him, arching a brow.

"Why go back so soon? Mr. Pruitt said to take care of you until he got in, and that won't be until two, maybe three

o'clock. Besides, I'm enjoying your company, *Ms.* Redmond,"
he said, deliberately emphasizing the word, *Ms.*

"Please, call me Danika," she blurted out, suddenly trying
to put him at ease and perhaps soften her rejection. "I appreciate the invitation, but I can't take the time right now."

"Okay. Well, Danika, then...we'll go back. However, I'd be
happy to show you around another time. Mr. Pruitt wouldn't
mind. I'm sure he wants you to feel welcome."

I'm not so sure, she thought, a fluttering sensation starting
up inside as it hit her that Carlos actually *wanted* to spend time
with her. It had been a long time since any man had told her
that, let alone a sexy youthful hunk like Carlos, and the sincerity of his invitation was not lost. She laced her fingers
together in her lap, thinking, then replied, "I'm sure that's true,
but I have a ton of paperwork to take care of and I've already
taken up enough of your time. I'd feel better if you took me
back to the plant."

With a tilt of his head, Carlos watched her as he considered
her reply, and then placed his hand on the back of the car seat,
very near her shoulder. "All right, but only if you agree to let
me take you out to Great Mountain Park before you leave,"
he prompted, dark eyes boring into hers. "On Saturday,
perhaps?"

A subtle curiosity swept over Danika as she gave his invitation more thought. What else did she have to do on a
Saturday afternoon in Bolan, Texas? Sit in her motel room
and watch one of three local television stations or read maga-
zines all day? Carlos was polite, intelligent and a very
pleasant man. Why not let him show her around? Anyway,
after this assignment at R&P was complete, she'd never see
him again.

"Perhaps," she impulsively replied, settling back in her seat,
wondering if a man like Carlos would have looked at her twice,
let alone want to take her sightseeing, a month ago—before her
miraculous makeover.

* * *

After returning to the plant, the long afternoon became an emotionally draining struggle as Danika worked with Raymond to find common ground on which to deal with the announcement of the merger. After many terse discussions, Danika managed to convince him to schedule the employee meeting for the following day.

"However, I must be the one to explain Cranstar's new staffing requirements," Danika insisted, hoping to move things along at a much faster pace. There was no way she was going to drag this out any longer than necessary. All she wanted to do was finish with the assignment, get away from Raymond Pruitt and go back to her relatively calm office in Houston, though Carlos's unexpected interest in her had created a bright spot in this otherwise problematic task.

"I don't think that would be wise," Raymond protested, much too curtly for Danika's taste. "I know my employees. They will not take the news well from an outsider. Best for me to tell them that pink slips will be coming. I'll answer all their questions about employment termination and give them an idea of what to expect." He paused, then said, "Just give me the information on Cranstar's severance packages. I'll need that for tomorrow."

"Sorry, I can't do that," Danika replied, sensing the beginnings of a major power struggle. "My instructions are to personally handle that subject, as well as how the voluntary terminations will work." Danika patted a folder on the table that had the Cranstar logo on the front.

With a short laugh, Raymond stood up and moved away from Danika, glowering over at her from across the room. "Voluntary terminations? I can tell you right now that very few, if any, of my employees will willingly depart. We're a tight-knit group...and in case you haven't noticed, there aren't many other places in this area that can offer salaries and benefits to match those at R&P. No one wants to leave my company," he added with assurance. "Tomorrow, you'll see that I'm right."

"Well, yes...we'll see," Danika answered vaguely, not wishing to press the subject. He seemed to be deliberately baiting her, as if trying to shatter the professional cool she was working hard to maintain. He had a way of rattling her with his voice, his manner, his very presence, but she was determined not to let her annoyance show. Why did he have to push so hard to make his point? To have his way? He had always been this way and Danika still wondered why.

"Raymond, I don't want to fight with you," she finally stated, eyeing him with a dispirited sigh. "I simply want to help you, and when I am finished here, I plan to go back to Houston as soon as possible."

"Fine with me," he tossed back. "You really didn't need to come in the first place. I can handle my people."

"You know," Danika went on, deciding to flex a bit of muscle herself. "I have instructions from headquarters that I *must* follow, but if you insist on blocking me—and as I said yesterday—I have the authority to recommend *your* termination. I ought to, for more reasons than I want to get into right now. Don't force me to do that."

Raymond broke into a lopsided grin, before telling her, "I am sure you won't." Turning his back to her, he studied the expansive view of his sprawling plant for a few seconds, as if gathering his thoughts while surveying his domain. Then, looking back at Danika, he went on. "I'd like to ask you something. Will you give me an honest answer?" His voice had become uncharacteristically calm.

Surprised by this sudden change in demeanor, Danika slowly nodded. "I have no reason to lie to you about anything, Raymond. What do you want to know?"

"Does management at Cranstar know that I am your ex-husband?" he spoke slowly, enunciating each word very carefully, emphasizing his point.

Danika swallowed the lump that sprang into her throat. Her mouth grew dry, and her lips remained tightly sealed, preventing her from speaking. Slowly she shook her head, giving Raymond the answer he wanted.

"So. I was right," he stated, with the slightest touch of triumph. "They don't know. What do you think Jim Planker would do if he knew you were threatening to fire me in order to punish me for personal reasons?"

A silent beat. Danika blinked, and then replied, "But that's not true."

"How would he know? You just said that..."

"I know what I said," Danika threw back, her patience growing thin. She silently cursed herself for having lost her temper and for baiting him with her reference to their past. Now, he was trying to threaten her? He'd better not go there.

"I'm sure your credibility at Cranstar would be shot to hell and your boss would be furious to learn that that you kept a possible conflict of interest situation secret," he pressed ahead with his theory. "I put in a call to Planker yesterday. He had already left for the day, but I can call him back. Do you think I should? Should I tell him what you just said? Fill him in on our brief, but ill-fated marriage?"

Struggling to regain her composure, Danika recalled the promise she had made to her boss when he congratulated her on her promotion. *I won't let you down,* she had told him, and there was no way she was going to allow Raymond Pruitt to mess things up for her.

"I'd rather you didn't speak to Jim about us," she acquiesced. "It would only cause unnecessary complications."

Raymond nodded, slowly. "I agree. So, what about the staff meeting tomorrow?"

Realizing it would do more harm than good to back him into a corner, Danika gave in. "All right. You break the news about the merger, but I must handle the discussions about Cranstar's severance packages. I don't want any misinterpretations or allegations of false promises that might negatively impact my handling of this assignment."

"Fine," Raymond reluctantly agreed.

Sighing, Danika picked up the stack of folders from the table, relieved that she and Raymond had managed to come to a satisfactory, though forced, compromise.

CHAPTER 10

At the staff meeting on Friday, Raymond announced to the three hundred plus employees that R&P had, indeed, been sold to Cranstar Oil and Gas International, and then launched into a lengthy discourse about how much he valued and needed each employee, expressing his regret that a small number might have to be released. He bragged about the low turnover rate at his company, puffing up his chest when he reminded them that he had never fired a single employee. He assured all in attendance that he would do everything in his power to help them remain on staff, even alluding to retraining sessions and reassignment of duties to ensure that as few people as possible would get pink slips.

Danika cursed silently under her breath, aware of how much more difficult Raymond was making her job. Jim Planker expected her to achieve an immediate fifty percent cut in staff, and Raymond was all but promising his employees that he would go out of his way to help them stay on board. How dare he undermine her like that?

When he finally turned the floor over to Danika, and questions erupted about what was coming next, everyone clamored for details about financial compensation, if they should be among those released.

Danika provided thorough explanations of what to expect, and once she had handed out packages detailing the generous severance offerings from Cranstar, it became evident that quite a few of the employees were eager to sign up for voluntary termination, discarding all thoughts of loyalty to their boss.

From the corner of her eye, Danika caught the thunderous expression darkening Raymond's face, and knew what he was thinking. His staff was abandoning him! The reductions that Danika had hoped for would most likely take care of themselves through attrition, and few, if any of his staff would have to be fired. As Danika continued to extol the benefits of leaving voluntarily, Raymond slipped out a side door and left the room.

When the meeting broke up, Danika left the briefing area and headed into the employee lunchroom to get a cold soda from the vending machine. She was exhausted from all of the tension and the questions and hoped a serious jolt of caffeine might help her get through the remainder of the day. Now, she needed courage to face Raymond, who had clearly not appreciated the manner in which his *devoted* employees had rejected his plea to stay. He had to be upset that they were embracing her—the enemy.

Danika went over to the vending machine, decided on a Dr. Pepper and dropped three quarters into the machine. She pressed the appropriate button, and was bending to retrieve her drink when she heard someone call out her name.

"Danika?"

Grabbing her soda, she quickly turned around and saw Carlos watching her from the doorway, one eyebrow arched in an unsettling stare. He walked toward her, a too-familiar smile lighting his features. "Good job, in there. Boy, it seems that everyone wants to leave now. Cranstar really knows how to trim down staff without firing a soul."

"That's what we wanted," Danika replied in as even a tone as she could manage, while a flush of heat passed up her neck and over her cheeks. *What is it about this guy?* she thought, aware of how foolish it was for her to have such a silly reaction to a simple greeting. Yes, he was brash, and damn good-looking, but he was sixteen years her junior! She should not be having this kind of a reaction to small talk from a man she barely knew. Should she? Danika clutched her cold soda can more tightly, attempting to remain calm.

"May I join you?" Carlos asked, approaching.

"Sure," Danika replied without a second thought, inclining her head in a quick nod as she slipped into a chair. She lifted her can of soda to her lips and waited for Carlos to settle down across from her.

"Damn good meeting," he commented again.

"I'm glad things went so smoothly. I think Mr. Pruitt expected more anxiety and protest about the proposed cuts," Danika added. "It is always good if staff reductions take care of themselves through attrition."

"Sure are plenty of folks ready to grab the cash and go. A severance package like Cranstar's won't come along again," Carlos commented, going on to explain to Danika that many of R&P's employees had been with the company since Raymond Pruitt started it, were in their midfifties and eager to retire. The buyout and Cranstar's attractive severance packages were precisely the kinds of motivators they had needed to make up their minds to leave. "New, younger blood is exactly what the company needs," he stated. "Though Mr. Pruitt would never admit that."

"I gathered as much," Danika replied, then added, "Thanks to good planning on Cranstar's part, my job was much easier than I had expected." She finished her soda and pushed back from the table, realizing that she ought to go. She wanted to talk to Raymond about arranging office space for her, so she could process the voluntary terminations. And she would need some clerical support, too. Hopefully, he'd be gracious enough to help her out. "Better get going," she said.

Carlos came around to her side of the table and bent close. "Have you made up your mind about going to the park with me tomorrow?" he asked.

"I'm still not sure," Danika stalled. "Let me get back to you, okay?"

"All right. Call me at home. Tonight. My number is in the book. The only Carlos Golan listed."

"I'll do that,"' she replied, wondering why she had not been able to simply tell him no.

As Danika exited the lunchroom, her cheeks were aflame, her pulse was racing, and she could feel the intensity of Carlos's eyes as they bored hotly into her backside.

Raymond burst into his outer office, told his secretary to hold all of his calls and stomped into his private suite, slamming the door behind him. Pacing the room, he placed one hand across his lips and strode back and forth as he struggled to sort through the flood of emotions that were assaulting him. He was humiliated, irritated and perplexed.

Danika's approach to his staff had gone over perfectly! Her calm, professional demeanor, her friendly tone and her extensive knowledge of the staffing requirements for the *Eco Quick-Valve Cleaner* project had impressed everyone—even Raymond—who now reluctantly admitted that he envied her ability to communicate with his employees. They had listened closely to every word she had spoken, as if she had been some kind of a celebrity handing out awards, not a cutthroat district manager from the new owner of the company. She had charmed them. Seduced them into thinking that leaving was their best option. He had expected an uproar of protest as soon as she opened her mouth, but that was not what had happened.

What had she done to make his staff so agreeable to her way of thinking? At the end of the session, it had been clear that the majority of the attendees welcomed the opportunity to leave R&P, felt no loyalty to him and were more than happy to turn their backs on his generosity and kindness.

How badly he had underestimated his staff's reaction to the news. Danika had inexplicably turned what he had assumed was going to be a tragically negative situation into a win-win proposition for all involved. Cranstar would get the numbers down and his employees were happy to walk out on him.

She was right, he thought morosely, his mind abuzz with the voices of his employees as they'd clamored for applications to accept Cranstar's offer. He was no longer in control of the company he worked so hard to launch. If not for his sons, he never would have sold out to Cranstar in the first place. But with two very bright boys who deserved the best education possible, the huge cash buyout, while leaving him in place as general manager, had been too attractive an offer to refuse.

Now, the sense of abandonment that hit Raymond made him slip weakly into his executive chair and give up a heavy, deflated groan.

It is happening all over again, he realized, staring morosely at the clean desk blotter, his head propped on his fist. A frightful emptiness filled his heart as flashes of long ago flitted through his mind. *My father...my brother, Danny...Danika... and even Julie, too. People I loved who didn't care enough to stick around for my sake. Why should my employees be any different? Everyone leaves me sooner or later. Daddy didn't even have the nerve to tell me goodbye when he got in the car and drove away, leaving me and Danny and Mom all alone. And Danny...running off to join the army without as much as a handshake or a slap on the back for his little brother. And now, Danny's bones are turning to dust in a desert somewhere in the Middle East. Danika? Ha. She abandoned me for her career the day after I married her, and even Julie...poor delicate Julie. At least, her departure left me two sons to remember her by.*

With a shake of his head, Raymond attempted to chase away the depressing ache that was beginning to rise inside, his mind fastened on Danika—the cause of this unexpected turmoil that was eating at him now.

He had loved Danika so much, but she had emotionally abandoned him for some crazy dream of being a famous entrepreneur, ignoring his requests to let it go. She had forced him to strike first and walk out on her before she could leave him. He had known it was coming. Only a matter of time. He had managed to escape that awful moment when the realization would hit him that she didn't need him at all. However, leaving her to marry Julie had been a mistake. If only he had been more patient, had not assumed that he was doomed to lose Danika. If only he had given their marriage more time. Who knows how differently his life...and hers...might have turned out?

He knew he had hurt her deeply when he left her for Julie, a woman he had hoped would never want more out of life than to be his wife and be there waiting for him when he came home from work. He had not wanted a busy entrepreneur like Danika for a wife, but look at him now. What did he have? No control at the company he had built from scratch. A lovely, but empty home. Two children, whom he only saw on weekends. And a master bedroom that was the loneliest room in his house.

When Raymond's secretary buzzed through on his intercom, he snapped back to the moment. "What do you want? I told you to hold all calls."

"It's not a phone call, Mr. Pruitt," his secretary replied. "Ms. Redmond would like to see you."

Danika. The last person he wanted to see right now. He needed time to put this turn of events into perspective and formulate his approach. She had made him look like an old-fashioned, paternalistic, small-thinking manger—a man who had selfishly tried to keep his employees under his control and ignorant of the benefits of leaving R&P. What did she want to see him for now? To gloat? Well, he was not in the mood.

"Tell her I'm leaving for the day. I can't see anyone," Raymond shot back, flicking off the intercom to fling back his head, eyes closed.

At least it was Friday. His sons would be at the house when he got home, and he always tried to spend as much time with them as he could, but he'd also have to find time to work on a plan to repair the damage Danika had done. He had to convince his most loyal employees not to leave him. Not now, when he needed them most.

He yanked open the middle drawer of his desk and was about to pull out his car keys, when a soft tapping at his door stopped him. He looked up, frowned and called out, "Yes?"

Danika poked her head into his office. "Got a minute?" she asked, entering before he could answer.

With a jerk of his chin, he straightened his shoulders and composed himself, now curious to hear what she had to say.

"Just wanted to thank you for arranging the meeting. I think it went extremely well," Danika started.

Leaning forward with his hands flat on his desk blotter, Raymond gave her a quick hunch of his shoulders, and then said, "Cranstar got what it wanted. Right?"

"Right," Danika agreed. "I don't think you will have to circulate many pink slips, after all. That's good, isn't it?'

Swallowing hard, Raymond paused, allowing her remark to settle. In one way, she was absolutely right. Now, he would not have to play the heavy. He would not have to lie awake and wonder if he had pulled food off the table of some single mom, or dashed the retirement plans of an elderly couple. Let them all go. It was their choice, not his, and there was no way to stop them from abandoning ship. Now, his job was to hold on to his position as general manager at R&P and turn the company into the best investment that Cranstar had ever made, ensuring his, and his son's futures.

"Good?" he repeated, taking a deep breath as he came back to the conversation. "It's progress," he admitted bleakly. "And now I know what I have to do." Rising, he circled his desk and perched on the corner, hands folded in his lap, prepared to level with Danika. After all, there was nothing to do now but go forward.

"And what's that?" Danika asked.

"If I want R&P to succeed within Cranstar, I have to change my approach." Raymond traced a finger over his bottom lip as he waited for her reaction.

Danika drew in a slight gasp, but said nothing.

"I know. I know," Raymond admitted. "You never expected to hear me say such a thing, did you?"

"No. I have to admit that I didn't."

"I want to put my energy into shaping a new R&P, not holding on to people who want to move on."

"My thoughts exactly," Danika agreed, giving Raymond a reassuring nod.

"I've got a lot of work to do," he sheepishly confessed.

"Raymond," Danika began. "I'll help any way I can."

"I appreciate your offer, and I will take you up on it. With your help, I can get a jump start on smoothing the way for the merger. On Monday morning, I plan to do everything I can to move this transition along."

"Good to hear," Danika agreed. "Let me know what I can do."

The silence in the room settled over Raymond like a calming force and he was certain that Danika was genuinely interested in helping him.

Maybe I ought to get reacquainted with this woman who is so familiar, yet still so unknown to me, he thought, and then impulsively offered, "Would you be willing to come out to my house tomorrow? I want you to fill me in on everything I ought to know about working with Cranstar. We could get an early start, maybe have lunch...a working lunch, if you'd like." Fingering his watchband, he mulled her reaction, then caught her gaze and held it until she quickly averted her eyes. Raymond felt as nervous as he had when he'd first asked her out on a date, and his heart was pounding just as fast. "Unless you already have plans," he rushed on, thinking he had asked too much of her and had overstepped his place.

"Well," Danika started, "I'd love to work with you, but Carlos invited me to go to Great Mountain Park with him tomorrow. I'm not sure if I'll be free in the morning. Maybe we could get together later?"

"What?" Raymond shot back, lifting both hands, palms up in question. He peered curiously at Danika, squinting. "Carlos Golan? He asked you out on a date?"

"Well I wouldn't call it a date exactly," Danika stammered, now looking directly at Raymond. "He suggested the outing and I really had nothing better to do tomorrow, so I told him I'd let him know…"

"Sounds like a date to me. And aren't you a bit…" Raymond groped for a way to make his point.

"Too old?" Danika prompted, then paused.

"Well…mature," Raymond finished. "Carlos is only thirty-three. I've known him since he was a teenager. Why would he want to spend his Saturday with you?"

"Perhaps because he finds me attractive? Interesting? Fun to be with?" Danika shot back, as she crossed her arms and gave Raymond a withering look.

"You'd better call him right now and tell him you can't make it," Raymond decided, reaching for the handset to his phone, which he held out to her. "Tell him you have to meet with me. He'll understand. Speed-dial number sixteen."

Danika drew back her shoulders in obvious affront. "Why should I do that?"

"Because Carlos Golan is well-known around town, and at the plant, as a player who has dated just about every single female within a twenty mile radius. I hate to tell you this, but he treats every attractive woman he encounters as a kind of test…to see if his charm holds up."

"Is that so?" Danika replied, skepticism thickening her voice.

"Yes. So, call him and tell him you have something more important to do than to boost his ego."

Without responding, Danika got up, walked to the door and then turned around to stare back at Raymond, who was still extending the phone to her. "I will see you on Monday morning, Raymond," she told him. "Have a nice weekend." Then she left.

Staring after her in surprise, Raymond slammed down the receiver and cursed Carlos aloud, a bitter taste of jealous anger rising in his throat.

CHAPTER 11

Danika was incensed. Where did Raymond Pruitt get off, trying to tell her who she could or could not spend time with? He wasn't her father, her boss or even her husband—not that she would have taken orders from any of them anyway.

She yanked open the door to her rental car and threw her briefcase into the backseat, and then got in and slammed the door. Sitting in the excruciatingly hot vehicle, she fumed in silence while perspiration darkened the front of her blouse and fused her thighs to the vinyl seat covers.

Just when I was thinking that Raymond had learned how to compromise and was lightening up on the control button, he pulls this crap. Stupid me...I was beginning to think that perhaps we could be friends, or at least civil to one another. But no. Same old Raymond. His way, or no way. Well, I'll call Carlos all right, and I'll accept his invitation, she decided, jamming the car key into the ignition.

When the engine started, she flipped the air conditioner on full blast, slammed her foot down on the accelerator and sped off down the driveway toward the entrance gates of the plant.

As soon as Danika arrived at her motel, she grabbed the local phone book and located Carlos's home number, which she immediately dialed. His voice mail took her call.

"Carlos. Danika Redmond here. I would be happy to tour the mountain park with you tomorrow. I have a map and a rental car, so I will meet you at the park entrance at ten o'clock.

Okay? Call me back if that won't work. The number here is 555-9099. See you in the morning."

Hanging up, she went into the bathroom and stared at her image in the mirror, a surge of satisfaction bringing a smile to her lips.

Danika was downright infuriating, Raymond thought as he drove home on the highway, *but she sure as hell has maintained her looks.* He was still trying to come to terms with the fact that Carlos Golan had actually asked Danika out on a date. *Awfully bold of Carlos to test his romantic charms on my ex-wife! But Carlos does not know who she is,* Raymond rationalized, keenly aware that Danika did not look more than a few years older than Carlos. Her skin was smooth, her eyes free of wrinkles and that body! What a shape! In fact, she was more attractive to him now than she had ever been, even when they were married. Raymond had to admit that seeing her so unexpectedly had stirred up feelings and memories that he had hoped would never surface again.

"Yes, I am jealous," he muttered into the windshield, teeth tightly clenched. *Yes, I want to spend personal time alone with her. And yes, I have missed her for a long, long time.*

Visions of how she had looked on their wedding day came over him. She had been so young, so happy to be marrying him and so easy to please. He had loved her then, and had expected to be with her forever, but somewhere down the line she had grown independent, had pulled away from him, frightening him into abandoning her. It had happened all too quickly, and his life had gone downhill after that, leading all the way to Julie's death. If only Danika hadn't been so stubborn. If only he hadn't been so afraid.

But we have so much more in common now. We work for the same company. We're older. Wiser. Now I understand what she needs—space to fulfill her dreams and my support. Could we possibly start over? he wondered, the thought bringing on a sense of euphoric anticipation that he had not experienced in a long, long time.

CHAPTER 12

At ten fifty-five, Danika dialed the number to Carlos's house and was greeted by his voice mail for the second time. She had gotten up early, eaten a larger-than-usual breakfast at the café next door to the motel and then set off to Great Mountain Park, looking forward the outing. But now, after sitting in her car for nearly an hour, she was beginning to doubt that he planned to show up.

"Where is he?" she murmured, glancing around the busy parking lot inside the park's entrance, where a family was unpacking picnic baskets, several couples were placing infants into strollers and a group of Boy Scouts were racing toward the trail leading to the lake, fishing poles in their hands.

Her mind slipped back to Raymond's less-than-flattering assessment of his employee, and though she hated to admit it, maybe he'd been right. Obviously, Carlos had not taken his invitation seriously or he'd be there. Had he been testing her? Setting her up to see if she would fall for his line? Surely not. Why would he want to embarrass her this way?

With a shrug, Danika got out of the car, stretched her arms over her head and studied the sky. It was a beautiful day, and the sun, though already shining hot and steady overhead, had not yet heated the mountain air to an unbearable temperature.

"Might as well walk around and enjoy the scenery since I'm here," she decided, pulling on her sunglasses and locking the car. She was wearing a pair of comfortable denim capris, a lightweight sleeveless shirt and sneakers. After showering this morning, she had left her hair wet and simply run a bit of gel through it, creating a mass of fine ringlets, over which she now placed a bright-red, deep-brimmed baseball cap.

"If Carlos shows up, let him come looking for me," she grumbled, starting down the walkway toward one of the many well-marked hiking trails that had been carved into the craggy rocks.

"Danika!" a voice called out.

She turned on the gravel path and squinted back into the parking lot, only to see Raymond stepping out of a red Cadillac Escalade, promptly followed by two teenage boys. "Damn!" she cursed in a loud whisper, wishing she could blend into the nearby tangle of bushes and disappear. Carlos was nowhere in sight and here she was setting off on a hike in the mountains all alone. How was she going to explain *this* to Raymond after the way she'd reacted to his warning yesterday? Maybe she should lie and tell him that she had canceled on Carlos, or that she had never confirmed the date, or that she had decided to come out alone for a hike. Or say nothing. After all, she didn't owe Raymond any explanations about what she did with her free time. And what was he doing here anyway? Spying on her?

"Hold up," Raymond called out, waving to her. He spoke quickly to the two boys, then hurried in her direction.

Biting her bottom lip, Danika waited for him to catch up with her.

"Hi," he said, slightly breathless, though in Danika's opinion he looked to be in very good shape. He was wearing black tight-fitting biking shorts, a white T-shirt with a single red stripe across the front and was holding a silver biker's helmet under one arm.

"Hi," she replied, tugging her cap lower over her eyes.

Raymond glanced around. "Where's Carlos?"

"He didn't show up," Danika blurted out, deciding not to play any games with Raymond. Who cared what he thought about her nonexistent date?

"Oh?" Raymond remarked rather smugly. "So you're alone?"

"Looks that way, doesn't it?" she shot back. *And I want to be left alone,* she thought, wishing he'd go away. She was not about to suffer through one of his paternalistic lectures.

"Would you like to join me and the boys?" he asked, gesturing back to the two teenagers who were busy unloading two bicycles from the back of the SUV. "We're going to ride over to the lake. It's really pretty over there. Cooler, too. Why don't you come along? There's room for you on the back of my bike."

Danika simply stared at him, thinking, *Where is the I-told-you-so lecture? Why isn't he hitting me with Didn't-I-tell-you-that-Carlos-was-full-of bull?* While she pondered this chance encounter, two boys approached, walking their bikes.

"Hey, guys," Raymond called out. "This is Danika. My first wife. You know, I told you she was working with me on the merger, and all." He made these remarks with a surprising casualness.

"Oh, yeah. Danika. Well, hi! I'm Eddie," the taller of the two said, giving Danika a big smile and a quick wave. "This here is Carl...my *baby* brother."

The younger boy slapped at Eddie, and then nodded briefly at Danika. "Hi. Nice to meet you."

"Hello," she managed. "Nice to meet you, too." The boys were as handsome as their father, tall and lean and strong, with gorgeous skin and lightly muscled bodies. And they had good manners, too!

After a few uncomfortable moments of silence, Eddie spoke up. "Dad, we're gonna go ahead. Catch up, okay?"

"Yeah. Good. Go on. I'll meet you at the lake," Raymond promised.

"Bye!" the boys cried out in unison as they mounted their bikes and sped off.

Danika watched them disappear around a curve in the biking

path before glancing back at Raymond, only to catch him watching her. "You have two very handsome sons," she remarked, not hiding her admiration as she stared at him.

"I know," Raymond murmured, meeting her gaze with unflinching pride.

She pressed her palms together as if to steady herself, feeling nervous and off balance. Why was she so emotional? she wondered. What was going on with her? "And they knew who I was," she added. "You told them about me? About us?"

"Sure." His voice was low, the word softly spoken.

"When?" she wanted to know.

"A long time ago. After Julie died, I think. And why not? I'm not ashamed of having been married to you."

"Well, no. But I'm...surprised that you would discuss your former wife with your sons."

"Of course, they don't know *everything*," Raymond clarified. "They know who you are, why you are here in Bolan and that you once played a very important part in my life."

"I see," was all that Danika could think of to say.

Raymond went on. "The boys have heard my life story more than once, including how I met you, proposed to you and convinced you to marry me. I haven't held back much from them...except how much I regret the way I treated you," he finished in a genuine tone of contrition, eyeing Danika closely, clearly watching for her reaction.

Danika tilted her head to one side, shocked by this unexpected admission of regret on his part, thinking he must be putting her on. "Raymond, please don't say things that you don't mean. Not now. It's way too late."

"But I do regret the way I treated you," he insisted. "I was wrong to put my needs before yours, and to assume that your dreams had no value."

From behind her dark glasses, Danika squinted skeptically at Raymond, trying to assess the honesty in his answer, recalling how hard it had always been for him to admit a mistake.

Never had she expected for him to admit culpability in their failed marriage, and the confession threatened to bring tears to her eyes. In a flash, she realized that she had been subconsciously waiting for this moment for a long time, and for it to come under such strange circumstance was beyond all expectation. But was he for real? she worried, afraid to let down her guard.

"I mean what I just said," he reassured her, stepping nearer. "I owe you that much, Danika, and I should have told you this a long time ago. I should have been more patient, and I should have trusted my love for you, and not given in to my fears."

"Should-haves and if-onlys don't count for anything, Raymond. I appreciate your attempt to apologize, but let it go. You did what you felt you had to do, and I guess it was for the best. We've both moved on with our lives, so what use is there in dredging up the past? Nothing can be changed."

Taking Danika by the arm, he guided her toward a small concrete bench beneath the low hanging limbs of a vine-covered oak. "That's not true. Change *is* possible. I know I've changed, just in the past three days." He laughed, shaking his head in wonder. "All because of you, Danika. Now I see how much I need you, how much I have always needed you."

Danika sat down on the bench, and then blinked up at Raymond, who settled beside her and took her by the hand. She did not pull away, though she was startled by this unexpected move, as well as the gentleness that now cloaked Raymond's words.

"But you left..." she began.

He lowered his chin, then glanced up. "Yes. And the only thing good that came out of my leaving you for Julie is that I now have two wonderful sons."

"You must be very close to them," she replied, floundering for a way to move the conversation away from their failed marriage. Rehashing that scene would do nothing more than initiate a load of bitter memories and unsettling emotions, which she would rather not face at the moment.

"I am close to them," Raymond confirmed. "They're my best friends, even though they are teenagers." He laughed, shattering the tension for a moment. "We don't keep secrets. When Julie was diagnosed with cancer, I tried to keep the news from them, but it backfired and they hated me for not telling them the truth. After that, and after going through her illness and eventual death together, I made up my mind never to keep secrets from my sons. I don't hold anything back. They know their father is imperfect and has a ton of flaws, and can be a bit of a jerk at times, but they are patient with me. We manage. I love them very much."

Danika nodded. "Yes. I can see that. And they love you, too."

"You can tell?"

"Sure. Love is difficult to disguise, Raymond. Especially when it radiates both ways."

"Did you know how much I loved you?" he ventured.

She nodded, afraid to talk. "I think so," she finally said.

He shifted on the bench, positioning himself in her line of vision, blocking out the sunshine that now bathed one side of his face. He took her other hand in his and held it tightly as he went on. "Danika. I have had years to think about what happened to us, and for some reason, I believe that this unexpected reunion might be my only chance to tell you what I should have told you long ago. Will you hear me out?"

"Yes, of course," she whispered.

"You were so beautiful and smart and willing to love me when we married. I never believed that I deserved you, and every day of our marriage I would wake up and look over at you and thank God that you were still there. When you became so absorbed in your business and began traveling around with that graphics-arts guy, spending so much time with other men and staying out so late, I got scared. I worked myself into such a state of insecurity, that I could not control my fears. I had to get out before you left me."

"But, Raymond, I never had any intentions of leaving you. I was simply busy, trying to do everything. If I ignored your needs to satisfy mine, I apologize." Danika pulled her hands away, but placed them on his bare arm. "I thought I was strengthening our marriage by working so hard. I wanted to safeguard our future, not tear it apart. Didn't you understand that?"

"I do now," Raymond admitted, "but back then, I was too bullheaded and selfish to look that far ahead." Sighing, he went on to tell Danika how Julie's death had only served to solidify his belief that he had been destined to lose all whom he loved.

"Raymond, you're a good man, a good father and I'm glad you told me this. All I ever wanted was for us to be happy and to stay in love forever." Danika closed her eyes, beginning to relax as she began to tell Raymond about her life—how she had focused on her career at Cranstar to fill the emptiness after their divorce. She could tell that he was finally actually listening to her, showing interest in what she had to say and he was actively considering her point of view. She had never seen him so attentive and patient to hear her out.

After their devastating breakup, she had buried Raymond deep within her heart, desperate to recover and move on. For too long she had allowed her failed marriage to influence her decisions about romantic commitments, preventing her from trusting another man with her heart. She wished he had been able to unburden himself of his fears while they had been married. If so, they might have been able to hold on to their love.

"It makes me feel sad to know that I not only cheated you out of a happy marriage with me, but I ruined your chances of happiness with someone else," he confessed.

Danika nodded in understanding. "Well, when we're young, we don't think about the fact that our actions will reverberate far into the future and affect us for years. Life takes us down many different paths, Raymond, and we never know where each one will end."

"Maybe that's for the best," he replied. "Some paths will bring us happiness, while others are destined to end in tragedy, and I do believe that paths exist that are never intended to end," he said thoughtfully. "They go on and on, pulling us through ups and downs, around rough patches, testing us with dangerous curves in the road."

Danika lifted her chin and sighed in agreement. "Like a lifelong marriage, a journey of true love?"

"Exactly," he responded with a whisper.

A quiet hush hung between them, disturbed only by the soft rustle of a bird as it moved among the tree branches overhead.

Danika felt the undercurrent of an electrifying attraction begin to pull at her senses, threatening to crack her restraint. When Raymond reached out to touch her cheek, she started to pull back, wanting to slow things down, but then she relaxed and allowed her resistance to dissolve. He splayed the fingers of one hand across the side of her face and pulled her to him, caressing her lips with his and then placed both of his hands at her waist and slowly moved them up her back into the curve of her shoulders. Braced against her, he deepened his kiss, moment by moment, until she knew that she was lost.

His lips, so soft and familiar, sent a wave of desire through Danika, who deepened the kiss as his tongue touched, then swept lightly over hers. Shifting slightly, she edged closer, as if trying to banish the empty years that had passed unfulfilled between them. A resurgence of her love for Raymond swelled in her veins and raced through her body, igniting the dormant ache that she still carried for him.

Though her mind warned her not to kiss him back so passionately, or press her breasts so firmly against his chest, or entangle her fingers in the sensuously wavy hair at the nape of his neck, she clung to him, unable to stop herself from melting into his arms. It had been a long time coming, and Danika knew in her heart that this time their love could not falter. This time, neither could let it slip away.

Breaking off the kiss, she removed her cap and shook out her curls, as if clearing her mind of a muddle of emotions.

Raymond reached up and touched her hair, drew the tip of his little finger along the side of her face and gazed longingly into her eyes. In a whisper, he asked, "How can you still be so damn pretty? You have only gotten better in all this time we've been apart."

"That's my best kept secret," she murmured. "Besides, you're holding up pretty darn well yourself." She chuckled, not flinching when his hand slipped to the small of her back and he gently pulled her to him, brushing his lips over the exposed skin at her shoulder.

"Would you be willing to think about…a…future together?" he murmured, his breath warm against her skin.

Pausing to take in Raymond's request, Danika felt her heart begin to pound. She wanted to say yes, but did she dare? Should she be wary of this sudden change in Raymond's personality? Could he really have become a different man since their youthful marriage twenty-five years ago?

When they had been married, he had been possessive, chauvinistic and had rarely spent his free time with her or taken an interest in what she had wanted to do. He had dismissed her needs, and had scoffed at the company she had been determined to build, so she had built her career at Cranstar. Her determination, focus and dedication had paid off, without any help from a husband. What did she need from him now? She had achieved her goals without him by her side, but the road had been a lonely one to travel. Was it possible to try again? Would it work? She really did not know.

It had taken Danika a long time to recover after Raymond walked out and now she was exactly where she had hoped to be at this crossroads in her life. She was unencumbered by a husband or children, in a management position with her company and more confident and attractive than she had ever thought she would be at the midcentury mark of her life—even attracting the attention of a much younger man. Her answer to Raymond's question would set the course for her golden years, so why complicate her life by taking on the challenge of mothering two teenage boys, and being a wife to Raymond Pruitt, whose faults she knew too well? Or did she? Danika wondered, fighting her attraction to the first man she had ever loved. If she had really gotten smarter and more practical with age, then she had better make the right decision.

"I can't answer you right now," she finally told Raymond, pulling out of his embrace. She saw disappointment flicker across his face and settle in the shadows around his eyes, but knew it would do no good to give him an answer she might later regret. "We both need to be cautious, Raymond. I think this reunion has taken us both by surprise and we might be overro-manticizing the possibilities of a future. Let's take some time, get to know each other again," she said. "I don't want to move too fast and make the same mistakes again. This time has to be forever."

CHAPTER 13

"Will that be all, Ms. Redmond?"

Melissa's question did not completely penetrate Danika's wandering thoughts, but it did force her to look over at the pretty administrative assistant who was helping her process the R&P Manufacturing voluntary termination packages.

Raymond had been quick to arrange a temporary office and clerical support for Danika to help her complete the task she had come to do, and Melissa had been a good choice. The young woman was bright, efficient and smart enough not to ask questions about the rumor that had been circulating through the company all day—Danika Redmond was the boss's ex-wife and he was still in love with her.

Danika had no doubt that Raymond had leaked the news himself, in hopes that it would make its way to her...and to Carlos, who had buzzed her that morning with a lame excuse about having had problems with his voice mail over the weekend. He had apologized profusely for the miscommunication, but she had blown him off, nearly thanking him for not showing up since his absence had made it possible for her and Raymond to reconnect.

"Anything else?" Melissa asked again.

"Oh, no, Melissa. That's all. I think we've accomplished enough for today," Danika told the young woman, closing the folder that she had been working on. She glanced at the clock on her desk, and then gasped to see the time. "Is it six o'clock already? It can't be!"

"It is," Melissa replied, bending down to reach into the bottom drawer of her desk, which was on the opposite side of the room. She removed her purse and took out her car keys. "Mondays *never* fly by this fast! It's sure been fun working with you."

"Thanks," Danika replied. "And you're right, it's time for both of us to get out of here."

Melissa snapped off her computer monitor and stood. "See you tomorrow?"

With a nod, Danika replied. "Yes. And we ought to be able to finish up the remainder of the applications by midday, so I'll have time to train you on the software to process the dependents' benefits, too. You'll have to handle those after I leave."

"Are you still heading back to Houston on Wednesday?" Melissa asked.

"That's my plan," Danika replied with conviction, though she had not yet made a flight reservation nor told Jim Planker when she would return.

After Melissa left, Danika remained at her desk, toying with an ink pen as her thoughts continued to drift—almost with a will of their own—over the past two days. She had spent almost every waking moment in the company of Raymond and his sons.

After their encounter at Great Mountain Park, she had gone to lunch with them and later attended an amateur rock concert in an outdoor amphitheater on the outskirts of Abilene. It had been a wild, spontaneous and fun-filled day. Not like any she had ever experienced before, and the adventure had left her with a stark realization of how boring and predicable she had let her life become.

The boys had welcomed her company, chatting easily with her about their school, their friends, their love for bike riding and the annual river rafting trip to the Texas Hill country that they would be taking with Raymond next weekend. When they had asked Danika to come along, she had quickly declined, using her impending return to Houston as an excuse.

After the concert on Saturday night, Danika had driven back to the motel in a daze, unable to believe how quickly her feelings for Raymond had shifted in the span of one day. Her attraction to him was as strong as it had been when she first met him, and her thoughts about a future with her ex-husband had become as excitingly consuming as those of a young bride about to set off on a brand new life. He had awakened feelings and sensations and hopes that had been absent far too long. It was time to rectify that.

He has gotten better with age, she decided, acknowledging that the uncanny way they were now reconnecting had initiated a luscious sense of anticipation that raced through her soul and kept a smile on her lips.

On Sunday, she had driven out to Raymond's home, and been pleasantly surprised—and impressed—by his beautiful, well-manicured property. He had proudly shown her around while the boys grilled hamburgers by the pool, making her feel more than welcome. In fact, all three men were embracing her as if she belonged with them.

When the day ended, and she had been heading to her car, Eddie had ambushed her at the carport and pulled her aside.

"My Dad has not smiled this much in years," he told her, a tinge of relief coloring his words. "Please stick around for a while. A long while. He... Well, no... We all need you here. And think about going on the river rafting trip with us, please?"

"I promise to think about it, Eddie," she had vowed, "but I do have to get back to Houston, you know? I have a job I want to keep."

He had nodded, then slipped off into the shadows and disappeared into the house.

During the drive back to her motel, the young man's plea echoed in her ears like thunder. *We all need you.* Those four little words carried a great deal of weight.

When Monday morning arrived, Danika had made it a point to remain ensconced in the Human Resources office with Melissa, even eating lunch at her desk and only venturing out to the ladies' room a few times. She had not wanted to see or speak to Raymond all day, but now she wondered what he was doing. Was he thinking about her? Embroiled in a complicated business matter? Or in his car and on his way home?

Her assignment at R&P was nearly complete and she had briefed Jim Planker on her progress. He had been extremely pleased and had congratulated her on the way she had handled the situation. Now, she ought to be preparing to leave, but was deliberately putting off making the arrangements. Why? Was it because Eddie and Carl wanted her to stay through the weekend to accompany them and their father on their river rafting excursion? Or was it because she really didn't want to leave Raymond? Either way, she was torn, and knew she had to be careful. The last thing she wanted to do was build false hopes by inferring that she was going to be a permanent part of their lives. She had a job, an apartment and a life to get back to in Houston, didn't she?

With a start, an e-mail message signal popped onto her computer screen, interrupting her reverie. When she clicked it open, she saw that it was from Jim Planker and hurried to open it.

Good job, Danika. All of the voluntary termination paperwork you e-mailed to me is now in process and the fifty percent staff reduction has been met. You really came through. More good news! Don't worry about rushing back to Houston. Your new assignment is to stick around R&P and work with them to streamline the design of the Eco Quick-Valve Cleaner containers. Pruitt has assured me that he has office space under renovation for you right now. We'll work out the details next week. Take a few days' vacation and keep up the great work.

Grinning, Danika hurriedly typed, Thanks for the new assignment. Just what I needed to hear.

With the decision about leaving made for her, she immediately buzzed through to Raymond, hoping he was still at his desk. "Hi," she said when he came on the line. "Is the invitation for a river rafting trip still open?"

"Most definitely," he told her, then added, "Hold on."

While Danika held the phone to her ear and waited for him to come back on the line, she could feel her heart pounding, her blood racing. She was actually going to stay in West Texas! And she was actually looking forward to jumping into a rubber raft to slide down a rocky river with two wild teenagers and her ex-husband. Was she out of her mind?

"Probably," she murmured. "But it feels so damn good."

Suddenly the door to her office burst open and Raymond was standing there, a mischievous smile curving his lips. "Sticking around, I understand?" he quizzed.

"So, *you* are responsible for my new assignment?" She hurriedly slammed down the phone. Damn it! Here he was taking control of her life again. "*You* postponed my return to Houston?" she blurted, pulling an exaggerated frown.

Raymond said nothing as he walked toward her, his eyes boring hotly into hers. With a strut that set her pulse afire, he approached, a serious expression replacing his quizzical smile.

"Seems that Cranstar *can* get along without you for a little while longer," he told her, bending to take Danika by the arm and urge her to her feet. "However, *I* don't plan to get along without you in my life a moment longer." He smothered her with a kiss that more than made his point, communicating his decision to keep her with him always.

A low moan of pleasure escaped Danika's throat as she felt herself responding to his nearness, the insistent pressure of his body against hers and his all-consuming request to let him make love to her. At last, he was making a command that she was eager to follow.

Holding her close, he whispered against her neck, "Will you have dinner with me tonight?"

"I'd love to," Danika sighed.

"And every night thereafter for many years to come?" he pressed.

"Without question," she whispered back, realizing that her life would be complete—not complicated—if she opened her heart to Raymond once more.

Enjoy the early *Hideaway* stories
with a special Kimani Press release...

HIDEAWAY LEGACY

Two full-length novels

ROCHELLE ALERS

Essence Bestselling Author

A collectors-size trade volume containing
HEAVEN SENT and HARVEST MOON—
two emotional novels from the author's
acclaimed *Hideaway Legacy.*

"Fans of the romantic suspense of Iris Johansen,
Linda Howard and Catherine Coulter will enjoy the first
installment of the *Hideaway Sons and Brothers* trilogy,
part of the continuing saga of the *Hideaway Legacy.*"
—*Library Journal* on *No Compromise*

Available the first week of March
wherever books are sold.

KIMANI PRESS™
www.kimanipress.com   KORA0650307TR

"Robyn Amos dishes up a fast-paced, delectable love story…!"
—*Romantic Times BOOKreviews*

BESTSELLING AUTHOR

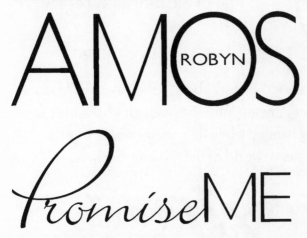

AMOS ROBYN

Promise ME

After taking a break from a demanding career and a controlling fiancé, Cara Williams was ready to return to her niche in the computer field. It looked like clear sailing—until AJ Gray came on the scene. As the powerful president of Captial Computer Consulting, AJ offered Cara the expertise she needed—even as his kisses triggered her worst fears and her deepest desires.

Coming the first week of March,
wherever books are sold.

ARABESQUE®

www.kimanipress.com   KPRA0070307TR

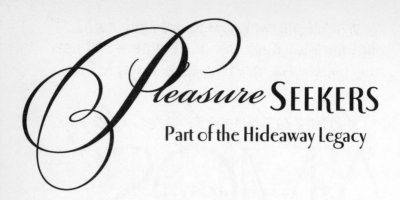

Pleasure SEEKERS

Part of the Hideaway Legacy

A sizzling, sensuous story about Ilene, Faye and Alana—
three young African-American women whose lives are
forever changed when they are invited to join the
exclusive world of the Pleasure Seekers.

Rochelle Alers

NATIONAL BESTSELLING AUTHOR

"Fans of the romantic suspense of Iris Johansen,
Linda Howard and Catherine Coulter
will enjoy [*Pleasure Seekers*]."
—Library Journal

Available the first week of January wherever books are sold.

sepia™

www.kimanipress.com

What if you met your future soul mate…
but were too busy living in the here and now
to give them the time of day?

friends: a love story

ANGELA BASSETT &
COURTNEY B. VANCE

An inspiring true story told by the celebrities themselves—
Hollywood and Broadway's classiest power couple.
Living a real-life love story, these friends-who-became-lovers
share the secret of how they make it work with love,
faith and determination.

Available the first week of January wherever books are sold.